House of Dreams

Novels by Jean Morley:

Black Pearls
ISBN 0-595-28804-9

Talley Girl
ISBN: 0-595-31776-6

Cotton Candy
ISBN 0-595-35107-7

Walking the Imp's Path
ISBN 0-595-40775-7

Intrigue and Elegance
ISBN 0-595-50463-9

The Reluctant Squire
ISBN 978-1907294259

House of Dreams

Jean Morley

DB

DIADEM BOOKS

House of Dreams

All Rights Reserved. Copyright © 2011 Jean Morley

No part of this book may be reproduced or transmitted in any form or by any means, graphic, electronic, or mechanical, including photocopying, recording, taping or by any information storage or retrieval system, without the permission in writing from the copyright holder.

The right of Jean Morley to be identified as the author of this work has been asserted in accordance with the Copyright, Designs and Patents Act 1988 sections 77 and 78.

Published by Diadem Books
Distribution coordination by Spiderwize

For information, please contact:

Diadem Books
16 Lethen View
Tullibody
ALLOA
FK10 2GE
Scotland UK

www.diadembooks.com

The views expressed in this work are solely those of the author and do not necessarily reflect the views of the publisher, and the publisher hereby disclaims any responsibility for them.

This is a work of fiction. Names, characters and incidents are products of the author's imagination. Any resemblance to persons living or dead is entirely coincidental.

Cover painting by the author.

ISBN: 978-1-908026-19-4

Chapter One

LONDON LAY BASKING in the sun of a warm spring day. The leaves on the trees were unfurling, giving a delicate and fresh touch of green, and the flowers in the parks were in bud and beginning to open, their petals showing new and clean. It was a lovely time of year to lift the spirits after the dreary winter days and to give the feeling of hope for the future.

In contrast, however, those who dwelt in a dour looking corner house in an old part of London had seen the death that morning of Mr Abraham Elliss. Now, as William, the elderly servant, fixed the black crepe to the doorknocker, Miss Katherine Elliss, the daughter, sat in the morning room facing old Dr Roberts. She ran her hand over her face as if to remove the tiredness and exhaustion she felt from the last demanding few weeks and managed to give a wan smile to the kindly gentleman sitting opposite her.

'I have known you a long time, my dear, and I feel I should give you some advice,' said the doctor. 'I know it has all been a struggle for you, being alone, but I must tell you that you have nothing to reproach yourself for in any way. You looked after your Mama and now you have looked after your Papa, which was no easy task, I know, especially with his drink problem. But at long last he has departed this world and when you have recovered, I hope you will enjoy yourself. You are still a young woman, you know.'

Kate smiled. 'I'm not, Dr Roberts, although it is kind of you to say so. I'm twenty-eight years of age.'

'There is still time for you to get out and about and enjoy yourself. I don't know, of course, but I expect your father will have left you this house and whatever money he had. So do something *you* wish to do for a change. Go abroad, travel, go out and about.'

'My father always said he had made provision for me but what it is, exactly, I don't know.'

'Well,' said Dr Roberts, getting to his feet, 'I expect that lawyer, Mr – er – Fawcett, will let you know in due course. Watch that he doesn't line his own pockets. He should see to everything but if I can be of any help to you, let me know.' He left, shaking his head and thinking of the attractive young girl Miss Elliss used to be. He hoped when all was normal again she would regain her good looks.

Kate was grateful to him. He was such a dear, she thought. She had known him since she had been a little girl, and she had always confided in him and told him her troubles. In fact, she had turned to him rather than her father, who was much older than the doctor. The problem had been that she was the youngest child of six, the rest being boys. The brother nearest to her in age was Daniel. He was married to Fanny and they had numerous offspring. Some ten years ago they had invited Kate to stay in their home in Lincolnshire, but she soon returned home telling her mother that all they had wanted her for was to look after their children while they went out enjoying themselves. She hadn't seen them since. None of the other sons had visited and where they were she had no idea. In fact, Kate had banished them from her thoughts a long time ago. They hadn't been concerned about their parents or a young sister. As far as she could, Kate felt she had done her duty to her parents and now she had to see that the elderly and faithful servants, William and his wife Matty, were also comfortable in their old age. She had known them all her life; they had always been there like the grandparents she had never known.

She now went to the kitchen where they were sitting waiting for her. 'Come and sit down, Miss Kate. Can we do anything for you? How about a cup of tea or some of Will's whisky?'

'A cup of tea would be good if we have any left,' said Kate, sitting down.

'Do you wish me to see Mr Fawcett and tell him the news so he can make the necessary arrangements?' asked Will.

'Oh, would you? Thank you. I'm afraid my brain isn't working very well at the moment.'

'That's all right, Miss Kate. It's not to be wondered at the way you've had to toil up and down those stairs day after day, apart from all the other aggravation from your Pa.'

'Hush, William,' said his wife.

'It's true,' said William. 'The poor lassie is worn out and it's not right. And while I think of it, Miss Kate, before that Mr Fawcett comes round, do you gather up any money in your father's pockets and desk and anything else of worth.' And with these words he left for the lawyers.

'There isn't anyone else to tell about your Pa, is there, Miss Kate?'

'No, I don't think so,' said Kate, feeling she couldn't concentrate on anything at the moment. 'A notice will be placed in the paper, I suppose by Mr Fawcett, but that is all. My brothers haven't been near for years. I can't imagine we shall see them, thank goodness.'

'Will said he'd go to the funeral on your behalf. At least, as ladies we are spared that,' said Matty. 'We can sit together and then I suppose the solicitor will call after he has attended the funeral to read your father's will. You have to think what you will do, dear, won't you?'

'Yes, and so will you, dear Matty. I know you would like to retire and I hope Papa has left you a large amount of money. You and Will have been with us for ever and I have been so pleased with the support you have given me. The house can be sold so that the three of us can benefit.'

'Have you any idea what you would like to do?' asked Matty. 'You could be married, you know.'

'I shouldn't think anyone would want someone my age apart from an old man, and I've had enough looking after Papa, let alone a complete stranger. No, what I would like is to have a nice little cottage somewhere in a pretty village and sit in a garden full of flowers. That would be a dream. You and Will could come too if you wished or have a cottage next door.'

Matty smiled to herself, thinking Miss Kate would be bored to tears if that was all she wanted, and it would be a shame to bury herself away in the country. When she had recovered from looking after her father she hoped Miss Kate would once more have her good looks and go out and enjoy herself. Matty remembered her when she was younger and a lively, lovely young lady going to the assemblies with her friends. As her mama had been a sickly person after bearing six children, mothers of Kate's friends had been her chaperone. Eventually, as Miss Kate had taken over the running of the house and nursing her parents, her friends had disappeared and her social life had ground to a halt. Now Miss Kate didn't look her best but Matty was sure that when she had her life back again, she would still be an attractive lady. Her features were delicate, her skin creamy and her eyes were still a greeny-blue that sparkled when she laughed. Her hair was wavy, inclined to curl and still gloriously auburn. True, her slim figure was thinner and her dresses hung loose on her but no doubt after more rest and relief from the responsibility of the sickroom, she would return to her attractive self even if she was a few years older.

'You know,' Kate said, pausing in between sipping the strong brew of tea Matty had given her, 'I don't feel like weeping, just a sense of relief it is all over. I suppose it was because there was no real love between us, not like Mama and I. But it isn't right, is it, Matty?' She looked anxiously at her.

'My dear,' said Matty bracingly, 'don't you worry about all that. Giving love to a person, whoever it may be, has to work both ways and if you'll pardon me for saying so, your father was always selfish, you know. He thought himself the Lord of the Manor, although he wasn't a lord and there was no manor.'

This at least made Kate smile. 'No, indeed,' she said. 'I suppose we can't make plans until the will is read and Mr Fawcett won't do that until after the funeral, although why not I can't imagine.'

'I think you should do as Will says and find all the money there is in the house and anything else of worth. The undertakers will need paying as well as Mr Fawcett, but I suppose he will see to all that. But you will need money for your immediate use, you know, and you don't know what extra expenses there will be.'

That night Kate slept fitfully, waking to listen if her father needed her and then realising he didn't any more. She would then sigh and cuddle down again. Consequently, the next morning she felt slightly better for the longer sleep. The undertakers came to lay Mr Elliss in his coffin, which was then placed in the front parlour, as was the custom, so that any mourners could visit before the funeral on the third day. William went in to see that all was right and as it should be but Kate stayed away and at Matty's suggestion she went for a walk in the nearby park. How good it was to be in the fresh air, which felt soft and healing, and as she took deep breaths the smell of death was replaced by the delicate scents of flowers. As she walked back to the house she felt more relaxed and better than she had done for a long time.

Later, Kate and William went through the house finding anything they could of value, which could be sold if necessary. There were some silver snuff boxes and card cases, also rings which were heavy and ugly but set with rubies and other precious stones. Kate couldn't think she would have use for these and so placed them in a large bag to take to be sold in the future. She found some money in her father's desk and papers relating to the house but nothing more. There were no safe or secret drawers. After the funeral she would have to ask Mr Fawcett about the money her father had in the bank. If he wasn't helpful, she would have to go there herself, which a young lady should not do, but perhaps William could accompany her, which would make it less shocking.

The day previous to the funeral dawned and Matty thought Kate was looking a lot better and told her so. 'I suppose a more restful sleep and walks in the fresh air help to clear my mind and I am more relaxed. Thank you for your support, dear Matty.' Kate placed her arms around her. 'If I hadn't you and William, I don't think I could have managed.'

'I'm pleased we were here, dear, to help you. Things will be better now, you'll see.' Matty smiled at her and patted her hand.

They sat down to an early evening meal. Kate had long ago foregone the privilege of dining alone as she usually helped with the cooking anyway. It was easier to eat with Matty and William in the kitchen and good to have company, too. They had nearly finished when they heard the doorknocker being applied with vigour.

'Gracious, whoever can that be?' asked Matty.

Chapter Two

'OH, DEAR,' gasped Kate, moving her chair back, 'someone's in a hurry.'

'It's all right, Miss Kate. Finish your meal, I'll go,' said William, pushing his chair back and getting to his feet, then treading slowly to the front door.

As he opened it a voice said, 'Oh, there you are.' The man who stood there was tall, wearing a black cloak and hat. 'Tell me where my man can stable the horses and coach,' he said abruptly.

William took his time and looked at him. Then he said: 'I'm sorry, sir, but there isn't any room, and what name shall I give Miss Elliss?'

'Tell her it is her brother and I need to know…'

'I will ask, sir,' William interrupted and walked slowly back to the kitchen.

'Who is it?' asked Kate sharply, as she saw the expression on Will's face.

'It's your brother, Miss, asking where he can stable his coach and horses.'

'Daniel? Oh, no, not now.' She pulled herself together. 'Right,' she admonished herself, 'you will be strong and hold your own, *not* weak.' With a determined look on her face and taking a deep breath, she went to the door to meet her brother. When she saw him, she said as acidly as she could: 'Good gracious, it is you. What are you doing here after all these years?'

'Never mind that,' Daniel said, with no smile on his face. 'Where does the coachman take the…?'

Kate interrupted. 'He can take them to wherever you will be staying. There is no room here.'

'But we shall be staying here, of course,' said Daniel, 'and why we are talking on the doorstep, I don't know. Fanny is in the coach and in need of...'

'Oh dear, she hasn't come as well, has she?' asked Kate, not hiding her distaste.

'Look, can we come inside and discuss what is to be done?'

After a pause, Kate said: 'Very well, you may enter the morning room but you are not staying here, either of you.'

Daniel returned to the coach and helped Fanny down, a lady in her late thirties and now dressed in funereal black.

Kate was thinking that she expected Mr Fawcett had let Daniel know about his father's death. But why? Had something been left to Daniel in the will and was Mr Fawcett being over zealous in letting him know? Did he think a little money on the side might be possible? Kate's thoughts were interrupted as Fanny came up the steps. She looked at Kate and said: 'Oh my dear Kate. How sorry I was to hear the news. He must have suffered so.'

'Not as much as I did,' thought Kate but she said nothing and stood back, ignoring her. She indicated the morning room and noticed as Fanny entered that a look of disapproval crossed her face as she sat on one of the chairs. Everything, as Kate knew, was shabby and in need of replacing, but as she hadn't had the time, money or inclination, she hadn't bothered about it. It was also decidedly chilly in spite of the spring sunshine outside.

Daniel stood, saying: 'The horses cannot be kept standing for long, so can we come to some arrangement?'

'There is no arrangement to come to,' said Kate quickly. 'You haven't been here for at least ten years. You never came near your father in all that time or contacted me. I have had to cope all on my own. So now it is all over, do not think to come in here demanding stabling for your horses and accommodation for yourselves.'

'I would have thought...' began Daniel huffily.

'Thought?' interrupted Kate crossly, 'That's been always the trouble. You never think.'

'Never mind, dear,' said Fanny, 'we don't want to be any trouble but if you show us a bedroom, we can easily make the bed between us. And do I smell dinner cooking?' She smiled sweetly.

'Well, of course, if you want a room with dust all over it and unaired bed linen, I'm sure you're welcome. But as far as dinner is concerned, it is all over and finished. We keep country hours here. There wouldn't have been enough anyway, we only cook for three people.' And if that doesn't deter them from staying, I don't know what will, Kate thought.

'So who are the three?' enquired Daniel, a gleam in his eye.

'The two servants, Matty and Will, who have always been here. You will remember them, I expect,' said Kate.

'Well, there you are. What is all the fuss about? They can prepare us a room…'

'Daniel, they will do no such thing at their age. And you are not ordering things as you want them. Just go and find a hotel, you had better not keep your horses waiting any longer.'

'Very well,' said Daniel, drawing himself up to his full height. 'Come, Fanny, we know when we're not wanted. But before we go, where is Papa?'

'In the front parlour. You may visit on your way out.'

At last the front door closed and Kate sat down. Her knees trembled and she felt sick. She didn't know whether to swear, which would relieve her feelings but would be unladylike, or to burst into tears. She did the latter as she was tired and not used to having to stand up to someone whilst in such a vulnerable state. If only her brother had been loving and sympathetic to her, she would have felt different. But why would he be? He had never been so before. She supposed she had taken the burden of looking after both parents and running the house on her shoulders and now she could do with some loving care and attention herself. 'But you are not going to get it,' Kate told herself sadly.

There was a tap on the door. It opened and Matty appeared. 'Are you all right, Miss Kate?' Then seeing her mopping her eyes she went to her and folded her into her arms. 'Shush, everything will be well, you'll see. You didn't expect your brother to be of any help, did you? Anyway, he's gone now, so we can be by ourselves again.' She went on talking until the sobs subsided and eventually Kate looked up with a watery smile.

'Thank you, dear Matty. I suppose it was just that I was disappointed he wasn't kinder to me.'

The following morning, Kate, looking heavy eyed, was up early, having slept fitfully. She found a blue grey dress, the only subdued one in her collection suitable for the solemn occasion. She hadn't enough money to buy a new one or the time to shop for anything black, but no one had visited all the time she had nursed her father so they wouldn't bother to come now. If they did, Matty could take a message. No one, apart from Mr Fawcett, Daniel and Fanny would see her so she wasn't bothered whether they approved of her dress or not.

While the men went to the funeral, Kate, Fanny and Matty sat in the kitchen. Fanny, decked out in her deepest black, looked out of place and felt it. She had asked if they could sit somewhere else, to which Kate had said she could sit anywhere in the house she liked but Matty and herself would stay in the kitchen. So she had sat with them thinking that being with servants was so very degrading. Also, when she learnt that only wine and macaroons were to be served to the mourners on their return, she protested.

'If you are so concerned,' said Kate forthrightly, 'you should have done something about it. How did I know you and Daniel were coming anyway? Incidentally, how did you know about Papa?'

'Mr Fawcett wrote to Daniel, of course.'

'I see,' said Kate, not at all pleased.

The front door knocker sounded. 'I'll go,' said Matty. 'I expect the mourners have returned.'

Kate stood up.

'Thank goodness,' said Fanny, 'now we can sit in another room and meet dear Mr Fawcett again.' She sailed out, all smiles, to greet the gentlemen and Kate was left to follow as though she was nobody.

Evidently, according to Daniel, the service and internment had been in order. He had thanked the vicar who said he would call on them during the following week. Fanny welcomed Mr Fawcett with smiles and an outstretched hand. Kate cut short her words by saying loudly: 'Good morning, Mr Fawcett, please come inside,' to which he bowed and followed the ladies into the morning room. Will and Matty hovered in the hall, not knowing whether they were to be included at the will reading or not, but Kate turned to them with a smile and said: 'Yes, do come in, Mr and Mrs Stokes.'

Mr Fawcett looked surprised but said nothing.

Glasses of wine were handed round by Kate and, as Mr Fawcett took his place at the table; everyone took their seat there too.

Mr Fawcett cleared his throat and said: 'This will not take long.' He took out papers from his case, cleared his throat again and began to read. 'This is the last will and testament of Abraham Elliss.' His voice droned on until he came to the important part for those listening. 'To my youngest son, Daniel, I leave my house and any money I have left on the understanding that he will look after my only daughter, Katherine. To my other sons I leave nothing.'

There was silence. Daniel had a smile on his face and Fanny looked round, very pleased with herself. But Kate was as white as a sheet. She couldn't believe her ears. All her hard work over the years evidently had meant nothing. Even if everything had been divided between Daniel and herself, she wouldn't have complained. Matty's cold hand crept onto hers. Kate managed to look at Mr Fawcett.

'Is that all?' she asked baldly.

'Yes, Miss Elliss.'

'So am I to understand that everything I have done for all these years counts as nothing and I am to be my brother's pensioner?'

'Er – I'm afraid so, Miss Elliss,' said Mr Fawcett.

'And what about Mr and Mrs Stokes, who have worked for years for my parents? Are they not mentioned?'

'No, Miss Elliss.'

'In that case, Daniel, I think you should settle a considerable sum on them out of your own pocket.'

Fanny gasped. 'Why should he? He hasn't known them!' she said.

'Yes, but I have and as I haven't been left anything it is up to Daniel to make all right.'

'Oh,' said Daniel, with a laugh, 'I don't think Papa expected that of me.'

'No, he wouldn't,' said Kate, her temper starting to rise, 'but I thought you'd have some finer feelings, even if he never had any.'

'Well, really!' began Fanny.

'Oh, be quiet,' snapped Kate. 'May I see the will, Mr Fawcett, please?' She held out her hand imperatively.

Mr Fawcett shrugged. 'I suppose so – if you can read it,' he smirked. As he offered her the papers she was so cross that she snatched them from him. She read the document but unfortunately it was all too true. It was just as the lawyer had read. The house and money were left to Daniel.

As she handed the will back she said, 'While Mr Fawcett is here I shall make this statement. In no way will I be beholden to my brother Daniel. I will not live with him or be at his beck and call. He hasn't worried one jot about me during the last ten years so I don't need him now. And if he hasn't the common decency to give something to Mr and Mrs Stokes, I just don't want to know him. Come.' She moved away from the table with a nod to Matty and Will to follow her to the door.

'But Kate,' called Daniel, 'what will you do? Where will you go?'

Kate turned and looked at her brother with scorn, then shocked everyone by saying: 'Like you, I don't bloody care!'

She turned and marched out of the room, followed by gasps from those left behind.

It was some time later that Daniel entered the kitchen. If Kate had expected him to knock, she was disappointed. She sat at the table, her chin resting on her steepled fingers. Daniel cleared his throat but Kate didn't move. She had nothing more to say to him and it was pointless discussing things any further. She felt disappointed, unwanted, unloved and above all, used.

'Fanny and I are going now,' Daniel said. 'We have decided to return in about two week's time when we shall assess what needs doing to the house and its refurbishment. Your rude remarks we will ignore. You can have which room you choose, of course, but as we shall eventually need to present our daughters to society we shall have to accommodate their wishes too.' He paused, then said with what he thought was to be a conciliatory gesture: 'You will be a great help to them, you know.'

Still Kate stared before her, giving no indication she had heard him. All she wanted was for him to go and not see him or his family ever again. Daniel felt out of his depth. He didn't know how to handle this wall of silence. He just shrugged and said: 'We're going now.' There was no answer or movement from Kate so he turned and left. A few minutes later the front door slammed shut, echoing through the house and making Kate wince. She buried her head in her arms and sobbed.

Some minutes later Matty entered the kitchen, saying: 'We heard the door... oh, Miss Kate what is it?' She sat next to her at the table and placed a comforting arm around her.

Between her sobs Kate said: 'Daniel has gone. He is coming back in two weeks' time to take over the house. Oh, Matty what are we to do? I cannot stay here if they are here. I really can't.'

'No, dear, of course you can't, but have you any idea where you can go? Any other relations or...'

Kate shook her head. 'Well, then,' went on Matty, 'Will and I have been thinking what we can do and I shall write to my sister to see if she can help us. She lives alone in a little village in Hertfordshire. Shall I ask if you can come too? We could stay there until we find somewhere else to go, couldn't we?'

'Oh, Matty, how could I? There wouldn't be room for three extra people. You go, of course, but...'

'Miss Kate, we are not leaving you. We could manage for a few days anyway. Emma, my sister, is out most of the time, I think, as she works in a large house somewhere.'

'But what about money? I have a little but...'

'Will said he'd try and sell those things of your Pa's which you found, so that will be a help for a start. Also, Will said, Mr Fawcett said only the house was left to your brother and not the contents. So any of those you could sell. If you let Will know what you want him to do about this, he'll do his best.'

'Perhaps there would be enough money for you to have,' said Kate.

'Don't worry about that at the moment. Let us see how much we can sell your things for first. Shall we have another look round and see what there is?'

Kate dried her eyes, took a deep breath and followed Matty round the house. They found the desk, which her father had used. It was a good solid piece of oak, also his chair. A harpsichord was pushed into one corner and Kate ran her fingers lovingly over the discoloured keys. 'This was Mama's, you know. Her Papa gave it to her. She played it when my Papa went out, as he never liked music. She taught me to play a little when I was young.' Kate smiled as she ran her fingers over it again. 'This could be sold, I suppose. I can't take it with me, can I?' she said sadly.

Kate noted down the furniture that was special, including a country long cased clock and the mahogany dining table and chairs. It was suggested that Will would find someone from a reputable second hand shop to come and view the furniture, take it away and hopefully pay a reasonable price for it.

'Matty?' asked Kate, 'do you think that Will would take me to Child's Bank tomorrow to see if the manager can help me? I don't know if any money is still there but it would be worth a try. Then we could see where it would be best to sell our items.'

'He will take you wherever you wish to go, Miss Kate, you know that. Shall we say that is what you will do tomorrow, and I will write a note to my sister. She is very obliging and will help us, I'm sure. It will all sort itself out, you'll see.' Kate sighed. She certainly hoped so.

The next morning, visiting the Bank, however, was a waste of time as the manager stated that Mr Fawcett had written to him saying the money would be held until Mr Daniel Elliss would let him know if he wished to take over the account. When Kate asked how much money there was, he said unpleasantly that was for him to discuss only with Mr Elliss.

Kate and Will went to the silversmiths next and then the jewellers, where they fared slightly better and managed to negotiate reasonable prices for the pieces they had brought. Will said he would deal with the furniture problem so Kate thankfully returned home.

'Well,' said Kate later as they sat round the kitchen table, 'at least there is a little money for us to begin with. We shall have to book our seats on the stagecoach, I suppose, as that will be the cheapest way to travel to Hertfordshire, and we shall need some food and then for you...'

Matty interrupted. 'Miss Kate, why don't you keep the money for the present? You'll have to pay for our journey. Then when we get to my sister's, we'll find out the situation and go from there. You keep it all safe until it's needed.'

'Yes, Matty, thank you, but I do want you and Will to have something. I intend to find work of some kind so I shall certainly give you some then, I promise.'

'That's all settled, then,' said Matty, trying to sound positive so as not to worry Kate.

Chapter Three

IT WASN'T UNTIL THE MIDDLE of the second week that Kate, Matty and Will found themselves packed and ready to leave London at an early hour. Matty had received a reply from her sister saying she would be delighted to see them again, and poor Miss Elliss too. The accommodation would be no problem, which cheered Kate as she didn't want to be a burden to anyone. No doubt, in time she could find some work and then she would perhaps buy a small cottage of her own. With these vague plans in mind and hoping the future would be a happier one, Kate left her home of twenty-eight years without a backward glance.

They were to travel by public stagecoach, which was the cheapest way possible, but before they arrived at the coaching inn Will visited Mr Fawcett's office, where he left the keys to the house. He gave them to a clerk working at the desk, telling him that Mr Fawcett would know about them and he could hand them over to the new tenant who would call for them in due course. Probably, Will thought, Mr Daniel Elliss would be expecting the house to be made ready for his arrival and that Miss Kate, for all her bravado of saying she would not be there, would be waiting meekly for him. What a pleasing thought that he would be so wrong. It was with a satisfied smile on his face that he joined his wife and Miss Kate.

Kate had never been on a stagecoach before but it wasn't long before she vowed to herself that she would never do so again. At first it was a slow journey as the London streets were busy with the usual horses and carts, street vendors and people hurrying to and fro, laughing, shouting and blocking the roads, but eventually this was all left behind and a more rural scene took its place. It was then the coachman whipped up his horses, resulting in the coach swaying from side to side and bouncing up and down over the rough roads. All the occupants of the coach, which included besides themselves two plump ladies with baskets full of shopping and a thin gentleman who continually sniffed, hung on for dear life. At least Kate couldn't think about anything else while she concentrated on not being thrown off the seat. Eventually the pace slackened and everyone felt better but this was only while the turnpike was negotiated and then they were off once more. Eventually the passengers were able to alight when a coaching inn was reached, where the horses were changed and refreshments could be taken. Will went into the inn and brought Kate and Matty some lemonade, which they drank gratefully. Will, of course, had ale. After ten minutes they were back on the coach as the coachman said he had to keep to time. There was not much opportunity to see the countryside as they had to concentrate on holding on but eventually they reached Hertfordshire and, as the horses slackened speed, Kate had a chance to see that springtime had arrived here too and everywhere was looking fresh and green.

As they drew up into the inn yard, Matty said: 'Thank goodness we haven't any further to go. My insides are all shaken. Are you all right, Miss Kate?'

Kate, feeling quite sickly, managed to smile and say: 'Yes, Matty, thank you. It's nice to be in the air, though, isn't it? What time is it, do you know?'

Will came up just then. He had been sorting out their baggage before the coach went on its way. 'It's late afternoon and we could do with something to eat. What about it, Miss Kate?'

'Will, I'm so churned up I don't think I could, but I would like a drink.'

While Kate and Matty stayed with their things, Will went inside and found some drinks as before. 'Now we wait for the cart,' said Matty.

'Oh?' said Kate.

'Em is sending someone over to take us to the village. It isn't far. Ashleigh should be looking pretty this time of year,' began Matty, conversationally. 'From what I can remember, as it's a few years since I visited, it is small but pretty, with some Elizabethan houses and more modern ones too, of course. The church is dedicated to St. Peter and is quite old. There is the green and some little shops. What else is there, Will?'

'There's the Old Bull,' said Will.

'Miss Kate isn't interested in that,' sniffed Matty.

'No, but I am,' Will grinned.

Ignoring him, Matty went on: 'Em lives in a house near to the church and she works ... Will, what is the place called where Em works?'

'It's just known as The Hall.'

'Oh, yes, that's right. It is away from the village, though. Em's been there quite a while.'

'Who lives there?' asked Kate, not really wanting to know but trying to be polite as she knew Matty was trying to take her mind off things.

Matty shrugged. 'I don't really know, no one of importance, I think.'

No more was said but Kate wondered that if there was only The Hall and a small village, there wouldn't be very much work to be had and if there was, the local people would expect to be employed. Still, perhaps she could travel a little further afield. However, it was no use worrying until she knew more. No doubt Matty's sister would be able to suggest something.

The cart arrived and it wasn't long before Kate and Matty were sitting on the wooden seats facing one another with their baggage stacked between them, while Will sat with the driver. He was a friendly man of about fifty, who looked as though he worked on the land. The cart was reasonably clean but as they bowled along the track to the village Kate wondered if her stomach would be ever normal again.

The village of Ashleigh looked calm and pretty in the spring sunshine and the cart slowed down and eventually stopped at the end of a row of charming small houses. Their gardens showed signs of new growth, with early flowers mixed in with the large leaves of the remaining winter cabbages and the ungainly bush of rosemary. Emma Moss must have been watching from the window, as the door opened immediately and there stood a little lady with her arms outstretched as Matty approached, her face wreathed in smiles. They embraced, chattering all the time.

'We shan't be able to get a word in edgeways,' said Will quietly to Kate as they slowly went up the garden path. Emma gave a little curtsey to Kate and said, 'Welcome, my dear. Do come inside. You must be shaken to bits travelling like you have and nothing to eat. We must do something about that, you know, but come inside and take off your cloak and bonnet and make yourself at home and we'll see what we can do.'

'Thank you, but it is quite all right, really it is,' said Kate smiling. 'I would just like…'

'To go to your room. Of course. Come with me.' She led the way up a small flight of stairs. 'I've put you in the little room at the back of the house overlooking the garden where it is quiet. I expect you're used to a bigger room but I hope you will be comfortable. If there's anything you want, let me know. I may not have thought of everything.' She then whisked herself out of the room, leaving Kate to sit down on the little bed feeling somewhat dazed.

For a time she just sat there, hoping her stomach would settle and now also her mind. Mrs Moss, for all her small size, was a little overpowering but it was a wonderful welcome and no doubt she had been nervous at having a stranger in her home. Kate thought, eventually, all would be well and she felt that after all those years spent in London she would find this was an entirely different life. She still sat on the bed; it was soft and smelled of lavender. She decided to stretch out on it for a few minutes to help calm her aching body and her pounding head. The pillow was cool and soft. She closed her eyes, gave a sigh of relief and fell fast asleep.

She was awakened some time later by Matty, who tapped on the door and opened it slightly. 'Miss Kate, are you all right?'

Kate opened sleepy eyes. 'Oh, oh, yes. I'm sorry, the bed was so comfortable I fell asleep. Thank you. I feel much better.'

'I did look in earlier but didn't like to disturb you. Em has prepared a meal for us. Would you like to come down or…?'

'Of course I'll come down, how kind your sister is. Could I just wash my face and tidy myself first?'

'There's no need to rush, dear,' Matty said as she closed the door.

Kate looked out of the window. Unlike London, all was quiet, and the back garden, which her window overlooked, was neat and tidy and would no doubt be full of colour later when the flowers bloomed. There was an apple tree just starting to show its leaves, beneath which stood a wooden seat. How lovely it would be, when the sun shone, to sit there, Kate thought. And for the first time in weeks she smiled and her spirits began to lift.

When Kate appeared downstairs, she found an appetising aroma drifting in from the kitchen. 'Mm, something smells good,' she said, as Matty appeared in the doorway.

'Come and sit down,' Matty said, leading the way into a small dining room. She indicated a chair. 'Will you be all right there, Miss Kate?'

'Yes, thank you, but why is the table set for three people only?'

'Well, Em had to go to The Hall,' said Matty as she disappeared once more into the kitchen. She came back again with Will, carrying dishes of oxtail soup, chicken in a butter sauce and a simple salamagrundy, which was a salad mixture of vegetables, hard boiled eggs and pickles. William and Matty sat down, and when they all had their plates of food in front of them, Kate asked why Emma had to go to The Hall.

'She has to feed the staff there. There aren't many at the moment as it is a skeleton staff, as the owner isn't in residence. They are eating the same as us, I expect,' said Matty, tucking in to her food.

'Oh, I see. But when will she be back? Won't it be dark by then?'

'She has a room there if she needs it. It has worked out quite well, really, as there are only two bedrooms here, you see. She will be back with us again during tomorrow morning, I expect.'

'Oh, dear,' said Kate. 'Have I caused problems for her? I really am sorry, Matty. It's like turning someone out of their home.'

'Nonsense. She said it would be all right for a while until we sort ourselves out. It's only temporary, isn't it? Besides, she said before she went that now she had seen you she's had an idea.'

'Really? Did she say what about?'

'No,' said Matty, 'but I think it was in the way of work you could do, if you wished to, of course.'

'Sounds intriguing,' said Kate, with a smile.

She went to bed that night in an optimistic frame of mind, wondering what Emma's thoughts were. She would find that out in the morning. She felt better for the food, of course, and she had met with kindness and was free of the drudge and worry that she had previously known. Daniel wasn't aware of her whereabouts either, thank goodness. She stretched and smiled to herself. A new life was about to begin. What a pity she wasn't eight years younger – but she told herself she would make up for those lost years somehow.

Next day Emma came back home. She looked tired, Kate thought, and wondered why, but when she found out that she had cooked the breakfast at The Hall and left everything neat and tidy before walking back home, she felt this wasn't surprising. At the earliest opportunity Kate said: 'Mrs Moss, I feel responsible for you being so tired as I've taken your bedroom. Can something be arranged so that you are not walking to and from The Hall all the time? I don't know your arrangements, of course, but…'

Emma smiled at her. 'You are very caring about others, aren't you? No wonder Matty and Will stood by you all that time. Now, Matty told me how you wish to find some work you can do and I wondered if you could take on mine at The Hall?'

'Take on your work at The Hall? But I couldn't, I mean you are a cook and – and besides what would you do?'

'Come and sit at the table, and if you don't object, Matty and Will can join us too and I will explain.'

When the four of them were seated, Emma began. 'The Hall is a reasonable sized house set in parkland, which is not extensive but there are lawns and fruit trees and vegetables. It is very pleasant. The owner, Mr Sheldon, lives in London most of the year. He usually comes here in the summer for a short time and his nieces visit occasionally from up north. Otherwise there is just a few staff to keep the place going. There's Mrs Sharpe, the housekeeper, and the butler, Mr Figgis, and a young boy, Tommy, who runs errands and things. Old George from the village looks after the vegetable garden and has the occasional meal. Two girls from the village also go in twice a week to keep the rooms clean, just in case Mr Sheldon might take it in his head to visit. But he has never done so yet except in summer since I've been there, and that's quite a few years.'

'And when this Mr Sheldon does visit, what happens then?' asked Kate.

'Well, he brings his secretary with him and his valet, and, of course, his coachmen. So there are about another six mouths to feed.'

'And more when he has visitors,' said Kate.

'Yes, but it's not often and if you wanted help I'm always here.'

'But what will you do, Mrs Moss? I mean, how will you manage money wise? I would be quite happy to give you and Matty some of what I earn if I could do the work but…'

'No, no, dear, how kind you are, but if you feel you could cook satisfactorily I shall be able to go and work for our dear vicar. He always wanted me to go and cook for him and look after him, you know. Perhaps Matty could help me out with some housework there and I would be next to my little house, wouldn't I? It would be so much easier for me to go home when I wanted to. Will could always help somewhere in the village, I'm sure. So what do you say, Miss Kate, will you give it a try?'

'Well, what can I say, you've been so kind to have thought it all out. I will try my best but, please, if I am not good enough, please, please, tell me. I would be so embarrassed if Mr Sheldon came and I couldn't reach your standards.'

'How would it be if I showed you the recipes I use for us, the servants, who are there now, and when you can work confidently for them, we can go further with more elaborate meals. They don't have to be too involved, though, as Mr Sheldon, thank the lord, doesn't like too much rich food.'

'Well, I hope I can learn quickly,' said Kate with a sigh.

'You have cooked a little back in London, Miss Kate, haven't you?' said Matty. 'I'm sure you have a basic knowledge.'

'I can only try. What worries me, though, is can I just take over from you eventually, Mrs Moss, without telling anyone? I mean, we surely have to let someone know that you're leaving and have someone come to see if I'm suitable?'

'Well, yes, but I thought if you tried it first for the present staff, under my guidance, of course, we don't have to tell anyone. Then, later, if you wish to stay, Mr Figgis will write to Mr Sheldon's secretary and he will deal with your appointment. But let us see how you get on first, shall we? My bedchamber there is very nice, too. It's quiet and you would be most comfortable in it.'

So it was agreed that Kate went to The Hall to be introduced to the staff. She and Emma took the path from the village and then through the park, and when Kate saw the house she stopped and gasped. 'Oh,' she said, 'isn't it beautiful?' She saw before her a three storey William and Mary house, built in the previous century. It stood looking proud and glowing in the sunshine surrounded by swathes of green lawn and trees against a backdrop of blue sky.

Emma looked at her. 'Oh, the house,' she said offhandedly. 'Now come along.' Kate's spirits lifted. To work in such a house must be wonderful. She found the staff a little wary of her and she wondered why, but when she was alone for a short while with Mrs Sharpe, the housekeeper, she realised that Emma had told them that she had been mistress of her own house in London.

'Mrs Sharpe,' Kate said to the rather angular lady with bony features sitting opposite her in the kitchen, 'I expect Mrs Moss has told you of my changed circumstances. So please could I ask you to treat me as you would any cook. I am Miss Elliss or you can call me Kate if you prefer. And can I please ask you questions when I'm not sure of things, also where I'm allowed to go and where not. I mean to try very hard with the cooking. This is a beautiful kitchen, isn't it?'

Mrs Sharpe smiled and seemed to relax. 'Yes, it's a lovely house and I will show you over it if you wish to stay. If you're not sure of anything, please ask and I will help if I can. When we are by ourselves we usually assemble in the kitchen for meals and often sit here afterwards. Otherwise, Mr Figgis and I have our own rooms.'

'It all sounds very homely,' said Kate, with a smile. 'It also occurs to me that I shall have to wear something different, but no doubt Mrs Moss will advise me.'

Kate met Mr Figgis next who was a stately gentleman in his late fifties and no doubt would be friendly when he had known her longer. The preliminaries over, Kate was shown the large larder where the food and dishes were. She was given an apron and she received her first lesson from Emma on cooking lunch for five people, which included Tommy, the young odd job boy.

That night, tucked into her bed at Emma's, Kate was pleasantly tired. She had shown that she could cook with Emma's help and knew she would improve. In fact, she told herself she was determined to be the best cook possible. She would show Daniel Elliss that his sister was capable of running her own life and was not beholden to him in any way. On the other hand she hoped she never set eyes on him ever again. One person she did hope to please was the as yet unknown Mr Sheldon. She wondered what he was like. Emma said he was living in London and visited The Hall very rarely. Perhaps he didn't like journeys and he was an elderly man. How wonderful if he had been the handsome, fair haired, blue eyed young man in her dreams of youth and who in her imagination loved her and swept her off her feet! She sighed. She knew it would never happen now. She wasn't young any more and she had a living to earn, she told herself. She was soon asleep, but with a smile on her lips.

Chapter Four

BROOK STREET was situated in the most fashionable and desirable part of London in which to live – that is, of course, if you had plenty of money. It was well away from the odours and sounds of everyday life that emanated from other less salubrious parts of the city and usually it was quiet, with only the sound of carriages rattling over the cobbles and the snorting and clip clop of horses to disturb the peace. The houses were large and well built with mews behind, and were not far from Hyde Park and Westminster.

On this particular morning in one of those houses, Mr Laurence Ward had received a letter. He usually had many bills, business letters and papers of one sort or another to deal with but this one, he thought, merited a consultation with his employer. At the age of twenty-four he was secretary to Mr Alexander Sheldon and felt himself lucky to have such a prestigious position at so young an age. Mr Sheldon was a well-known figure in society and he could have chosen anyone. It had come about when his father, Hugh, had died just as Laurence had finished his schooling, leaving his widow to bring up the four younger children as best she could. Mr Sheldon had been Hugh's friend, and had kindly offered the position of secretary to Laurence, as he was in urgent need of employment. He had been overjoyed to take it as he had always admired Mr Sheldon, and he had been initiated into the work by the previous secretary who was leaving for a higher position elsewhere. Laurence had to cope with the various problems that arose but he found that Mr Sheldon was patient with him when he was asked any questions, and didn't lose his temper when, as was inevitable, he made mistakes. Now, this morning, Laurence left his office to find his employer before he departed to join his friend, Sir Michael Forest, on a riding expedition. After looking in several rooms, he found Mr Sheldon at last in the library. He was busy turning the pages of a book on ancient writing which he had purchased the previous day.

Laurence saw before him a tall, broad shouldered man in his late thirties with dark hair neatly tied back. He dressed well and at the moment was ready for riding. As always, the cut of his coat was superb, fashioned by a leading tailor, and the material was of the very best quality. He wore no lace, fobs or jewellery, apart from a signet ring, and he certainly never used powder or patches. He considered these things were not for a man of his size, but for all that he was the epitome of an elegant gentleman. Laurence knew that he was also someone to whom friends could turn in times of trouble, and those brown eyes under their dark brows could look warm and friendly, but he could as easily give a heavy set down if you were unfortunate enough to get on the wrong side of him, when those same eyes turned to dark chips of obsidium.

As his secretary came into the room, Alexander looked enquiringly at him. 'Yes, Laurie, what is it?' He had a pleasant, rich voice and on occasions he had been known to sing.

'Mr Sheldon,' said Laurence, 'I think I should go to Hertfordshire next week.'

Amusement shone in Alex's eyes. 'Oh? You think you need a vacation or that a change of scenery would be nice, or…'

'No, no, sir,' Laurie interrupted. 'Sorry, I began badly. I've had a letter from Mr Figgis and…'

'Who the devil is Mr Figgis?'

'He works at The Hall, sir,' said Laurie, looking puzzled.

'Oh, that Mr Figgis.'

'Yes, sir,' said Laurie, frowning. 'Is there another one, then, sir?'

Alex's lips twitched. 'Somewhere, I expect, but what has this Mr Figgis got to say?'

'That there is a change of staff and I should go and…'

'Surely they can deal with it. Mrs – er – Hatchet Face is up to that, isn't she?'

'Sir, do you mean Mrs Sharpe, the housekeeper? She is a very nice lady, sir, and…'

'I'm sure she is but she is decidedly hatchet faced.'

Laurie sighed. Mr Sheldon was in one of his funning moods, evidently, and he would leave without getting an answer unless he persevered. 'Please be serious, sir,' he said.

'I am serious. What I want to know is why there is a need for you to trouble yourself about a change of staff?' He lifted a dark eyebrow.

'Well, sir, it is the cook, Mrs Moss. She wants to leave but she has found a replacement.'

'Ah, the cook. That is different, isn't it? We don't want to be poisoned, do we?'

'No, sir, but I don't suppose it's as bad as that. Also Mrs Moss has been at The Hall for some time now.'

'Ah, I see. Write a letter to her for me to sign, thanking her for her - er -wonderful meals over the years. Then see the new candidate and taste his or her cooking. I'll leave it to you to employ them or not but remember although I don't visit The Hall very often, we do entertain when we are there.'

'Yes, sir.'

'If he or she is no good, say so. When will you go?'

'Two days next week, sir, when you have nothing of importance in your diary and when you don't require my services.'

'Everything I do is of importance and I always need you, Laurie.'

'Of course, sir,' said Laurie, keeping a straight face.

'You have my authority to engage the new cook or not. If there is no one there when we go later in the year, we can always take Pierre from here…'

'He wouldn't like that, sir,' Laurie broke in quickly. 'I mean, being French and…'

'No, I suppose not,' said Alex, rapidly losing interest. 'How difficult everything is.'

'Yes, sir. And do you want me for anything else today?'

'No, I don't think so. Why?'

'I need to visit the shops for various items of clothing and…'

'Ah, yes, by all means, Laurie, by all means. Perhaps the new cook will be young and beautiful and…'

'I doubt it, sir. They never are.'

'Look at the time,' said Alex, glancing at the ormolu clock on the mantelpiece. 'I must go. Sir Michael will be waiting.'

'Will his daughter be with him, sir?' asked Laurie, giving him an innocent look.

'Oh, God, I hope not,' said Alex as he left the room.

Alas, Alexander's fears were realised. Although he had enjoyed riding in Sir Michael's company, he hadn't expected his wife and daughter were to join them. Lady Forest had taken every opportunity to keep her daughter in Alex's view. He wouldn't have minded if she had been a beauty but the poor girl wasn't even attractive and only nineteen anyway. Towards the end of their ride Sir Michael suggested the gentlemen galloped ahead, and when at a safe distance, he apologised profusely for his wife's actions and promised it wouldn't happen again.

Alex returned to his house sometime later, in not quite such a sunny mood. He was met by his butler, who took one look at his master's dark face and tactfully suggested that he should bring wine to the library immediately. He also sent a message to the kitchen to Pierre to prepare something especially tasty for Mr Sheldon's evening meal.

Alex drank his wine and relaxed with a book until his mood improved. Then, after a delicious meal consisting of beef cooked in Pierre's special way, he began to feel much better and decided to visit his club for a while and meet his friends over a game of cards, and depending on his mood afterwards, perhaps visit one of his lady friends.

Laurie set forth on his journey to Hertfordshire the following Wednesday morning. He had sent a reply to Mr Figgis's letter, telling him of his arrival on that day, and as it was a mild and sunny one Laurie sat back in the carriage ready to enjoy his journey and his brief stay in Ashleigh. He was travelling by himself in a hired conveyance, which was paid for, of course, by Mr Sheldon. Although it wasn't as comfortable as a private carriage, it was the next best thing and certainly a far cry from the stagecoach that poor Kate, Matty and Will had had to use. Laurie had packed his clothes, including his new ones, and he also had the letter he had written for Mrs Moss, which Mr Sheldon had signed, and some money for her as a thank you for her past services. Laurie hoped the new cook was suitable, as he didn't relish the thought of telling her that she wasn't good enough. However, he could have a word with Mr Figgis before he interviewed her to gauge his reactions. After all, a lot rested on Laurie's decision. If Mr Sheldon wasn't pleased when he visited, Laurie's head would be on the block.

Laurie felt in a happy state of mind, as it was good to be out of London for a while and to breathe the fresh air of the countryside. He felt, too, that it wouldn't be long before Mr Sheldon would take this journey as he was showing signs of boredom, Laurie could tell. Mr Sheldon had plenty of friends, male and female, and he was a popular gentleman, being single and reasonably pleasant and charming if he chose to be. Also he had plenty of money. He was a hostess's dream but the despair of the matchmaking mamas. For the life of him Laurie couldn't think why he wasn't married. He certainly wouldn't be bored then, as Laurie knew, coming from a large family.

It was early afternoon before he was set down at the front door of The Hall. Mr Figgis was there to greet him and after Laurie had paid off the driver he followed Mr Figgis inside the house. Although much older than Laurie, Mr Figgis knew just how to talk to him, a mixture of respect as he was secretary to Mr Sheldon, and friendliness, as to a younger man. Laurie was shown to his usual room, after which he was taken to the dining room where a cold collation was set before him. When he had finished and was feeling much better for the food, he was taken by the servant who had waited on him to Mr Sheldon's study, where Mr Figgis joined him once more.

'I thought you could send for whosoever you wished to see, sir. I expect you have to interview the new cook and see Mrs Moss and...'

'Yes, I'll do that now as I'm expected back home tomorrow. So, Mr Figgis, what do you think to the new cook?'

'She is a very nice lady and her food is good as far as I'm concerned, but if you speak to Mrs Moss first she will explain things to you.'

'Very well. Is she available now?'

'Yes sir, of course.'

Mrs Moss came in, a little apprehensive, but Laurie held his hand out to her saying: 'How nice to see you again, Mrs Moss. Do please sit down.'

Emma smiled and sat facing Laurie across the desk. 'I hear you wish to leave us?' he said.

'Yes, sir. I'm getting old now and I have found a good replacement, I think. I did say that if there was a problem I could always be called upon as I live in the village, sir.'

'Well, first of all, Mr Sheldon has written this letter to you and charged me with the office of thanking you and presenting you with this for all your work at The Hall over the years.' He handed the letter and the purse of sovereigns to Emma, who thanked him rather shakily as all of a sudden she had become emotional. All she could do was smile through her tears and murmur 'How kind,' and 'Thank you,' and dab at her eyes with her handkerchief.

When Laurie thought she had recovered a little, he asked her about the new cook. 'In your opinion, is she good enough to cook for Mr Sheldon?'

'I believe so, sir. The staff are pleased with the food she cooks and I have shown her the type of food Mr Sheldon likes. If there is a problem, I'm near enough for her to contact me. But she is doing very well, sir.'

'What about when Mr Sheldon visits and invites his friends and neighbours to dinner? Will she be able to cope with quantity as well as quality, do you think?'

'I don't see why not. Two girls from the village are usually brought in to help.'

'Right, thank you. I will see her soon but perhaps I had better have a word with Mrs Sharpe, the housekeeper, first.'

Laurie stood and so did Emma. He shook her hand again, hoped she enjoyed her retirement and as she left, Mr Figgis appeared once more.

'I'll see Mrs Sharpe next, please.'

When Mrs Sharpe sat down, Laurie remembered Mr Sheldon calling her hatchet faced. He was wrong, Laurie thought, looking at her. Her face was long, it was true, but she was a pleasant looking lady for all that. Laurie had always thought that his employer had a small, unkind streak in him and wondered why. Laurie had found he was always pleasant to him, though.

'How are you, Mrs Sharpe?' he now asked.

'Very well, sir, thank you. Everything is as it should be.'

'How do you get on with the new cook?'.

'Miss Elliss? Oh, very well, sir. She doesn't mind being told if things are wrong and when I have a problem she helps me out too. We get along well, sir.'

'I'm pleased to hear it,' said Laurie, a little taken aback by this accolade.

'Yes, sir. The food she cooks for us is delicious, so I hope you and Mr Sheldon will agree with us. Do you know, sir, she decided to ask us, the staff, even including Tommy the boy that helps out, what our favourite dishes are, and then we have that dish at least once a week.'

'Oh, I see. And what dish did er - er Tommy ask for?' asked Laurie.

'Well, he's only a boy and not quite with it, you know, although he works well. He asked for jam tarts.' She smiled.

Laurie thought this new cook knew just how to keep everyone happy, evidently. A clever ploy. He thanked Mrs Sharpe and as she left said: 'Right, Mr Figgis. I will see Miss Elliss next.'

'Yes, sir.'

'By the way, Mr Figgis, what is your favourite dish that is cooked for you?'

'Oh, that, sir,' laughed Mr Figgis. 'Why, I like a good potted cheese, sir.'

When the new cook, Miss Elliss, came in, Laurie could hardly believe his eyes. He wasn't expecting anyone so young, attractive and elegant. Kate had come into the study dressed in her black skirt and white blouse with a demure cap over her red hair as befitted a cook. She had taken off her apron.

'You wish to see me, sir?' she asked, her greeny-blue eyes looking at Laurie seriously.

Laurie cleared his throat. 'Yes, please sit down.' He noticed she didn't just flop on to the chair but moved with grace as she sat. 'I have to ask you a few questions, you know, as you are new.'

'That's quite all right, sir,' she said.

'How do you like it here, and how do you get on with the rest of the staff?'

'Very well, thank you. They are all very kind and helpful.'

'Good, and do you feel competent cooking for Mr Sheldon and any friends he may invite?'

'I believe so, as long as I'm told in advance how many I'm required to prepare for.'

'Ah yes. If that isn't done it will be my fault.'

Miss Elliss smiled at him. She had a pretty smile, he thought. 'No doubt, between us, we can keep Mr Sheldon happy, then,' she said.

Laurie wondered if Mr Sheldon would be happy to employ such a pretty cook. Perhaps, though, it would be best if he didn't know. Laurie cleared his throat.

'Could I have your full name please,' he asked, as he drew a blank sheet of paper towards him.

'Katherine Elliss.'

'And is it Miss or...'

'Miss.'

'And would you mind telling me your age?'

'No. I'm twenty-eight years old.'

'And how long have you been a cook?'

This was a tricky one but Kate answered without a blush: 'I've always cooked but not professionally. This is the first time...'

'I see. I don't think I need ask anything else, thank you.' In fact, Laurie had felt quite uncomfortable asking the questions he had. Somehow it hadn't seemed right, although Miss Elliss hadn't made any demur about it. He felt he couldn't ask any more personal questions and wondered, as she was so well spoken, if she had fallen on hard times as she looked to be from a better class of family than the others. Fortunately, the few times Mr Sheldon came to The Hall, he seldom saw the staff other than Mr Figgis as he brought his own valet with him, and as long he was fed and comfortable he did as he pleased and troubled no one else, least of all taking interest in his staff. Anyway they were always 'below stairs,' apart from when the chambermaids went about their work, and not allowed in the rest of the house unless invited as today, when Laurie had been using Mr Sheldon's study. Otherwise they kept to their own quarters. So Laurie dismissed from his mind any more thoughts of the new cook, apart from sending her his compliments after he partook of his meal later in the day. As far as

Laurie was concerned, Miss Elliss could cook and fitted in well with the other staff, and that was all that was needed.

When he returned to London the next day, he felt he had checked everything with Mr Figgis so that all was in order whenever Mr Sheldon wished to visit.

Chapter Five

AFTER THE DEPARTURE of Mr Ward, the staff were summoned one by one to Mr Figgis's private room to receive their payment for the next six months. Kate joined the rest of the servants, and when it was her turn Mr Figgis said he was glad that Mr Ward was pleased with her cooking. Kate smiled and said she was relieved too, and pleased that her meals had earned his approval. She hoped Mr Sheldon would also be pleased.

'If Mr Ward says it is good, so will Mr Sheldon. Don't worry, Miss Kate, we are all enjoying you being here.'

Kate experienced a feeling of satisfaction. No one had ever complimented her as Mr Figgis had just done. Tears of pleasure came to her eyes. True, she was a servant now like the rest of them, but they were friendly and she was appreciated, which was something that had been lacking in her family life. Emma was delighted with her too, as Kate had fulfilled her expectations so now she could live comfortably in her own little home and look after the vicar of St. Peter's next door. Matty and Will still lived with her, but they helped her and were finding work around the village, which brought in a small wage.

During the day Kate was busy and she concentrated on her work so that she had no time to think of other things. But when she returned to her room for the night, other thoughts crept into her mind of what might have been. If only she had been able to sell the house and use the money for herself and Matty and Will, she could have had a much easier life. She sighed. Perhaps she was meant to be a menial and that was her role in life; a dismal thought. Then her usual fighting spirit told her it was all her father's and Daniel's fault. At this point, angry tears pricked her eyes, but she determinedly dashed them away and began to prepare for sleep by thinking of the morrow's meals.

Laurie might well have thought Mr Sheldon would soon be travelling to The Hall, as he was showing signs of being tired of the hustle and bustle of town life and needing a break from the fetid smells that multiplied as the weather became warmer. However, on arriving back in Brook Street, he was informed that Mr Sheldon had visitors who would probably be staying for a while. He was curious to know who they were but first went to his room to change after his journey, before going down to the office to see what messages there were, if any. He could tell someone had been in and that his pen had been used. Laurie prided himself on keeping everything neat and tidy so that he could lay his fingers immediately on anything that was needed. Now he found a note in Mr Sheldon's handwriting, which said that he was to join him and his visitors as soon as possible. As Laurie had left The Hall at an early hour that morning and as it was now nearly lunchtime, he hurried to see where his employer was and what was expected of him. He found him in the library with two other gentlemen and recognised Mr Sheldon's brother-in-law, Matthew Johnston, with a younger man.

'Laurie,' said Mr Sheldon, 'you're back early. Well done. Do you remember my brother-in-law?'

Laurie bowed. 'Yes, sir. How are you, Mr Johnston?'

Matthew smiled. 'Thank you, I'm well. How are you, Laurie? Alex keeps you busy, I see. But may I introduce my son Christopher to you, whom I don't think you know?'

Laurie saw before him a tall fair-haired, good looking young man of nineteen years of age. 'No,' said Laurie with a smile, 'but that can be rectified, I hope.'

Chris grinned back at him and returned his bow. They talked together and Laurie found out that Chris and his father had come down from their home in Derbyshire to stay for a week in London to introduce Chris to London life, while his mother and two sisters visited an aunt in Yorkshire.

'We haven't found anywhere to stay here yet,' said Chris, 'but we are hoping that my uncle will know of a suitable place.'

Alex heard, although he had been speaking to Matthew, and Laurie wondered how he could manage to do the two things together. 'But of course you must stay here,' Alex now said, 'we have enough room. See to it, Laurie, will you please?' Laurie left the room.

'I don't want us to inconvenience you, Alex,' said Matthew. 'I'm sure you must have commitments, but...'

'I'm pleased to see you both and I can easily miss a few invitations. In fact, some of them were beginning to bore me. However, we can visit the theatre if you would like, have a flutter, or do whatever you wish to do. I can always ask Laurie to accompany us if you would like him to.'

'Thank you, I would,' said Chris.

Eventually a servant took Matthew and Chris to their prepared rooms while Laurie waited for Mr Sheldon's questions.

'Well, how did you find things at The Hall, Laurie?'

'Very well, sir. Mrs Moss was very emotional regarding her letter and the money. She shed a few tears, sir.'

'Good God.'

'Yes, sir. But they all seem to be happy and I had no complaints.'

'And the new cook?'

'The food she cooked for me was very good and according to the rest of the staff she is well liked. Her name is Elliss.'

'What?' Alex snapped as he turned swiftly to look at Laurie. In his turn Laurie looked surprised at the sharpness in Mr Sheldon's voice.

'Elliss, sir,' he repeated, wondering what he had said to make Mr Sheldon react in this way.

Alex had stiffened, and his face was tense as he asked: 'Is she married or...?'

'No, sir, it is Miss Katherine Elliss. Is anything the matter, sir?' Laurie frowned. For the life of him he couldn't make out what was wrong. He felt sure he hadn't said anything out of place.

Mr Sheldon seemed to relax so Laurie went on: 'She seems a very nice lady and the rest of the staff like her and...'

'Is she about my age?'

'No, no, sir she's...' Laurie was about to tell him her exact age but Mr Sheldon seemed to lose interest.

'Good, good,' he said and quickly left the room.

Laurie frowned, then shrugged, but still he wondered what it had all been about. The name of Elliss certainly had triggered off a memory of some kind. Perhaps it wasn't a very pleasant memory. Laurie felt intrigued and hoped he would find out in time what had upset his employer.

Later, at dinner, the conversation was mostly about the family. Alexander's sister, Amelia, was well and busy, and the two girls, Chloe and Phoebe, were now seventeen years old.

'Ah, yes,' said Alex, 'the terrible twins. I wonder if I shall tell them apart now they are older?'

'We can, of course,' said Chris.

'Will they be coming down to Hertfordshire this year?' asked Alex. 'I'm quite happy to have them again if they would like to come.'

'Oh, yes,' said Matthew, 'I'm charged to give you a message from both girls asking if they could visit you again. Mind you, they are older now and quite lively. I can send them with their nurse when it is convenient, if you are agreeable.'

Chris cleared his throat. 'Do you think I should accompany them, Papa? Nurse is getting old and the twins are sometimes too much for her and – and I would love to visit The Hall too. I haven't been for a long time and I could bring my sketch pad and…'

Alex laughed. 'If you won't be bored, Chris, you are very welcome. Laurie will be free occasionally and will have some time to spare if you wish for a friend. But tell me about your drawing. Is it of anybody or anything in particular?'

Chris looked eagerly at him. 'No, it is only that I'm trying to build up a folder of buildings. That's one reason we came to London, so that I can draw some of the great buildings here. I am studying architecture and I'm working for someone in Derby already, but I would like to move to London eventually. For fun I draw people, but only quick sketches, of course.'

'Oh dear, I shall have to be careful, won't I?' grinned Alex. 'But I'm pleased you are putting your talent to good use. I will have a word with a few people I know who could be helpful.'

'Oh, sir, thank you,' said a delighted Chris, his face flushed with pleasure.

Alex didn't mind helping his nephew and was quite willing to help a little with the monetary side too for his sister's sake. Amelia had married Matthew simply because they loved each other. As Alex had once remarked, even if they were both paupers, they would still have married. Matthew was far from being without money, but he had to work hard for it and he was in a firm of lawyers in Derby. He liked his work and did his best to provide little luxuries occasionally for Amelia and the children. Amelia was eighteen months older than her brother, attractive and very capable, and she loved her family, and both she and Matthew had agreed that his coming to London with his son was important. Chris particularly wanted to better himself and Matthew thought the loss of a week's wages was worth it. Alex always helped where he could in having the children down at The Hall, which was a treat for them and a chance for their parents to have a few days completely on their own. Also, Alex never minded sharing some of his inherited wealth.

Matthew now looked at his brother-in-law and saw again a tall, well built man, attractive, when he was in a good mood, but Amelia said he could look 'devilish' when in a bad one. Matthew had always seen him in a good mood, fortunately, as now, but he was aware of a restlessness about him. Matthew wondered why he didn't travel more or why he wasn't married, as he was sure Alex could have chosen whomever he wished and she, whoever she was, would have been delighted to be his wife. Still, Matthew thought, it wasn't his business and he had always found Alex pleasant enough, as now. He appreciated him wishing to have the children at The Hall with him, but it crossed his mind that it might be because he was lonely. What Alex really wanted, Matthew thought, if he was to stay single, was to have a project in mind such as helping budding architects like Chris, or something similar.

Matthew's thoughts were interrupted by Chris turning to him and saying: 'Papa, you are deep in thought. Uncle Alex thinks it best for us to organise a few things, otherwise we shall find the week gone without accomplishing anything.'

Matthew cleared his throat. 'Sorry, I must be tired, but you both are quite right. Tomorrow morning, perhaps we should go and see a few buildings like Westminster Abbey and Wren's St Paul's, and then in the afternoon take things a little easier. What do you think, Alex?'

'By all means. If you wish, I will go with you and we will take the carriage. We might visit the Tower or the Naval College. Did you know it was built over King Henry the Eighth's Palace?'

'That's interesting,' said Chris, always having a thirst for knowledge in this particular field. 'And I must find houses of different designs, too.'

'Laurie could be free in the evening, I expect. Would you like to go to the theatre? No doubt Laurie will know what is on.'

'You rely a lot on your secretary,' smiled Matthew.

'That's what I pay him for,' was the curt reply.

The following week was organised so that Chris would work on his drawings until he had enough in his folder to present to a future employer, but he couldn't resist sketching some of the people too. When he joined Laurie and two of his friends one evening, they visited a few rather more lowly places, where the wine was cheap and the entertainment was card playing or watching scantily clad young ladies dancing. His sketch book, of course, was at the ready, but Chris thought he had better not show these particular pictures to his father. His head, the next morning, didn't feel too good but after a drink of some concoction ordered for him by Laurie he felt much better and able to face his breakfast. His father and uncle noticed he was quiet and a little pale but they didn't make any comments apart from a knowing wink between them.

By the end of the week Chris and his father had enjoyed their time spent in London. As promised, Alex introduced Chris to some gentlemen who certainly were interested in his work, and promised to help him in the future. It was also arranged that he and his sisters would visit The Hall at the beginning of July.

When they had departed, Laurie thought Mr Sheldon had enjoyed their company, as he seemed back to his normal self once again, less restless and more satisfied with his lot. But no doubt, by the time the end of June came, he would be pleased to have Laurie visit The Hall to make arrangements for his youthful visitors and himself.

Chapter Six

IT WAS THE MONTH OF MAY, the sky was blue and the sun was shining. Kate had visited Matty, Will and Emma briefly that morning to see that all was well, and then she had shopped in the village. Everyone knew her now and it was pleasant to chat, if only for a short while as, of course, her work always beckoned. She noticed some almond trees already in blossom and she smiled to see the abandoned maypole still standing on the village green. She walked back through the grounds of The Hall, breathing in the fresh air, which was unlike anything she had ever known in London.

She saw and waved to the gardener who, with extra help from some of the villagers, was scything the grass. Others tended the vegetables and fruit trees and, nearer to the house, the stable hands were washing and cleaning everything in the yard and stables where, at the moment, only two work horses and a cart resided. She heard the blackbirds and saw with delight two baby birds sitting together on a bush, wings flapping, chirping away to tell their mother they were hungry. She flew in to feed them as Kate passed.

Kate entered the kitchen and put away her purchases. She said as Mrs Sharpe came in: 'It is so beautiful out there I didn't want to come indoors.'

'You sound as though you haven't seen Spring before.'

'Not like this I haven't. There are no foul smells here as in London.'

'Do you have time this afternoon to sit outside?' asked Mrs Sharpe. 'If so, we could sit under the trees over there. There is a seat and I have some mending to do.'

'I suppose I could,' said Kate, 'for a little while at least. That would be lovely and I can help with the mending if you would like.'

Kate realised that in a small way she was happy, and the sunshine made a world of difference. She could cope easily now with the cooking and she was free to go out when she wanted as long as she did her job and the meals were on time. She felt happy and relaxed. Life wasn't perfect, of course, but it was good.

This idyllic situation continued for Kate until nearly the end of May. It was shattered one morning by Mr Figgis announcing to them all that he had received a communication from Mr Ward. This informed him that Mr Sheldon would be arriving sometime in June and all must be made ready for him. At the beginning of July, young Mr Johnston would be arriving from Derbyshire with his two sisters and their nurse. It wasn't known for how long they would all be staying.

Consequently, there was a hive of activity over the next few weeks airing bed linen, cleaning rooms and allotting the right bedchambers to the right people. Mr Sheldon and Mr Ward had their usual ones but Mr Johnston hadn't visited recently so one had to be organised for him. A large one had to be found for the two girls and a suitable one nearby for the elderly nurse.

In the kitchen Kate found her notes she had taken from Emma for the eventuality of a 'house full', as she had termed it, and sent Tommy with a message to the village butcher asking him to let her have certain cuts of meat at specified times. Other fresh food would have to be shopped for daily but the shopkeepers were quite happy to acquire extra stocks to supply The Hall, which boosted their sales for a few weeks, and to await the arrival of the most important man in Ashleigh. Two girls came in daily to help with the preparation of food and to help Kate generally. She soon found they were capable and took quite a lot of the basic preparation off her. They found Kate easy to work for and 'not a bit naggy' as one of them put it and they were happy to oblige her in any way.

Accommodation for the coachmen and the extra horses had to be arranged. Mr Sheldon usually came with two carriages, one for himself and Mr Ward, if he was accompanying him, and the other for his valet and luggage, and he also brought extra horses for riding. Laurie always thought it was a pity they didn't stay longer at The Hall to justify all the disruption caused at both ends of the journey.

He wasn't the only one to think this. It had crossed Kate's mind too. The skeleton staff at The Hall were paid full wages at all times so surely it would have been sensible to stay longer, but she supposed if one had enough money to do just as one pleased, these things didn't cross one's mind. She couldn't complain, anyway, as she had a generous wage just to feed the usually small amount of staff. Now she knew with all the extra people there would be to feed that she would really earn her keep.

It was during the third week of June that Mr Sheldon and Mr Ward arrived with their entourage. 'Do we all have to go out to welcome him?' Kate asked Mrs Sharpe.

'No, no, Mr Sheldon doesn't like shows of that kind. He just likes to come as though it's nothing special. There's no need for you to worry, you won't see him unless he wishes to compliment you on the food in person. But he doesn't usually. Just prepare the dishes like you know how and that's all you have to bother about.'

Kate was thankful for this at least. She had enough to think about with all the extra mouths to feed.

The weather had been reasonable with a mixture of sun and showers but there had been no respite for Kate, as in the previous month, for sitting outside, even for a short while. She had been too busy from morning to night providing meals and supervising the clearing up and helping the girls to keep everything clean and wholesome and away from the notice of flying insects. However, one day Mrs Sharpe told her that Mr Sheldon had gone visiting in the area for the rest of the day and wouldn't require a mid-day meal. Other meals could, therefore, be simpler and easier to prepare and so Kate left the two village girls to cope while she took the opportunity to have a break. She took some tablecloths that needed mending to her usual seat beneath the trees. She told Tommy to be sure and let her know when she had been there an hour, as she must return to start preparing dinner.

She breathed a sigh as it was good to relax and sit in the air, and as she sewed she felt the warmth of the sun. She took off her cook's mobcap, which she always wore in the kitchen to cover her hair, and shook her hair free. It was good to feel the cooling air through it. She breathed deeply and relaxed as she sewed. All was quiet apart from the stirring of the leaves and the occasional bird song.

Time seemed to go quickly as it always does when one enjoys oneself and when she heard a sound she thought Tommy had come to tell her the hour was up. She looked up with a smile but no Tommy stood there, instead there was a tall, dark man who looked frowningly at her. He was carrying his coat over his shoulder. Had he walked from the village? Kate, not liking the way he was looking at her, stared at him.

'Who the devil are you?' he asked abruptly. Then, not waiting for an answer, he said: 'Do you realise you are trespassing?'

'The question is,' began Kate, a martial look in her eye, 'who are you? I think you are the trespasser.'

'Oh, you do, do you? Then let me tell you, my girl, that my name is Sheldon and I own these grounds and house.'

Kate opened her eyes wide. 'Good gracious!' she said as she hurriedly stood and gave a small curtsey. 'I beg your pardon, sir, but I was led to believe you were quite elderly.'

'Really?' Mr Sheldon said frostily, 'And who was the miserable person who told you that?'

'No particular person, sir, it – it sort of came through what people said.' Kate wished she had minded her tongue.

'So, who are you?'

'I'm your cook, sir.' She looked quickly for her mobcap and put it on as best she could.

'I see,' said Mr Sheldon solemnly, but his lips twitched. 'Er – you've put that thing on back to front.'

'Oh, damnation,' said Kate, forgetting herself and taking off the offending cap.

'So,' said Mr Sheldon, moving nearer with a look of amusement on his face. 'Where do you come from?'

Oh dear, thought Kate, I hope he's not going to ask too many questions. All she said was: 'London, sir.' She continued hurriedly, 'Please excuse me, I must go and prepare the meal.'

'One moment. You were not in such a hurry before I came, were you? Why now?'

'Because I am sure it is time I should return.' Please, Tommy, come now, she prayed.

'Why hurry away?' Mr Sheldon came nearer until he stood in front of her.

'Mr Sheldon.' She tried to sound sensible, but the proximity of his large presence unnerved her. 'I must go if you wish your meal to be on time. The others don't know what to do unless I'm there.'

'Then we shall keep everyone waiting.' He put out a forefinger and lifted her chin so that she had to look up at him. 'And in future you do not argue or swear in my presence.' As she looked straight at him, he added: 'Or put poison in my food!'

Kate opened her eyes wide. 'I wouldn't, you know I wouldn't.' Then, as she detected humour in his face, she said innocently, 'Of course, there are other things I could add such as…'

He held her chin more firmly. 'You are trying my patience too far, you know, and if I'm ill after eating your food, I shall know who to blame and your punishment won't be pleasant.'

'Now I wonder what that would be,' said Kate. 'No one said anything about what happens to them if they cross you in any way.'

'But no one has, so far,' said Mr Sheldon. 'So be careful.'

'Perhaps no one dares. I wonder why?' said Kate thoughtfully.

'Perhaps because I pay their wages?' said Mr Sheldon, a glint in his eye.

Kate gave a sigh. 'Oh, well, perhaps I'd better do my work as usual and not upset anyone.'

'Much better,' he said grimly.

Fortunately, Tommy came running and interrupted them. Kate had never been so pleased to see him in her life.

'Who are you?' demanded Alex, moving away from Kate.

'T-Tommy, sir,' he said, looking anxiously at Kate.

'Thank you, Tommy. Is it time for me to return?'

'Yes, Miss.'

'Then, if you will excuse me, Mr Sheldon, I must go back to work.' She curtsied and gave him only a brief glance.

Alex still stood where he was, neither telling her to go or detaining her. As she walked beside the lolloping Tommy he wondered who she really was with that glorious auburn hair and her elegant figure. Before he went back to the house he bent and picked up her mobcap, which had fallen to the ground. He turned it over in his hand, frowning, then marched to the house and was lucky enough to find Laurie chatting to Mr Figgis. They looked at him in surprise, as they hadn't expected him home for some while to come, and they stopped their conversation.

Laurie looked at Mr Sheldon's dark face and wondered what was wrong. He said, unluckily: 'We didn't expect you home yet, sir. Is everything all right?'

'No, it isn't,' snapped Alex, nearly biting his head off.

'Excuse me,' murmured Mr Figgis, deciding to make himself scarce.

'Before you go, you had better return this to its owner.' He handed Kate's mobcap to him.

'Whose is it, sir?' asked Mr Figgis, somewhat at a loss, turning over the now crumpled piece of cotton.

Alex waved his finger tetchily at him. 'The cook woman's. Laurie, in here,' he said sharply.

While Mr Figgis took himself off to the kitchen, Alex led the way into the library.

'I walked home from the village. Sir Arthur is getting old and forgetful but I feel I have to visit him when I came to The Hall, as he would be upset if I didn't,' Alex began.

'But I thought you would have been brought back by someone from Sir Arthur's, sir.'

'Yes, so did I. But he became ill after the meal, which was rather poor, anyway, so I said I would leave and it was quicker for them to set me down in the village.'

'I see.'

'No, you don't. As I said, I walked home from the village to find a woman sitting mending something on a seat under the trees. I told her she was trespassing and she told me I was. She was surprised when I told her my name, as she said she had thought Mr Sheldon quite old. Who has been saying such things and where did you find her?'

Laurie bowed his head to hide a smile. Oh dear, Miss Kate had rubbed Mr Sheldon up the wrong way, hadn't she? He hoped she wouldn't do so again. He said out loud: 'I've no idea where those thoughts of your age came from, sir, I'm sure. She was here when I came as you know, and introduced by the last cook, sir.'

'Well, find out who she is and her background.'

'I'll try, sir.'

'Otherwise you can give her her marching orders.'

'Very well,' was all that Laurie said. He knew that he would not tell Miss Kate to leave as she cooked well and the rest of the staff liked her. It was just that she had been unfortunate enough to catch Mr Sheldon in a bad mood.

Laurie was dismissed and went to see the housekeeper. He knocked on the door of her private room. 'How can I help you, sir?' Mrs Sharpe said when she saw who was there.

'Is it possible for me to have a word with Miss Kate or is she too busy at the moment?'

'Shall we go to the kitchen and see?' said Mrs Sharpe, leading the way.

There was a hive of activity as Kate and her two assistants were working quietly but busily and the aroma was something to die for, thought Laurie.

'Miss Kate, Mr Ward would like to have a word with you if you can spare the time.'

'Oh, yes, yes, of course. I can leave things for a few minutes. Where…?'

'Shall we go outside for a while?' How anyone could work in this hot kitchen on such a day Laurie didn't know.

Kate had a few words with the two girls about the food and went out of the door with Laurie. 'Is anything wrong?' she asked.

'Mr Sheldon found your hat or whatever it is called. Do you have it?'

'Yes, it will be washed. Is – is that all?'

'No, he is rather put out that you thought him elderly. Perhaps it is because he didn't enjoy his meal at Sir Arthur's,' he looked at her with a grin.

'Oh dear,' she said. 'No, I didn't say I thought him elderly. I didn't know who he was until he told me, and I said I didn't think it was him because I had the impression that he was older, if you see what I mean.'

'Why did you have that impression? Did someone say so?'

'Oh, no. It's just that he doesn't come here often, so I thought he didn't like travelling, and he lives alone apart from the servants. Obviously I put two and two together and produced the wrong number.'

'Thank you. I'll explain it to him.'

'Mr Ward, is there anything he particularly likes to eat? Perhaps I can…'

'Well, his outing this morning ended in a poor meal, so if he eats something good he'll be in a better mood. What are you preparing?'

'Sirloin of beef and a duck suet pudding with carrots and cabbage.'

'Oh, he'll enjoy that. He likes fritters too.'

'Then I will make some apple fritters. There are still some apples put by from last autumn.'

'Mm, lovely,' said Laurie, his mouth already watering. 'Thank you, Miss Kate. Don't worry, I'll explain to Mr Sheldon.'

Kate thanked him and returned to cook the rest of the meal while Laurie went to find Mr Sheldon in the library. When he explained how Kate had not known him, he just said: 'Oh!' and that was it.

But Kate took herself to task. She must remember, she told herself, that she was now a servant and she didn't talk to gentlemen as an equal. She shouldn't have said what she did even if it had not been Mr Sheldon. The trouble was she had been used to standing up for herself over too many years and it was difficult not to do so now. But, she consoled herself, Mr Sheldon had made her a little uneasy. He was so large when he stood over her and looked at her with those dark eyes.

As Alex had no visitors, Laurie was expected to dine with him, and later when he had joined Mr Sheldon at the dining table, the subject of Kate came up once more.

'Who is she, really?' asked Alex. 'Do you know?'

'No more than what I've told you.'

'How old is she?'

'She said twenty-eight, sir. Why?'

'Mm. I was just wondering if I had ever met her in London where she said she came from.'

'I did wonder if she had fallen on hard times for some reason,' volunteered Laurie.

'Could be but I'm not really interested.'

Laurie said nothing but thought Mr Sheldon was more interested than he would admit. 'The dinner is good, though, isn't it, sir?'

'Surprisingly so. I wonder how she knew I liked apple fritters?' He looked enquiringly at Laurie.

'Perhaps you looked as if you would like them, sir,' said Laurie vaguely, looking innocently at him.

'Now how does one look…?'

'I don't know, sir. Perhaps its women's intuition.'

'I've known many women in my time but none have had intuition and wouldn't know the meaning of the word.'

'Yes, sir.'

'What do you mean, yes, sir?'

'I was agreeing with you, sir.'

'Mm.' Alex turned to the servant who had served them and was on the point of departing. 'Please ask the cook to come here,' he said, much to Laurie's discomfort. He hoped he wouldn't say anything to upset her.

A few minutes later the door opened and Kate entered. She had taken off her apron but her hair was confined still to her mobcap. She looked tired, Laurie thought and felt concerned, so he smiled at her.

'You wished to see me, sir?' she asked, her eyes looking anxiously at Alex.

'Yes,' he said. 'Thank you for an excellent meal, in spite of our conversation this afternoon.'

'I'm pleased you enjoyed it, sir.'

'And how did you know I liked apple fritters?'

'I didn't, but perhaps someone mentioned it and I remembered.'

Alex looked quickly at Laurie, who was smiling at Kate.

'I see.'

'Is that all, sir?'

'Why, are you in a hurry?'

Laurie wished Mr Sheldon would stop playing games and let poor Miss Kate leave. Couldn't he see she was tired?

'I have to see that the girls finish their work before they go home, sir, and I have to be ready for tomorrow morning also.'

'Will you be able to manage when my visitors are here?'

'I – I hope so, sir.'

'If you wish to hire anyone else to help while they are here, have a word with Mr Ward. That's all.' He nodded and smiled at her.

Kate curtsied. 'Thank you, sir. Goodnight. Goodnight, Mr Ward.' She returned to the kitchen, surprised, pleased, and with a smile on her lips.

Chapter Seven

THE DAYS THAT FOLLOWED were busy ones for Kate. Sometimes she thought she hated the sight of food but Peg and Tilly, the two girls who helped her, were full of fun enabling Kate to get through the days and to think her life wasn't so bad after all. One day, she was able to find a short time to make a quick visit to see Matty and Will and take them some of her wages as she had promised. They were grateful and glad she was reasonably happy and managing well, but worried that she was still so slim. Kate was pleased to see them again and felt secure in the knowledge that if anything went wrong they were there for her to turn to.

She had hurried back through the park and hoped she wouldn't encounter Mr Sheldon, but she believed he had gone riding so she should be safe enough from meeting him. His dark eyes and face had unnerved her and she was pleased that after their meeting he hadn't bothered her again. Occasionally he had sent a message to the kitchen praising a particular dish of food but that was all. Mr Ward checked if things were going well with the kitchen staff from time to time, otherwise no one worried them.

One day Mr Figgis informed all the staff that Mr Sheldon's visitors from Derbyshire were on their way and expected to arrive any day. Kate was permitted the extra help as Mr Sheldon had suggested. Kate asked the girls if they knew of anyone who could cook. Tilly said her mama, Mrs Watson, would be pleased to help. Kate also learnt that she had expected to be the replacement for Emma when she had left, and because of this Kate wondered if Mrs Watson would be difficult to work with, but when she saw her she knew everything would be all right. Mrs Watson was a clean and tidy lady with a pleasant face and she said she would do whatever Kate wanted her to. She said she knew Kate was all right to work with as her daughter had praised her highly indeed. So with an extra pair of capable hands, work in the kitchen, however hectic it became, would be much easier and an older lady to talk to was a change for Kate, too.

One early Tuesday afternoon, a clatter of wheels and clip-clop of horses' hooves heralded the arrival of the visitors. Mr Figgis quickly informed Mr Sheldon, who was reading in the library, and then opened the great oak door through which Alex hurried to meet his guests. First to jump down from the carriage was Chris. He hailed his uncle with a great grin on his face. 'At last we are here, sir!' He turned to let down the steps.

Alex strode forward and clapped him on his shoulder. 'Good to see you, Chris. And who have we here?'

Two giggling girls managed the steps, then flung themselves at Alex. 'Uncle, Uncle, here we are at last! It was such a long journey. We stopped at...'

'Ladies, ladies,' Alex laughed. He saw before him two pretty young girls of medium height with fresh complexions and blue eyes full of mischief. 'It is lovely to see you both and you can tell me all about it presently. Miss Hunt, how are you?'

Alex stepped forward to greet the girls' chaperone and nurse who was being helped carefully down the steps by Chris. She was a frail looking little lady who had been with the family for many years. She smiled. 'Thank you, sir, I am well.'

Alex turned. 'Is Mrs Sharpe here?' As he asked, the housekeeper appeared at his side. 'Look after Mrs Hunt, please. I'm sure she needs refreshment and rest after such a journey with these young people,' he said. Then he turned back to the twins. 'Now you two, who is who?' he asked.

'I'm Phoebe,' said Chloe, 'and this is Chloe.'

'No, no, I'm Phoebe and this is Chloe,' said the other, amidst giggles from both.

Alex looked at them. 'I see,' he said. 'Chris, come here and tell me who is who.'

'This one is Chloe, sir. Normally she's a little quieter and if you look carefully her nose is a slightly different shape to Phoebe's.' Both girls lifted their faces for their noses to be inspected amidst further giggles.

'Mm,' said Alex, 'you're both trouble, I can see that.' One twin on either side of him tucked a hand within his arm and they accompanied him into the house. 'We'll behave, Uncle, really,' they assured him.

Following them, Chris asked: 'Is Laurie with you, Uncle?'

'He is. No doubt you'll see him presently.'

'Oh, good.'

'Who's Laurie?' asked Phoebe.

'My secretary,' said Alex as he left them so that they could go up to their bedchambers.

The servants brought in their baggage, which was taken to the appropriate rooms for the maids to unpack, while the coachman and groom drove round to the stables. Peg and Tilly were summoned by Mr Figgis and were given tankards of ale to take to them.

Chris was the first one to find Alex in the library. 'I am to tell you that Mama and Papa are well and send their love, well Mama does, and Papa says he gives you full authority over the twins and they have been told to behave.'

'Very well,' said Alex, a gleam in his eye. 'Now, have you eaten on the way or shall I ask for something to be prepared for you all?'

Just then the twins came in. They had changed their travelling dresses for simple white gowns decorated with pink stripes and small white daisies. Their wavy light brown hair was dressed with pink ribands threaded through. They looked a pretty picture between them.

Laurie knocked on the door and entered the room to have a word with Alex about a letter he had received. 'I – I beg your pardon, sir, I...' Then he saw the twins who, as he said afterwards, took his breath away.

'There is no need. Let me introduce you to this one who, I think, is Chloe and her sister Phoebe. You know Chris, of course.'

'Ladies,' said Laurie, bowing with a smile, then turning said: 'It's good to see you again, Chris.'

'I hope we can have your company some of the time, Laurie,' said Chris, looking at his uncle.

'When he's no work to do,' said Alex.

'Oh, poor Laurie,' said Phoebe.

'Not at all,' laughed Laurie.

'Did you wish to see me about something?' asked Alex.

'Yes but it isn't important. I didn't mean to interrupt.' He went to the door but Chris went forward to talk to him.

'Ladies,' said Alex, 'are you hungry? Would you like refreshment of some kind?'

The twins looked at one another. 'A drink would be nice, please,' said one.

'With a little something to eat, a – a macaroon or... but not if it's inconvenient,' said the other.

'Shall I see to it, sir?' asked Laurie, overhearing.

Alex nodded. 'And ask Figgis to bring three ales as well if you are going to join us, Laurie.'

'Thank you sir.'

Twenty minutes later a servant announced refreshments were on the dining room table. The girls were delighted with small pieces of rich seed cake, jam tarts, gingerbread and macaroons.

'You must have a good cook, Uncle,' remarked Chloe.

'Of course,' was the only reply from Alex. It flashed through his mind that he hadn't seen Miss Elliss lately but then, on second thoughts, why should he? He supposed she still worked in the kitchen, as he hadn't heard anything to the contrary. He shook his head and hurriedly dismissed the thought.

The summer days became warmer and the kitchen became hotter. Whenever they could, the kitchen staff took it in turns to sit outside in the shade. It was Kate's idea, of course, and it worked very well. 'We may as well be as comfortable as we can,' she had said. From Kate's point of view, if the staff were happy and she showed some concern for their welfare, they would work for her all the better.

The visitors, as far as Kate could tell, were enjoying themselves. The twins were frequently to be seen near the trees in the park, sometimes with their brother, who would sit and sketch them and whatever else he could see. One morning he came to the outside kitchen door and asked if he could draw the ladies at work. Kate gave permission, of course, and

Peg and Tilly thought it wonderful that in a few lines they could recognise themselves. Kate was surprised how quickly he could capture a likeness on a sheet of paper and when he showed her herself, she said she thought he had made her look nicer than she was.

'Not at all,' he told her seriously. 'If I had some colours I would like to paint you. Forgive me, but the colours of your hair and eyes are beautiful.'

Kate blushed. She had never had such a compliment from a stranger before but all she replied was: 'I fear you are a flatterer, sir.'

'No, no, I assure you,' Chris said. 'I hope I haven't offended you?'

Kate looked at his earnest face and smiled at him. 'Of course not,' she said, 'how could you?'

Peg and Tilly said, with giggles, when Chris had departed: 'We think he fancies you, Miss Kate.' Then they looked closely at her. 'But he was right, your eyes are a bluey-green, they are beautiful.'

'Nonsense,' said Kate, embarrassed. 'If everyone goes on like this I shall be so puffed up in my self esteem that...' But she didn't finish as just then the gardener appeared at the door with a basket of strawberries. He was an elderly man with grizzled grey hair and skin burnt as brown as a nut.

'Oh, how lovely,' said Kate, 'the first ones we've had. Thank you, Adam.'

'I thought I better let you have them fresh like. I've only just picked them.'

'Have you a few for yourself?' Kate asked, quite happily disposing of Mr Sheldon's fruit.

'Just a few, Miss, if that's all right?'

'Of course it is. Are they good?' She smiled at him

'Oh, yes, Miss. And you have some too, mind.' He touched his hat and went back to the garden where he proceeded to pick the vegetables for his employer's evening meal.

While Kate enjoyed the simple happenings of everyday, Alex decided that after the twins had settled in and Chris had amused himself enough, it was time he organised an outing for them all. Miss Hunt was not included in this, as Alex had said that if Chris came with them and he himself was present there was no need for a chaperone. Miss Hunt was relieved, as junketing around the countryside in a carriage in the hot weather was not her idea of enjoying herself, she said.

Alex was pleased to see the twins looking neat and tidy in their blue-grey riding habits. They were identical, with the same saucy hats and curling blue feathers over their ringlets. They had set each other's hair the previous night in dampened rags so that they would look their best for Uncle Alex, they had told each other primly, then spoiled it all by giggling. 'I think that Laurie might be impressed by you, though,' said Phoebe to Chloe.

'Oh, do you really think so, Phe?' said Chloe, blushing.

'Well, of course. I shall do my best to encourage him to think so, anyway,' said Phoebe importantly. 'Remember, I am the elder twin and…'

'By five minutes,' said Chloe.

'So I'm to be treated as your chaperone.' Then they both collapsed into giggles again.

The following morning the weather was perfect for an outing. When everyone was ready the horses were brought round. Alex had hired two special ones suitable for young ladies to ride from nearby stables for the length of time the twins stayed with him. Unlike them, the palfreys were docile and so were much petted by their riders.

'Where are we going, Uncle?' asked Phoebe.

'I thought we would ride to Hatfield House and walk in the grounds. It's not too far.'

'And what is Hatfield House?' asked Chloe.

'It is where Henry the Eighth lived at one time and where Queen Elizabeth was born.'

The journey to Hatfield House didn't take long but there was no hurry as it was a pleasant ride and the countryside was looking its best. 'This is all so beautiful,' Chloe said. 'The villages are full of pretty trees and flowers and streams. We have lovely countryside too but it's not the same, somehow.'

It wasn't long before they were dismounting outside the large gates of Hatfield House. This Jacobean building in the style of the original Elizabethan house was completed in 1611 and the owners were happy to let careful visitors walk in the gardens if the gentleman who stood guard outside gave his approval. On this occasion, he did, and with the twins smiling sweetly at him they were able to walk in the extensive gardens and the park and to admire the ruins of the original Elizabethan house of Bishop Morton of Ely.

Chris had his sketchbook, of course, and worked hard while Phoebe devoted her time to Alex. It seemed that Laurie and Chloe were enjoying each other's company. For all Phoebe's chatter, Alex didn't fail to notice this and said to her with a smile: 'Are you trying to take my attention away from your sister and my secretary?'

Phoebe grinned at him. 'No-o but Clo told me she liked him a lot so I thought I'd let her enjoy herself.'

'And you?' smiled Alex.

'Well I'm enjoying talking to you, aren't I?'

'You're a minx.'

Phoebe giggled. 'I know plenty of young men at home, more than Clo, as she's usually much quieter than I am, you see.'

'I see,' said Alex, hiding a smile.

Over lunch, which was taken at one of the town's gabled and timber framed inns, they looked at Chris's sketches. 'You really are talented,' said Alex, flicking through the pages, 'an architect you must be.' He smiled at his nephew. Then an arrested look came into his eyes as he saw the result of Chris's visit to the kitchen. Phoebe, looking over his arm, said: 'Isn't your cook pretty, Uncle? Chris said he would like to paint her.'

After a few moments Alex replied. 'Did he indeed? I don't suppose she would have time to sit for him otherwise we would have no food.' He calmly turned over the page. Phoebe made a face at Chris.

Laurie, sensing a little tension, diverted this by remarking on the food which had arrived and handing round a dish of pastries.

Chapter Eight

A FEW DAYS LATER Phoebe and Chloe decided they would like to walk to the village, which they hadn't seen before. Miss Hunt said it would be impossible for her to walk so far, particularly as the weather wasn't quite so pleasant, being a little overcast but still quite warm. The twins pulled a face at each other behind their chaperone's back, then whisked themselves off to find Uncle Alex. When they enquired of Mr Figgis where he was they were told he was talking business with Mr Ward and shouldn't be disturbed. 'But your brother is in the library, ladies, if you wish to know,' he said.

They thanked him politely and went to see if Chris would accompany them to the village. 'Well, I would rather not as I've found a rather good book here and the weather is a little humid today. Why be energetic? I'm sure there are some interesting books here for you to read.' They pouted at him, said that they didn't feel like reading and left him.

'What do we do, Phe?' asked Chloe, wrinkling her nose.

'Well, why don't we walk to the park and then we would come to the village and then perhaps we could...?' She didn't finish the sentence but just grinned at her sister with raised eyebrows.

'Why not?' said Chloe, 'After all, no one else is bothered about us and we can always scream if there is trouble.'

'Do you think we should put on our cloaks? It is a little dull.'

'But it is too warm for cloaks. Besides, someone is bound to ask us where we are going. Let's just go.' So quietly and with smiles on their faces they slipped through the side door into the park.

'Money. Have you any with you?' asked Phoebe.

'I have a little,' said Chloe. She went on: 'After all, we come here regularly and no one worries. Poor old Hunt, she's really not much use to us now, is she?'

'No,' said Phoebe, 'but Papa would never turn her off. She must be quite old. Besides, we won't need her in a year or two anyway as we shall be married.'

'Oh, Phe, do you really think so? Not everyone manages to do so, do they? I mean, look at Uncle Alex.'

'Well, that's his own fault, isn't it? He does the asking after all.'

'Perhaps he didn't meet anyone he likes in London.'

'Mmm.' A mischievous smile found its way on Phoebe's face. 'Have you met Uncle's cook yet?'

'No,' said Chloe. 'Have you?'

'No, but I think we should. She looks a lot prettier and younger than most cooks if Chris's drawing is to be believed. Whenever she is mentioned Uncle goes all disinterested and I'm wondering if he really likes her.'

'Does he go and see her, then?'

'He doesn't seem to,' said Phoebe, 'but men are peculiar, aren't they?'

'Laurie isn't peculiar,' said Chloe.

Phoebe looked at her sister. 'Oo-ooh, I bet he is really,' and she ran off as quickly as she could with Chloe chasing after her.

They came to the park gates and stopped to get their breath back. 'Phew! It's too hot to run. Do you think we shall have a storm?'

'Well, let's hurry to the shops and we can shelter there if it does rain,' said Phoebe. They proceeded demurely, straightening their skirts as they went. 'Oh look,' said Phoebe, 'they had a maypole. That would have been fun. What pretty little shops, too. Let's look in the windows.' The first one sold a variety of things for ladies like combs, ribbons and some materials. After saying how pretty one thing was and how others were not so attractive, they moved on to the next shop. Here, homemade confectionary was sold. After some deliberation the twins decided to enter the shop and buy a very few lemon flavoured sweetmeats. The lady behind the counter remarked on their likeness and guessed they were staying at The Hall. Outside, the twins each popped a sweetmeat into their mouths and pronounced them just the thing to refresh them on such a warm day.

They were about to visit the bookshop next door when a rumble of thunder could be heard. At the same time a lady dressed sedately in a serviceable cloak and an unfashionable bonnet walked towards them carrying a large basket. She looked up at the sky then stopped when she saw the twins. She smiled. 'It looks as if it will rain,' she said. 'Shall we hurry home or wait in this shop and see? I am Miss Elliss from The Hall.'

'Oh,' said Phoebe. 'Are – are you my Uncle's cook, by any chance?'

'I am. How did you know?'

'Well,' said Chloe, 'our brother made a sketch of you.'

'So he did,' smiled Kate.

By now large drops of rain were beginning to fall. 'Into the shop,' said Kate, shepherding them inside. 'Good morning, Mr Greaves, may we shelter here for a few minutes, please? Perhaps we could view the books on display while we wait?'

'Certainly, Miss Elliss. Do you have much more shopping to do?' He looked at the parcels Kate was carrying in her large basket. She had been to the butchers for extra supplies and next door for a few more groceries. She could have sent Tilly or Peg but the girls couldn't be relied upon to choose the best quality food.

'No, no, but the shopping is heavy and I don't want to get it rained upon if I can help it.'

While she chatted to Mr Greaves, Phoebe and Chloe looked on the shelves at the books and eyed Miss Elliss when they thought she wasn't looking.

The few drops of rain turned into a heavy shower with thunder and lightning. The twins were pleased they were in the shop and Miss Elliss was there. Eventually the worst of the storm passed and although it still rained it wasn't such a downpour.

'I think we should go home,' said Kate, eyeing the twins, 'before it all starts again. I think you had better take my cloak. Can you share it and cover your heads and then it will stop you getting really wet.'

'Thank you,' said Chloe, 'but what will you do?'

'Well, I have my bonnet and I shall just walk as quickly as I can.' Kate took off her cloak and the girls, with their arms around each other's waists, clutched the cloak holding it over their heads.

'When you've changed your dresses,' said Kate, 'bring them and my cloak down to the kitchen and I'll dry them where it's warm.'

'Thank you, Miss Elliss,' said Phoebe. 'Now Chloe, we have to step at the same time. Start with your left foot. Ready? Then off we go.'

'Thank you, Mr Greaves, for sheltering us,' said Kate. 'I must make haste otherwise the lunch will be late.'

'I do hope you can return without being too wet,' he said. He watched her go and shook his head. Why was such a charming young lady working in a kitchen?

Kate hoped she wouldn't get too wet but as she walked as best she could with her heavy shopping basket, she knew she would arrive soaked to the skin. When she reached the park gates it looked as though the rain was increasing and the thunder rumbled. She heard screams at a distance from the girls and she was pleased they had made good progress and were nearly back at The Hall.

The twins let themselves in by the side door, out of breath and with wet feet and wet hems of their skirts. They stood still waiting to get their breath back, then walked towards the stairs.

'And where have you two been?' They looked up quickly to see Alex standing there and not looking at all pleased.

'We went to the village,' said Phoebe, 'and we were caught in the rain.'

'And where is Miss Hunt?'

'She wouldn't go with us as it was too far,' said Chloe.

'So you both went to the village without asking and without a chaperone?'

'Well, not exactly,' said Phoebe, crossing her fingers behind her back. 'Miss Elliss was with us.'

'Oh, was she? And where is she now?'

'She told us to hurry back so I expect she is still on her way as she had parcels to…'

'Go and get dry and then I'll see you both in the library.' Alex strode out the door into the rain.

By this time Kate had reached the seat near the trees. She stopped to recover her breath and to change the heavy basket into her other hand. Then she began to walk as quickly as the rain allowed as it was descending in a steady stream. She felt wet through; her long skirt kept sticking to her and her bonnet had more or less collapsed. She felt a mess and was sure she looked one but with her head down she battled towards the kitchen door.

Before she arrived, however, Alex, looking like the thunderclouds above him, met her. In fact, she nearly walked into him as her eyes were concentrating on her feet. 'Good gracious, girl, you're wet through.' He snatched the basket from her, took her hand and pulled her along the rest of the way to the kitchen door. He pushed her inside, much to Mrs Watson's and the girls' surprise, then left the basket on the floor and walked over to the internal door. He opened it and, turning to look at Kate who just stood there recovering her breath and dripping on to the floor, said curtly: 'When you are ready, I'll see you in the library.' He didn't wait for a reply, which was as well as Kate was so out of breath and confused, she couldn't give one.

After she had recovered a little, she apologised to Mrs Watson and the girls. She said she must go and change but could they proceed with the luncheon as she would have to see Mr Sheldon before she came back to the kitchen. She went to her room and was pleased to discard her wet clothes, but the sight of herself in the mirror, bedraggled bonnet, wet hair hanging down and her blouse plastered to her body didn't add to her confidence. Had Mr Sheldon noticed the state she was in? Probably not, she told herself, he was too vexed and getting wet himself to notice.

She rubbed herself down with a cloth and tried to dry her hair, then put on fresh clothes and shoes. She rubbed her hair once more then tried to comb and pin it to make a neat style so her cap could be placed on top but her hair was too thick and needed drying further, so she gave it a last rub, combed it neatly and left it loose. It would soon dry then and by the time she had spoken to Mr Sheldon and gone back to the kitchen, she would be able to wear her cap. So with that item in her hand she asked her way from a servant to the library. She knocked on the door.

'Come in,' said Mr Sheldon's voice.

Kate opened the door to find the twins were with him too and were eyeing her anxiously. Kate gave a small curtsey and waited, but not without a reassuring smile at the twins which wasn't lost on Alex.

'So,' he said, 'tell me your version of what happened.'

'I had to visit the butcher for the meat I had ordered and...'

'Why? Can't one of the girls go or the other woman?'

'Well, no. Mrs Watson wouldn't be able to carry the quantity and the girls weren't too happy about the weather. And I like to look at the meat for myself to see if the quality is good.'

'I see,' Alex said but he didn't sound convinced. 'So these two didn't go with you?'

'There was no need. They are allowed in your park, are they not? I met them at the gates, so no harm was done.'

Relief showed on the twins' faces and they grinned at each other.

'Very well, you two, you may go,' said Alex.

Kate turned to go, too, but Alex said, 'Not you, Miss Elliss.'

Kate frowned at him. Perhaps, having noticed her hair not being tidy under her cap as it should be, she was in for a reprimand. She thought she must forestall him. 'I apologise for not being dressed properly but...' She indicated her cap.

Ignoring her words Alex interrupted her. 'Sit down,' he said.

'Sir?'

'I said sit down,' he repeated, pointing to a comfortable chair.

Kate didn't know whether to do as she was told or to try and argue that she was needed in the kitchen. She opened her mouth to say something and then as she saw Mr Sheldon was still waiting and looking at her, she went over and sat on the edge of the chair he had indicated.

He poured a glass of sherry and handed it to her. 'Th-thank you sir, but I shouldn't be here, I...'

Alex sighed as he sat down in a chair opposite her.

'Miss Elliss, whose house is this?' he asked wearily.

'Why, yours, sir.'

'Then I say what happens.' He paused but as she said nothing and only sat and held her glass and looked at it, he went on: 'I suppose what you told me just now was the truth?'

Kate smiled. 'Well, yes, although I didn't plan to meet the young ladies, exactly. But as no harm was done...' She looked anxiously at him.

He nodded. 'That sounds more like it and no more will be said, but I have to look after them.'

'Of course.'

'Now to yourself. Oh, drink your sherry,' he ordered, waggling an imperative finger at her.

Kate hurriedly took a sip and found it warming as it passed down her throat. Alex went on: 'In future when you have heavy shopping to do, take someone with you, that boy for instance. And that's an order,' he said as she was about to protest.

'Very well,' she said meekly enough.

Alex' lips twitched. For all her confidence, he thought she looked worn out with dark shadows beneath her eyes. Of course, having that colour hair she would be pale skinned but it was a creamy skin, like silk. He frowned at her. She hurriedly took another sip of sherry.

'Tell me,' Alex said, 'is something worrying you? Can something be done about it?'

Kate smiled a little. 'Thank you. I – I haven't been sleeping well because of the heat, I suppose. Now it has rained perhaps things will be better.' She glanced briefly at him.

'Mm. I wonder,' he murmured.

'Sir?'

'I wonder if you are being truthful?'

'Yes, yes,' she said, not looking at him. How could she explain that the treatment she had received from her father and Daniel still hurt and was difficult to forget, try as she might? Also the long working days were taking their toll. True, she was happy enough but she was also worried that her money would run out before she was paid again. She had quite happily given half of her earnings to Will and Matty as she had promised. They hadn't wanted to take it but Matty confided to Kate that Emma's wage from the vicar wasn't enough to keep three people. Will was doing his best to find work in the village but he was getting too old to do heavy work. Then this morning Kate had come home with very wet feet and discovered she needed a pair of new shoes. Somehow she must find a pair for outdoor wear but not until her next pay day in a few months' time. Mr Sheldon was being very kind, she thought, but she wondered why he was concerned about her. But she had been concerned for her servants so she supposed he was just doing the same with his staff.

She wished he didn't ask her awkward questions, though. She thought him a formidable person and in truth he frightened her a little.

'Very well,' he said at last, frowning at her, 'we'll leave it at that. I must see Mr Ward now but you will drink your sherry slowly and sit there until you are recovered. You understand?' Then as he thought she was about to protest said: 'And don't argue.' He left the room.

Kate blinked. She thought, to sit quietly with a glass if sherry in such a chair was luxury indeed. She couldn't remember the last time she had sat so comfortably and had been looked after. For once in her life she relaxed and sipped her excellent sherry while her eyes gazed at the shelves of books, the view of the garden and she listened to the steady rain outside. Eventually the sherry was no more and her eyes began to close.

Chapter Nine

LUNCHEON was a quiet affair with just Alex, Chris and the twins sitting at the table. Laurie had work to do and said he would have something later and probably visit the kitchen to see what was left. The twins, suitably chastened by their morning's adventure, were quieter than usual which Alex noticed and wondered how long it would be before they were back to their mischievous selves. It still rained so Alex asked Chris if he would like a game of chess that afternoon, to which he happily agreed.

'And what would you two like to do?' asked Alex. 'There is a drawer full of games collected by your Mama, so you may have a look there and see what you can find.'

Phoebe grinned. 'Thank you, Uncle,' she said primly, 'we are used to amusing ourselves, but perhaps you will show us some card games, you know, like faro or piquet or loo.'

'And are you so wealthy that you can afford to lose money?'

'No, no,' piped up Chloe, 'but we can have pretend money of some kind.'

'I see. Now, this evening I have to go to a meeting in the next village. It's an annual event so I should be there. I'm hoping I shall not be away too long. So you will have to decide what to do. Perhaps Laurie can join you, in which case Miss Hunt had better be present, too.'

The twins looked at each other and made a face. 'Promise,' said Alex.

'Yes, of course, Uncle,' the twins chorused demurely.

'If you are good,' said Alex sternly, but his lips twitched, 'next Saturday evening we are invited out to dine with Mr and Mrs Lucas and the eldest of their two children. They have a large house near Great Amwell, which is not far away. After we have dined there is to be dancing and young people whom they know from the village will arrive to join us.'

'Ooh,' said Phoebe, 'how lovely.'

'We can wear our new dresses, Phe,' said Chloe.

'That's all girls think about,' observed Chris to Alex.

'You would moan if girls didn't look pretty, now, wouldn't you?' said Phoebe. 'Besides, I expect you'll be all dressed up and your hair brushed just so.' She suddenly had a thought. 'We won't be expected to wear wigs, will we, Uncle?' She looked anxiously at Alex.

'No, no, we are not in London or Bath, you know.'

'Do you wear a wig like Papa sometimes, Uncle?' asked Chloe, looking at Alex's dark face and hair.

'Sometimes, when the occasion demands,' he said.

Chloe looked at him, trying to picture him in a powdered wig. Alex said nothing but was secretly amused.

'I don't think I'd like to wear a wig,' said Phoebe. 'Aren't they itchy?'

'Mama powders her hair sometimes which looks quite pretty,' said Chloe.

'That will do,' said Chris, 'it really isn't a subject to be discussed at the luncheon table.'

The twins made a face at him while Alex ignored them.

'Uncle Alex,' said Chloe presently, 'is Laurie invited to the dinner and the dancing afterwards?'

'Not as far as I know.'

'Oh, poor Laurie.'

'There will be plenty of other young men there, I expect.'

'Yes, of course, but...' Phoebe gave her sister a nudge and as Chloe looked at her, winked.

'Oh dear,' thought Alex, 'what are they planning now?' Aloud he said: 'You had better warn Miss Hunt she will be needed.'

'Yes, Uncle,' was the demure reply.

Meanwhile, Kate woke up. She was disorientated for a moment and then realised, with horror, that she had gone to sleep. She looked round and saw the ormolu clock on the mantelpiece. 'Good gracious,' she thought, 'luncheon should have been served long ago.' She looked round and found she was alone. Mr Sheldon had not returned, thank goodness. She picked up her empty sherry glass and quickly walked to the door. Outside stood a servant. He smiled at her. 'Do you feel better, Miss Elliss?'

'Thank you, yes.' She lifted her eyebrows. How had he known and why was he standing there? He answered her unspoken question.

'Mr Sheldon said you weren't well and I had to see that no one came to disturb you,' he said.

'Oh, I see. Well, thank you.' She smiled at him. 'I'd better go back to work, hadn't I? Have you had your luncheon?'

'Not yet, Miss Elliss.'

'Then I'll send you something special. What is your name?'

'Ben, Miss.'

In the kitchen she found Mrs Watson, Peg and Tilly. 'Is everything all right, Miss Elliss?' they asked.

'Yes, yes, thank you. What about luncheon?'

'We sent it up. There is no need to worry but we did wonder what had happened.'

'I'm so sorry, but Mr Sheldon made me sit in a chair with a glass of sherry because he thought I looked ill.' She placed the glass on the table. 'He left me saying I was to drink it and I went to sleep.'

'Do you feel better, though?' asked Mrs Watson, who was quite concerned.

'Yes, thank you, I think so. It was a bit embarrassing, really. Now,' said Kate, assuming a businesslike attitude, 'how has dinner progressed? Oh, and will one of you take Ben his luncheon as he will be hungry. He had to see no one entered the library while I was there, on Mr Sheldon's orders.'

'I'll go,' said Tilly with a grin. She placed some cold meats on a plate and a large slice of some special strawberry tart. 'I bet Ben hopes he has to stand guard again,' she said with a cheeky grin.

There was still plenty of preparation to do so Kate tied on her apron and began work.

While Kate prepared the next meal, Alex and Chris played chess in the library, where the only sound was a quiet 'check' and later 'checkmate'. The twins, looking in the drawer Alex had mentioned, found some playing cards which they put on one side for when the men could join them. They found another chess set but decided it was too serious a game to play on such an afternoon. They settled to play 'Fox and Geese' and then to chatter and discuss the forthcoming invitation to Mr and Mrs Lucas.

'A pity Laurie cannot go too,' said Chloe, dreamily.

'Never mind, you never know what might happen,' said her sister.

'Mm. You sound like Mama,' said Chloe. 'I don't see what could happen.'

'Well, don't harp on it,' said her sister brusquely, 'there are other fish in the sea.'

Chloe made a face. 'You might meet someone handsome there,' went on Phoebe, 'you never know.'

Eventually Alex and Chris joined them and they sat round the table to play loo. 'Come along, you two, where's all this pretend money?' said Chris.

'We can use these counters,' said Phoebe as she emptied them out of the box.

'Do you know how to play, Uncle?' asked Chloe.

'Er – no, I don't think so.' As Chris looked at him with raised eyebrows, Alex gave him a quick wink.

'Right,' said Chris, 'everyone has to place three counters into the pool. Now listen.' He explained for a little while and then they had a practice game. When the girls and Alex said they thought they understood what to do, they began to play with Chris's help and they progressed quite well. The twins liked the gambling part and were pleased with themselves when they had accumulated many counters.

'Gosh!' said Phoebe. 'How wonderful if it were real money. Look how much we would have, Chloe.'

'I know,' said Chloe sadly.

The next game Alex said must be his last one, as he had to see Laurie before dinner and his departure for his meeting. The twins excitedly began to play, intent on 'fleecing' the gentlemen, as Phoebe said, to which phrase Chris took exception. But as the game went on their play became worse until all their counters ended up in a pile in front of Alex.

'I thought you said you didn't know how to play, Uncle,' said Phoebe suspiciously.

Alex laughed. 'Well, that just shows you should never trust people when there is gambling. Fortunately, you didn't have to lose real money.'

'It's not fair, Uncle, we...'

Alex held up his hand. 'Sorry, I have to go. Rip up at Chris instead, he knew!' and he left the room.

'Oh, thank you, Uncle,' said Chris grimly, as his two sisters advanced meaningfully upon him.

The evening came. Alex had departed for his meeting and the twins and their brother were seated in the withdrawing room wondering what to do. They chatted for a while and then Phoebe had a wonderful thought, she said. 'Why don't we practice our dancing steps ready for Saturday?' She jumped up. 'Which dance shall we try first?'

'The minuet?' asked Chloe. 'Come along, Chris, you be my partner and we'll have to hum a tune.'

'I know,' said Phoebe, 'go and see if Laurie is free to come; then it will be better. Uncle said he might.'

'Oh, yes,' said Chloe, clasping her hands together.

Chris disappeared through the door to see if he could find Laurie. He knocked on the door of the room where he worked and was surprised to hear him call: 'Come in.'

'I'm sorry,' said Chris, 'Are you still working?'

'As I hadn't anything else to amuse me, I thought I would,' said Laurie. 'Why, is anything wrong?'

'No, no, but as the girls and I are on our own, they want to practice their dancing steps for next Saturday and we wondered if you would like to join us?'

Laurie grinned. 'I can dance a little, I think.'

'Oh, good,' said Chris, 'do come, it will be more fun.'

The twins were delighted to see Laurie, of course, but Chris, mindful of Alex and the proprieties, told his sisters to go and fetch Miss Hunt.

Phoebe pouted. 'But she'll only go to sleep,' she said.

'It doesn't matter. She will be present in body if not in spirit,' he said as an afterthought.

So Miss Hunt, complaining a little, came down and the twins sat her in a comfortable chair. 'All you have to do,' said Phoebe, 'is to watch us trying to dance.'

Miss Hunt nodded and smiled.

'We have to hum the tunes,' explained Chloe, shyly, to Laurie.

They led with Phoebe and Chris behind them. They started to hum the tune when Phoebe told Chloe to hold out her dress. Chloe made a face at her. 'Just hum,' she said. But as their humming wasn't very tuneful and timing not their strong point, their steps faltered and it all ended up a little chaotic.

'Can anyone play the harpsichord?' asked Phoebe suddenly. 'I'm sure Uncle wouldn't mind it being played. Dear Miss Hunt, you can play, can't you?'

Miss Hunt shook her head. 'So sorry, dear, not any more. My hands, you see.' They certainly looked a little twisted.

'I've an idea,' said Laurie. 'Wait a moment.'

It was a surprise to Kate to hear a knock on the kitchen door just as she had finished tidying up and was about to take off her cap and apron. Mrs Watson and the girls had gone home a while ago when there had been only light rain falling.

'Come in,' called Kate, wondering who she would see.

'It is only I, Miss Elliss,' said Laurie. 'I've come to ask if you play the harpsichord. I – I just thought you might.' Laurie hoped she wouldn't be offended.

'I used to be able to play,' said Kate slowly. 'May I ask why?'

'I'm sorry. You see, the young ladies want to practice their dance steps and they hoped someone could play for them. I – I thought perhaps you knew how.'

'Oh, I see. And Mr Sheldon, would he expect me to?'

'Oh, no, he has gone out to a meeting somewhere and won't be home until later.'

'Well, I can try. But could I ask Mr Figgis if he thinks it the right thing for me to do?'

'Yes, of course. Miss Hunt is present so we are observing all the proprieties.'

Laurie led the way to Mr Figgis's door and knocked. When he opened it, Laurie asked if he thought it permissible for Miss Elliss to help the visitors practice their dance steps by playing the harpsichord.

Mr Figgis said he could see no objection and his permission wasn't really needed, but privately he felt pleased that he had been consulted.

Laurie returned to the withdrawing room with Miss Elliss some ten minutes later. Kate looked round quickly and gave a small curtsey.

'Miss Elliss,' announced Laurie, 'has kindly agreed to play for us.'

'Oh, how wonderful!' said Phoebe, going up to her. 'We want to practice our steps, you see.'

'The trouble is,' said Kate, 'that I haven't played for some time, so I might not be very good.'

Chris stepped forward. 'Why don't you try and see what you can do, ma'am?' he said.

'But will Mr Sheldon mind me...?'

'He's out, he won't know,' said Chris. 'Besides, we'll take the blame if there is a problem.'

Kate consoled herself with the thought that she was a servant so she couldn't refuse to help.

Some music was found, a minuet amongst it, the harpsichord was opened and Kate sat down. It was a beautiful instrument and Kate began to play, slowly at first to get the feel of the keys again. She asked if they would listen while she played to see if it sounded right. After a few tries she found her stiff fingers worked once more and the twins clapped their hands saying: 'How lovely, that is just as it should be. How clever you are, Miss Elliss.'

'Well, I apologise in advance for any wrong notes I play,' she said.

'Please don't worry about it,' said Laurie kindly, 'as long as the timing is right, that is all that matters.'

A country dance was decided on next, and suitable music found. The girls had forgotten one of the movements. Chris said he knew it but eventually an argument broke out as Phoebe said he was wrong. As Kate sat listening, Laurie came over to her. 'Would you know the next move, ma'am?'

'I – I think so.'

Laurie clapped his hands to stop the bickering. 'Perhaps I can help?' said Kate.

They looked at her. 'Doesn't it go like this?' And she performed the steps using Laurie as her partner.

'Yes, yes,' cried the twins, 'how clever you are. Of course that is it.'

They progressed from one dance to another, smiling, laughing and thoroughly enjoying themselves. The music and laughter seemed to have penetrated the walls to the ears of Mr Figgis and Mrs Sharpe. To hear more clearly, they carefully opened the door a little so they could peep through to watch and listen to the music and see the young ones enjoying themselves. They smiled at each other and continued to look at the happy scene. It came as a great surprise, therefore, when they heard a discreet cough behind them. They turned and saw Mr Sheldon standing there. Mr Figgis recovered first. Carefully closing the door he said: 'We were just checking everything was all right, sir, with the young ones.' He bowed.

'And is it?' asked Alex at his driest.

'Oh, yes, sir. They are enjoying themselves.'

'I'm pleased to hear it,' said Alex. He nodded and while Mr Figgis and Mrs Sharpe bowed and curtsied before going back to their rooms, Alex quietly opened the door. The music had stopped as Miss Ellis was showing Laurie and Chloe the steps they should be doing. As she turned to go back to play for them she caught sight of Mr Sheldon standing quietly just inside the door. Kate stopped and then the others did the same. The twins, seeing him, rushed towards him with smiling faces. 'Uncle Alex, we're having such a lovely time. Come in and watch us.'

They took an arm each and escorted him into the middle of the room. 'And is Laurie having a lovely time?'

Laurie, slightly red in the face, said: 'It has been most enjoyable, sir, thank you.'

'Miss Hunt is here, as you can see,' said Phoebe, turning him to view the good lady. Unfortunately, she was fast asleep.

'Ah, yes,' said Alex blandly, 'no doubt she can keep an eye on you. Perhaps she has more than the two that are closed at the moment.'

The twins laughed. Laurie went to Miss Hunt and carefully woke her by placing his hand on her arm. 'May I escort you to your room, madam?'

'Oh, oh, yes, thank you.' She rose to her feet and, seeing Alex standing there, gave a little curtsey, saying: 'Thank you, sir, for a lovely evening.' Laurie placed her hand within his arm and led her out of the room. The twins giggled.

Chris was helping Kate to pack the music away. He spoke kindly to her, with a shy smile, as he could see she was feeling uncomfortable.

Phoebe saw Alex looking across at them. 'It was Laurie's idea to ask Miss Elliss to accompany us,' she said.

'And he has conveniently absented himself, I see.'

'Miss Elliss has been very kind in coming to our aid,' said Chris, coming over to Alex after the harpsichord and music were all tidy again.

Alex looked over at Kate. She didn't know whether he was vexed or not. She gave a small curtsey, said: 'Goodnight, sir,' and walked to the door where Chris had rushed forward to open it for her.

Alex's eyes followed her all the way but before she left the room he said imperatively: 'Miss Elliss.'

She turned and looked at him apprehensively. With a small bow all Alex said was: 'Thank you.'

Chapter Ten

WHEN JOHN, the valet, had brushed his master's coat and laid his garments flat in the press, he turned and saw the frown on his master's face. He asked him if everything was in order and was he needed further.

'No,' said Alex, his mind still elsewhere, 'no, thank you, John. You may go. Good night.'

John closed the door quietly. Mr Sheldon was worried about something. He was unusually preoccupied tonight and John wondered what was troubling him as he missed the conversation that usually took place between them. The valet shook his head and hoped his master would feel better in the morning.

Alex lay in his comfortable four poster bed with a frown on his face, pondering an annoying question. Who was his cook, Miss Elliss? He knew she came from London but that was all. Had she, like Laurie had suggested, fallen on hard times through debt or some such thing? She certainly wasn't the usual servant and she wasn't a young miss either. She was elegant, accomplished on the harpsichord, and she spoke well, apart from that time when they had first met and she had sworn. He smiled suddenly. She had certainly forgotten herself on that occasion; no servant would answer as she had done, even if they had felt like it, as it would have been instant dismissal. She could cook, though, and the food was really good. Should he just leave things at that? He would be returning to London soon after his visitors had left anyway. But Miss Elliss intrigued him. He thought of her wonderful red hair and how her face was quite beautiful when she didn't look so anxious and tired. Her eyes were a lovely greeny-blue, the colour of the sea. Alex gave a sigh.

Perhaps in due course he would find out more about her, but now, he told himself, he must sleep. He snuffed out the candles.

At the same time, on the floor above, Kate lay in her narrow bed. The room was stuffy as she hadn't opened the window all day because of the rain. But, for all that, she felt happy again. It had been lovely to play music once more and to dance a little, just by showing the steps to the girls. She very much appreciated the sound of happy voices and being treated like an equal by the young people; they had been very sweet to her, she felt. She thought the twins were lovely and funny, Chris was a kind young man and so too was Laurie. She wondered how he had guessed she might play the harpsichord. And to add the finishing touch, Mr Sheldon had bowed to her and thanked her with a smile. She stretched. She wouldn't think of her monetary problems for now, but would just close her eyes and think of the happy evening she had had. She blew out her single candle and slept.

The next morning Kate was up earlier than usual. She went to the kitchen to prepare breakfast with Mrs Watson and the girls. 'At least it is fine today,' said Tilly, 'and we can have the door open.'

'I hope it doesn't rain again for a while,' said Mrs Watson. 'I left the washing blowing on the line at home.' And so the conversation was of everyday things.

It was different in the breakfast room. Alex, Chris and Laurie were discussing what to do that day. Laurie had work to do, he said, so Alex asked Chris if he would like to go riding as the weather had improved.

'Yes, I would, please,' said Chris. 'After being indoors yesterday that would be just the thing.'

'Oh, here's trouble,' said Alex with a smile as the twins came in.

'You're late for breakfast,' said Chris, 'so we didn't save you any.'

The twins both made a face at him. 'We don't mind,' said Phoebe, her nose in the air. 'We will just go and ask dear Miss Elliss for something.'

'You only have to ring,' said Alex. 'Afterwards, what would you two like to do? Chris and I are going riding. Would you like to go with us or have you something else in mind?'

'No,' said Phoebe. 'Are you going far? We would like to ride but perhaps you would wish to go further than we are used to.'

'Well,' said Alex, 'how about if we take a groom with us, and he can accompany you back when you wish, if Chris and I go further.'

So that is what they decided to do and an hour later they set off.

In the kitchen, luncheon was prepared for the servants only, as, of course, Mr Sheldon and his guests would eat elsewhere. Mrs Watson would be able to take care of anything needed by Mr Ward or the servants and so Kate decided she had time to walk to the village. She found everywhere outside in the parkland smelling fresh after the rain, but she had to walk a narrow path to avoid the puddles that still lay around. Then the sun came out and Kate smiled and relaxed. Apart from buying one or two personal things, like some thread to mend her underskirts and some lotion for her chapped hands, Kate thought she would have time to visit Matty for a few minutes and tell her about the previous evening. She would be so pleased to know all about it. Also she hoped Will would be able to mend the holes in her shoes which might keep them in use until she was paid her wages again. All in all, the trip should be an hour at the most.

Her items purchased, and her money reduced further but only by a little, she saw the shoemakers and would have liked to indulge herself by looking in the window but instead she hurried past. She came to Emma's cottage and trod up the path and knocked on the door. Matty opened it, looking tired and anxious. 'Oh, Miss Kate, I am so pleased to see you,' she said.

'And I, you,' said Kate with a laugh. Then she saw Matty's worried face.

'Whatever is wrong?' she asked.

'Come into the parlour and I will tell you,' said Matty, leading the way.

'Now,' said Kate as she sat down, 'tell me.'

'It's Will. He's in bed with an awful cold and cough. He wants to get up but he has a high temperature and is so hot. He is far from well.' To prove her point Kate heard a wracking cough from above stairs. 'I've given him some medicine,' Matty went on, 'but it doesn't seem to do much good.'

'Can I go and see him?' asked Kate

'No, no, you might catch whatever he has.'

'Has he had a doctor visit?'

Matty shook her head. 'I don't like to say, Miss Kate, but we really can't afford…'

Kate stood up. 'Don't worry about money. I will call at the doctor's now and ask him to visit.'

'But Miss Kate,' said Matty, wringing her hands,' you don't have enough. It worries me…'

'Well, don't let it,' said Kate bracingly. 'I'll have to go as I must get back to The Hall but I will ask the doctor to call. Give my love to Will and try and let me know how he progresses, please.'

Kate retraced her steps to the village and found the doctor's house situated in a quiet street at the far end of it. She trod up the steps and raised the brass knocker on the door. A maid soon answered. 'Could the doctor call at the cottage next to the church, please, urgently?' Kate asked.

'Please come in, Miss. Dr Pearce is here.' She led the way to another door, opened it and said: 'Dr Pearce, here's a lady to see you.'

'Come in,' he said, standing up. He was tall and slim, with a gentle smile on his face. Kate thought he was about thirty years old but she was too worried to notice any other details about him. 'Do sit down,' the doctor said. 'How may I help?'

'I haven't come about myself, but could you visit an elderly gentleman who lives in the cottage next to the church? He has a very bad cough and cold but I didn't see him for myself.'

'Very wise,' said Dr Pearce, still with that smile. 'I will go now as I'm not expecting any patients at the moment.' He began to pack a bag with instruments and bottles.

'Oh, thank you,' said Kate gratefully. 'Could I ask when you wish me to pay you?' She crossed her fingers, hoping he didn't want any money at this moment.

'When I've finished the treatment.' He gave her a friendly smile. 'Shall we go?'

Outside Kate explained she couldn't accompany him. 'That is quite all right, but may I know your name and address?'

'I – I live at The Hall, and the name is Elliss. Your patient is called Mr Stokes.'

'Thank you, Miss Elliss.' He bowed and raised his hat.

Kate returned to The Hall much later than the hour, flustered and worried once more.

'It's all right, Miss Kate,' said Mrs Watson, when Kate briefly explained why she was late. 'I've sent the luncheon to the servants.'

'I really am sorry. I will cope with dinner later while you go home early, if you like,' offered Kate. 'Then you'll be able to take in your washing.'

'Are you sure that would be all right?' asked a relieved Mrs Watson. 'It would be lovely to get it all ironed and away today. The girls can help you, can't they?'

'Yes, of course,' said Kate, hoping that Peg and Tilly wouldn't mind the extra work.

It was Saturday and after breakfast the twins decided to try new hairstyles and check that their dresses were just as they should be for the coming evening when they went to dine with Mr and Mrs Lucas. Their dresses were charming confections of cream brocaded silk, the skirts of which were parted to reveal petticoats of cream decorated with a pattern of blue forget-me-nots for Phoebe and tiny pink roses for Chloe. The bodices were tight fitting with a scooped neckline, which must not be too low, had said their Mama, and elbow length sleeves all edged with froths of delicate lace. Ribbons of blue and pink respectively adorned their hair, each with a tiny spray of flowers to match their dresses.

'We must go and see Miss Hunt and remind her to go with us tonight,' said Chloe.

'I suppose so,' said Phoebe, 'but why we have to take her I don't know, she doesn't do anything but go to sleep.' They giggled.

'I expect Uncle doesn't want to risk not doing the right thing. I know when we're with Mama and Papa we don't take her but I suppose Uncle feels more comfortable about it if we do.'

'It would be better if we took Miss Elliss. She's more lively,' said Phoebe.

'But she's the cook. She wouldn't be allowed,' said Chloe.

'I agree, but I don't think she looks like a cook at all, do you? I think,' said Phoebe, her face full of mischief, 'I think there is a mystery. Uncle

Alex smiled at her quite nicely the other night, didn't he? I wonder if he likes her?'

'What do you mean?' asked Chloe. 'He doesn't see much of her, does he? I mean she's in the kitchen most of the time.'

'Well, we don't know what happens when we are not around, do we?' giggled Phoebe.

Chloe ignored her. 'Look, Phe, what do you think to my hair like this?'

That evening the twins, very pleased with their cream dresses and carrying the lightest of shawls, found Alex and Chris awaiting them in the hall. Miss Hunt, dressed sedately in a dark gown and with her greying hair neatly hidden under a lace cap, followed them. Alex, wearing a dark blue fitted coat edged with gold braid, an embroidered waistcoat and velvet knee breeches, bowed and smiled. 'Ladies,' he said, 'you both look delightful and good enough to eat.'

'Thank you, sir,' the girls chorused, curtseying and now on their best behaviour. But Alex noticed they had a mischievous twinkle in their eyes.

Chris laughed at them. He was dressed in a pale blue coat with a flowered waistcoat beneath. Like Alex, his fair hair was unpowdered and tied back.

'It will be a little crowded in the coach but we don't have to travel far,' said Alex, as he led the way to the waiting coach outside. 'Come, Miss Hunt, let me help you up the steps,' he said.

Miss Hunt thanked him and hurriedly sat down inside murmuring, 'So kind, so kind.'

As Alex had said, the journey didn't take long. Phoebe and Chloe were quieter than usual but with a suppressed excitement. Chris asked Alex if it would be permissible to perhaps sketch a little.

'Maybe,' said Alex,' but have you brought your paper and...?'

'That is what capacious pockets are for,' said Chris, indicating his coat pocket.

'Oh, but you will dance, Chris, won't you?' asked Phoebe.

'Of course,' said her brother surprised. 'What has that to do with it?'

'Well, you can't carry your book around with you and...'

'Oh, I shall give it to Uncle Alex to hold,' said Chris blithely.

'But you will be dancing, Uncle, won't you?' asked Phoebe.

'No, no,' said Alex obligingly, 'I shall just sit and hold Chris's sketchbook. That is why I came.'

Phoebe and Chloe giggled.

They were warmly welcomed by Mr and Mrs Lucas, who were a pleasant couple and elegantly dressed. Mr Lucas wore spectacles, which fascinated Chloe as they kept slipping down his nose. Miss Hunt was taken care of by the housekeeper who said she would be restored to them when the dancing began. Mrs Lucas introduced their two eldest children, a young man of seventeen called Richard and his sister, Lucy, who was a year younger. They were friendly and quite awed by the twins looking so alike. 'It's a good thing you are wearing different coloured ribbons in your hair,' said Richard with a smile, 'otherwise we wouldn't know who is who.'

They sat down to dinner, the company comprising just Mr and Mrs Lucas, their two children and Alex's party. The food was good and plentiful and the twins and Chris were asked how they were enjoying their holiday and what had they been doing. It was all very relaxed and pleasant.

During the meal a servant entered with a piece of paper, which he handed to Mr Lucas. 'I'm sorry to intrude, sir, but I thought you should see this.'

'What is it, dear?' asked Mrs Lucas. 'I hope no one is ill.'

'No, but it looks as though Miss Groves has had a mishap and will be late.'

'Oh dear,' said Mrs Lucas. 'Now what shall we do? Miss Groves was going to play for the dancing, you know. I can't tell all the young people not to come at this late stage, can I?' She felt her evening doomed. She did want it to be a success, inviting Mr Sheldon and of course, it would be such a disappointment for the children.

'We could all hum a tune and someone could beat time with a – a spoon or something,' said Richard, picking up his large soup spoon.

'We know someone who can play the harpsichord, Mrs Lucas,' said Phoebe helpfully, looking at her Uncle.

'Do you, dear?' Mrs Lucas sounded quite distracted. 'But it is so awkward.'

'If it would help, I could send a note to my secretary to bring Miss Elliss, if that is acceptable to you, Mrs Lucas,' said Alex. 'She may not be so proficient as your Miss Groves but she would be better than no one.' Alex smiled at Chloe.

'Oh, how kind,' said Mrs Lucas. 'They would be a little late, I expect, but we could play a game or two until they came, couldn't we?'

'Show Mr Sheldon to my study, Parker, so that he can write to his secretary,' ordered Mr Lucas.

'Yes, sir. This way, if you please, sir.'

So Alex interrupted his excellent dinner to write his note.

Laurie sat alone in his study. He thought perhaps he might read for a while. As he was pondering which of his books he should choose, he heard the doorknocker and wondered if it was Alex back again. He waited and the next moment there was a brief knock and Mr Figgis opened the door. 'A note for you, Mr Ward,' he said, 'and the messenger left.'

'Thank you,' said Laurie. He saw it was Mr Sheldon's writing and quickly opened it. It read:

> *Dear Laurie,*
> *Please bring Miss Elliss and music here as soon as possible. Come in my carriage. See that Miss Elliss is suitably dressed (no mention of a cook, if you please) also yourself as you are invited to join in the dancing.*
> *Yours A.S.*

'Is everything all right, sir?' asked Mr Figgis.

'Yes, I have to take Miss Elliss to the Lucas's, something about the music. Would you let someone know that I need Mr Sheldon's carriage in about twenty minutes, please?'

Laurie went in search of Miss Elliss. He found her tidying up in the kitchen. She looked up in surprise when the door opened and she saw Laurie standing there.

'Miss Elliss, please leave what you are doing and go and change into a – a dress suitable for the drawing room. You are asked to play for the dancing at Mrs Lucas's house. I am to take you. I've just had a note from Mr Sheldon.'

'But – but I can't, I…'

'It's an order, Miss Elliss, and I have to go too,' said Laurie ruefully. 'You are to be Miss Elliss with no mention of being a cook. I'll explain more on the way.'

'Good gracious, I don't know if…' She didn't finish the sentence as Laurie had gone.

Kate locked the kitchen door after her and quickly went up to her bedroom. She had to obey – she was a servant, but she would rather have been left alone after such a hectic day. She had two suitable dresses, which were not in the height of fashion and she expected them to be creased. She shook them out and laid them on the bed. Which should she wear, the blue one or the green one? The blue one was less creased but did it still fit? She hurried up, took off her kitchen clothes and washed quickly in the warm water that she had the forethought to bring upstairs with her from the kitchen. The blue dress was sedate and simply cut, with a neckline that was not too low and with only a small amount of lace edging the neckline and the sleeves. It fitted well into the waist and the skirt was plain, full and elegant. Kate brushed her hair but hadn't time to do more than tie it so that her curls fell over her left shoulder. She ought to wear a lace cap, as she was an older lady, she thought, but knew she hadn't one. She found her pointed shoes, the only pair she had other than her everyday holey ones, placed a shawl over her shoulders, which had seen better days, and hurriedly descended the stairs to find Mr Ward waiting for her.

Laurie was dressed in a smart coat of dark maroon. He smiled at her when she joined him. 'Well done,' he said, 'you look very nice. Shall we collect the music on the way out?'

Kate nodded anxiously.

Chapter Eleven

'I WOULD IMAGINE,' said Laurie, when he and Kate were travelling to the Lucas's house, 'that the lady they asked to play the harpsichord has not, for some reason, appeared. Whether Mr Sheldon suggested you, I do not know, but more likely, I think it would have been one of the Miss Johnstons. But Mr Sheldon specifically said there was to be no mention of you being a cook.'

'Well,' said Kate, 'I hope I don't disgrace them by wearing this old dress but indeed, it is the best of the two I have.'

'But you look very nice. I'm sure it won't matter anyway, for most of the time you will be sitting down and they all will be pleased you are playing for the dancing. Do your best and if there is a problem I will come and sort it out. Don't worry.'

'Thank you,' Kate said meekly, but it was Mr Sheldon she was worried about. Would he expect her to assume the role of a friend or just a passing acquaintance? She would have to wait and see. She also hoped that she wasn't needed for too long, no more than an hour at the most, as she had to be up early the next morning to bake bread and organise the breakfasts.

When they arrived there were more carriages bringing young people for the dancing. Laurie and Kate followed them in and they approached a large room specially set aside for this event. It was prettily decorated with swags of pink gauze and with pink and white flowers around the room. A large bowl of lilies stood near the harpsichord. They saw Mr and Mrs Lucas with their children, Richard and Lucy, and Laurie introduced himself and Kate.

'Oh my dear,' said Mrs Lucas, 'I am so glad that you could come. Thank you. I think you know Mr Sheldon, don't you? Oh, here he is'

Alex strode towards them, bowed to Kate and smiled. 'Thank you for coming, and you too, Laurie. Oh, here are your admirers, Miss Elliss.'

The twins, with Chris, hurried across to them. 'How pleased we are to see you,' said Phoebe. 'Now we can enjoy ourselves!'

Chloe smiled shyly at Laurie who promptly asked her for the first dance.

'Come along, Miss Elliss,' said Alex, and he led her to the harpsichord where there was some music ready for playing. 'If you feel more comfortable with the music you have brought, play that,' he said. 'You look a little anxious. There is no need to be. Play as you did before and everyone will be happy.' He turned as Mrs Lucas came up to him.

'Is everything all right for you? We are so grateful to you for coming at such short notice.'

'I will do my best,' said Kate with a smile.

Alex didn't know what to do. If he stayed near Miss Elliss perhaps to turn the music and give her support, would she be more nervous than if he left her? As he was debating the problem Mr Lucas came up to him.

'Mr Sheldon, would you join me for a game of chess? Dancing is not for me, I'm afraid.'

'I would be delighted,' said Alex. 'Do you require anyone to turn the pages for you, Miss Elliss?'

'No – no, thank you. I think I shall be all right.'

The two men retired to play chess and Kate didn't know whether to be pleased or sorry.

Laurie and Chris came to her as they saw she was on her own and trying to find the music for the first dance. 'Miss Elliss, are you all right? I saw Mr Sheldon go away and…'

Kate smiled at Laurie. 'How kind of you both,' she said. 'I think I am now organised so shall I play for a country dance?'

Laurie and Chris hurriedly took their places.

Once Kate began playing she forgot about her worries, Mr Sheldon, her old dress and her tiredness and smiled at the sound of the young people enjoying themselves. Later when they all found how friendly Kate was, they came to ask her to play for certain dances. Mrs Lucas was a good hostess and found partners for the shy girls and encouraged some boys to try and dance. Kate noticed Miss Hunt sitting with the other chaperones.

Later, as Kate was looking through the music for a minuet, Alex brought her a glass of wine, which he placed on a small table by her side. 'I thought you might be thirsty,' he said simply.

'Thank you,' said Kate, 'I am a little.' She smiled at him and gratefully sipped the wine. It tasted good. This didn't go unnoticed by a number of people. Mrs Lucas wondered if she was Mr Sheldon's latest flirt and the twins looked knowingly at each other and whispered to Laurie and Chris. Then Kate struck the keys once more and Alex walked away.

Kate had been playing for nearly an hour and she was beginning to feel tired. Oh dear, she wondered, was that excellent wine to blame or had her previous tiredness begun to take hold of her? She shook her head as if to clear it and played a wrong note in the process. The young ones didn't seem to notice but Alex heard and quickly looked over to Kate.

There was a diversion with the appearance of Miss Groves. She had brought some music with her but apart from that she was as different from Kate as could be. She was small, painted, patched and powdered with a ravishing low cut pink silk gown, which must have cost a fortune. Mrs Lucas rushed forward to meet her.

'Miss Groves, how pleased I am that you could come after all. I do hope you are well. As you see, we have Miss Elliss playing for us until you arrived.'

'Yes,' Miss Groves lisped, 'I heard the wrong notes.' As this wasn't said quietly, some young people made faces at each other and some looked annoyed. Miss Groves wasn't making a good impression.

'Yes er – well,' said Mrs Lucas, 'let us go over to the harpsichord. Here is Miss Groves, Miss Elliss, she has managed to arrive safely, after all.'

Kate looked up, a smile on her face but, as she saw the look that Miss Groves gave her in return, she rose quickly to her feet, picked up the music she had brought with her and moved away.

Alex, observing what was happening, quickly went over to her. 'Mrs Lucas, thank you for a lovely evening. I must take Miss Elliss home now.'

'Oh,' said Miss Groves, with a saucy look on her face, 'I thought you were coming to turn the pages for me, sir.'

'I'm sorry,' Alex replied shortly, 'I don't read music.'

Miss Groves pouted and sent another saucy look at him. Alex ignored her, bowed to Mrs Lucas and turned to Kate.

'Thank you, Miss Elliss,' said Mrs Lucas.

'It was a pleasure, ma'am.' Kate curtsied and turned.

'I think I must see Laurie before we leave,' said Alex. 'He can bring the others home, together with Miss Hunt.'

'I can go home by myself, sir,' said Kate.

'No doubt, but I prefer to go with you.' He walked over to Laurie, gave his orders and returned to Kate. Her shawl was collected and they were soon in the same carriage she had arrived in and on their way back to The Hall.

Kate wondered what she was to do. Did she try and make conversation or leave it to Mr Sheldon to decide? She needn't have worried, for as soon as they were on the open road he thanked her for coming at such short notice. 'I'm afraid it was the twins who suggested your coming and I couldn't do anything about it as Mrs Lucas was in such a dilemma. But I'm pleased you came, as I couldn't abide Miss Groves' looks or manners for a whole evening.'

'Perhaps she had problems that prevented her arriving on time which put her out,' said Kate, not wishing to discuss it further.

'But that is no excuse for bad manners, which many noticed,' said Alex severely.

'No,' said Kate.

'Where did you learn to play the harpsichord, Miss Elliss?' asked Alex, after a pause.

'It – it was a long time ago,' Kate prevaricated.

'Of course, you are in your dotage, are you not? Come, come, Miss Elliss, who taught you? And don't say you can't remember.'

'My mother taught me,' Kate said after a pause.

'And was she a lady of consequence?'

'Just to me,' said Kate with finality.

Alex sighed. 'Well, I suppose we are very lucky to have such a talented lady working at The Hall, one who cooks lovely meals and plays music. Is there anything else you can delight us with, Miss Elliss?'

The question didn't encourage Kate to talk as Alex had hoped. The only reply he received was, 'No, sir.'

He made no answer but smiled to himself.

A servant opened the door on hearing their arrival and Alex helped Kate down from the carriage. 'The others will be here in another hour, I expect,' said Alex. 'May I offer you a drink before you retire, Miss Elliss?'

'Thank you sir, but I have to be up early…'

Alex was just going to say something else, but seeing her white face and how she could hardly keep her eyes open, said instead: 'Of course, I can see you are tired. What time do you have to rise in the morning?'

'I have to be down by six, sir.'

'Would it help if I took the children out to lunch or…'

She smiled sleepily at him. 'Thank you but there are the servants to feed and…'

'Can't the other cook cope?'

'I – I don't know, sir, and I want it all to be done as well as possible.'

'I will ask you again tomorrow,' he said. Then, seeing her looking anxious, continued, 'Good night, Miss Elliss, I do realise the long hours you work, you know.' He bowed and turned, leaving her to hurry up the back stairs to her bedroom.

Alex went into his favourite room, the library, where he knew Figgis would have set wine ready for his return. The evening hadn't been to his taste but, of course, it had been kind of Mr and Mrs Lucas to invite him, especially as he had young visitors. The meal had been excellent and the games of chess with Mr Lucas were better than having to watch a lot of youngsters dancing. It was fortunate that he had to bring Miss Elliss home, a good excuse to leave. He frowned at the thought of her. She was a mystery to him. He couldn't fault her with her cooking, and her manners and speech were those of an educated lady, not a common servant. She worked hard and didn't look for kindness. Perhaps she had never been given any. She was popular with the young people and they treated her with respect, but didn't hesitate to request her to play a dance of their choice. Alex wondered if 'Miss Powder and Patch' would be as popular. He doubted it. His expression was one of dislike and he dismissed her from his mind.

He had no more time to mull over the evening as he heard the coach and horses outside and then the chatter and laughter of the occupants. A few minutes later his solitude was broken and first the twins came in, giggling away, followed by Chris.

'Oh, Uncle Alex,' laughed Phoebe, 'just now, coming home, we were talking about our lovely evening when Miss Hunt said that wasn't it funny but she thought the first lady to play the harpsichord looked like your cook! We were in whoops! We didn't tell her it really was.'

'So where are Miss Hunt and Laurie?'

'Oh, he's being a gentleman and seeing Miss Hunt up the stairs to her room. Chloe will be getting jealous!' Phoebe taunted her sister.

'Stow it, Phe,' said her brother inelegantly. 'And you two had better be off to bed as well.'

'Thank you for taking us, Uncle, it was a lovely evening. It's a pity Miss Elliss couldn't have played all the time for us, though. Everyone said how nice and friendly she was,' said Chloe.

'And wasn't Miss Groves nice and friendly?' asked Alex.

'No, she only played what she wanted to play – or could play,' said Phoebe.

'She wore such a pretty dress, though,' said Chloe dreamily.

'Well, Miss Elliss would have looked beautiful if she wore a beautiful dress, wouldn't she, Uncle?'

'I suppose so,' Alex replied gravely.

'We'll say good night, sir,' said Chris firmly. 'Come along, you two.'

Alex was left with his unfinished glass of wine and his thoughts of Miss Elliss in a beautiful dress the colour of her eyes.

Chapter Twelve

THE NEXT MORNING Kate awoke just before six o'clock. Old habits die hard, she thought. She dressed and prepared to go down to the kitchen. She looked at herself in the piece of mirror, which stood on the chest as best it could, and thought she looked good. She had been asleep as soon as her head had touched the pillow last night, so she had had over six hours of solid sleep. It would still have been nice to have lain longer in bed and think about the previous evening, as everyone had been kind and, surprisingly, so too had Mr Sheldon. She couldn't remember the last time anyone had been pleased with what she had done, apart from Matty and Will, and that one time when Mr Sheldon had complimented her on her cooking. She hoped, though, that she wouldn't have to talk to him again as it was obvious he realised that she came from a different background to the usual servants. She wondered if he would enquire about her today, or take his visitors out to lunch to relieve the pressure of work in the kitchen as he had offered, but at the moment she felt able to cope with everything.

Mrs Watson and the two girls arrived and everyone became busy preparing breakfasts for Mr Sheldon and his guests, the servants and themselves. Afterwards, of course, there was the next meal to prepare, as well as washing the breakfast dishes. It was while this was happening that there was a knock on the door. Tilly opened it to find Mr Ward standing there. 'Good morning,' he said, 'may I speak to Miss Elliss, please?'

Drying her hands, Kate joined him in the corridor outside.

'How are you after last night?' he asked with a smile.

'I feel well, thank you.'

'Mr Sheldon asked me to find out, but said he was taking Mr and the Misses Johnstons out for a meal anyway, so if you needed to rest more you would have time.'

'Please thank him,' said Kate, perversely a little put out that Mr Sheldon hadn't enquired in person as he had said, 'but I think I shall be quite all right.'

Laurie smiled. 'When you left last night and Miss Groves played for the dancing, it wasn't so much fun. Everyone said so. She played too quickly and no one requested anything. I thought you would like to know,' he said with a grin.

'Oh, well,' began Kate, feeling embarrassed, 'I – I'm pleased you enjoyed it, thank you.' She returned to the kitchen glad she had acquitted herself well on the previous evening, especially as she had been so nervous.

After the breakfasts were finished, Kate wondered if it would be possible for her to walk to the village to see how Will fared, as it was a pleasant day and she had a little spare time. She had had only one hastily written note saying the doctor had called but that was all. Mrs Watson said she would like to purchase some groceries to take home, so she and Kate decided to walk through the park together but return separately as soon as they had finished their errands. Peg and Tilly said they could cope, and as they would only have to peel the vegetables for the later meal and gossip, they would enjoy being by themselves.

Donning a shawl and her old bonnet, and replacing the screwed up piece of paper over the hole in her shoe, Kate and Mrs Watson sallied forth. It was good to be out of the kitchen and to walk in the fresh air. The temperature was warm and the smell of the outdoors was pleasant. Kate remembered to ask Mrs Watson to order various foodstuffs for The Hall while she was at the grocers so that Tommy could collect them the next day. At the gates they parted company and Kate hurried to the cottage to see Will and Matty. Matty was overjoyed to see her. 'Do come in, Miss Kate. You have time?'

'A little. I can't stay long but I do want to know how Will is.'

'He's a lot better, come and see. He is sitting in the parlour for a little while. The doctor said he could today but not for very long as it is the first time he has left his bed.'

'Miss Kate, it is lovely to see you,' croaked Will, but Kate was disturbed to see how drawn and poorly he looked.

'How are you feeling, Will? Did the doctor give you some medicine?'

Matty answered for him. 'The doctor has been so good and called every day at the beginning. It was the influenza, you know, and poor Will had it so badly.'

'So Dr Pearce is a good doctor, is he?' asked Kate. 'I knew where he lived, but I didn't know anything about his reputation.'

'Oh, yes, he is very good and caring. He says Will is recovering quite well and will gradually become stronger. Em says he is the best doctor around.'

Kate stayed a few minutes more, telling them a little about the previous evening and then she left, asking them to send for her if she was needed and saying she hoped to call again soon. She left with mixed feelings. She was pleased that Will was much better but was worried about the size of the bill she would be presented with if the doctor had visited a few times and supplied medication. She didn't begrudge Will anything, bless him, but it was a worry, as she had no money to spare at the moment. As she neared the park gates she was so engrossed with her thoughts that she didn't notice the figure striding towards her until she heard him say: 'Good morning, Miss Elliss.'

She looked up quickly into the face of the man she had been thinking about, Dr Pearce. She gave him a small curtsey. 'Dr Pearce, I have just been visiting Mr Stokes and he is sitting in the parlour for a while.'

'Good, good, but I hope you didn't stay too long. We don't want you ill, you know.'

'No, of course not, but I am so pleased for what you have done for him.'

'Thank you,' said Dr Pearce and he went on to tell her that it would be a while before Will was much better because of his age.

Just then Tommy opened the park gates and Dr Pearce took Kate's arm and moved her back as four horse riders came through. Kate saw Mr Sheldon followed by the twins, then Chris. As Alex looked down the road to see if all was clear for them to ride out, he looked straight at Kate and the doctor. Kate automatically gave him a curtsey and Dr Pearce a bow. Mr Sheldon didn't acknowledge either but looking beetle-browed proceeded on his way. The twins followed, managing to give Kate a quick smile before moving forward, and Chris only had eyes for his uncle. Kate smiled briefly at the doctor and said quickly that she must go back to the house. She thanked him again for his attention to Will and hurriedly passed through the gate which Tommy was still holding open for her.

Mrs Watson returned to The Hall having been to the grocers'. Here, evidently, was where all the gossips congregated, to buy their small provisions for the week and to spend more time learning everyone's news. This is where they were told who was ill, what their children, young and old, were doing, who had drunk too much and had got into a fight, and any other news, good or bad. The grocer, used to all this laughing and chatting, found it was good for business as the ladies often bought more so that they could stay and listen to any scandal related to the villagers. One lady asked if they knew of anyone who could read and write. She was the sister of an author of historical reference books. 'My brother needs someone who has a good hand to write out his manuscript so that his publishers can read it clearly.'

'I thought you did that,' said her friend.

'Yes, I do, but another person would be a help and they would be paid.'

The ladies laughed. Some said they couldn't read, let alone write, and some said it would take them until Domesday to finish it, but they all agreed they would ask around and let her know if they knew of such a person.

When Mrs Watson was back in the kitchen she found Kate sending Tommy off to the gardener for any fruit she could use.

'Why, what are we making with fruit this time, Miss Kate?'

'Fritters. I saw Mr Sheldon ride out this morning as I was returning and he didn't look very pleased about something, so I thought it diplomatic...'

'To make fritters,' they all chorused together and laughed. It had happened before, of course, but Kate, although she laughed with the others, wondered if Mr Sheldon was displeased with her about something.

While they were busy preparing the meal and chatting, Mrs Watson remembered about the conversation in the grocers. 'Mrs Berry was asking if we knew of anyone who could write a legible copy of her brother's book so he could send it to his publishers. I did wonder if Mr Ward would be interested, Miss Kate. Do you think he would? I know he can read and write and he would be paid for his trouble.'

'I don't know,' said Kate vaguely, her mind concentrating on the two chickens she was taking out of the oven to baste. It wasn't until she had made the fritter mixture and placed the bowl somewhere cool that Mrs Watson's words penetrated her mind. She could read and write, she thought, and the extra money would help with the doctor's bill. Maybe this was the answer to her problems. Mr Sheldon's visitors would soon be going home now, and Mr Sheldon and Mr Ward would then return to London, if what she had been told was true. So she would have more time to herself. 'I could help the author you were telling us about, Mrs Watson,' she said.

'Really?' said Mrs Watson. 'I mean I'm sure you can read and write as you are a clever person, but the writing would take some time to do and when would you be able to do it?'

'Well, after the last meal of the day. I can do it then. It wouldn't be too tiring as I'd be sitting down and the work will be totally different. How can I find out about it?'

'Well, if you're sure, I can see Mrs Berry on the way home and let you know tomorrow.'

'Thank you, Mrs Watson. That is kind of you.' Kate felt lighter hearted. She would cope with the extra work somehow, she told herself. The money she earned would help to defray the doctor's bill and that would be a load off her mind. She might even have enough to spare for a pair of new shoes. She felt more cheerful and continued preparing the meal with renewed vigour.

Alex and his visitors returned to The Hall during the late afternoon. He suggested to them that they could take tea in the withdrawing room if they wished after they had changed. He had to see Laurie, he said, so he wouldn't join them.

'Thank you, Uncle,' said Chris, 'for a lovely day and the lunch.'

'Oh, yes,' said Phoebe, 'and letting us all go round those dear little shops. We bought a little needlecase for Mama because it was so pretty, and a bookmarker for Papa, and we bought this one for you, Uncle, to say thank you for such a lovely time. Oh, there is one for Laurie, too. I think someone must have painted them.'

'We also bought this little card. Isn't it pretty? It has forget-me-nots painted on it and a space for a message and this dear little bow of blue ribbon. We thought we would give it to Miss Elliss for being so kind to us,' said Chloe, 'and as she had a blue dress on the other evening.'

'That certainly is a kind thought,' said Alex seriously. He hoped Miss Elliss would appreciate it too. Somehow, though, he thought she would.

'Shall we include your name on it, Chris?' asked Chloe.

'Er, no,' said her brother, 'I shall give her one of my sketches, the one of you two dancing. I thought she'd like that. Would you like to see what I was drawing, too, sir? Perhaps you would like to choose any you would like to have?'

Alex was touched. 'Thank you, girls, you know how much I like to read, and I certainly want to see your drawings, Chris,' he said and he caught the twins in either arm and kissed them. 'I'm pleased you enjoyed your stay,' he smiled. 'Tell your parents I will be happy to have you all again.'

'Thank you,' they chorused.

'You will probably see me later on in London, sir, anyway, if that is all right. I am hoping I shall be sent for to start my training as an architect.'

'You will be welcome, Chris, and you can always stay with me if you wish. You only have to let me know,' said Alex.

After they had left him for tea, Alex decided that he had found the day rather irksome, apart from the riding, of course, which he always enjoyed. He didn't know why. The twins and Chris were no trouble and easily pleased, the weather had been pleasant and the lunch at the Mitre Inn had been very good. He frowned. What did worry him, he decided, was why was Miss Elliss talking to the doctor? Was she ill or was she friendly with him?

Laurie had been busy, as the post from London had reached him that morning. It was mainly bills that wanted paying and some private correspondence for Mr Sheldon.

'Well, Laurie,' said Alex, waving him to sit down again, 'I see you have had some post. Anything interesting?'

'Only bills, sir, just the usual ones, and these private letters for you.'

'Mm,' said Alex, opening one. 'This is an invitation to dine with the Forests. I think not. A similar one from ...' He threw the rest back to Laurie. 'Open them, dear boy, and say I'm on vacation or whatever you think, but don't accept them.'

'Yes, I will, of course,' said Laurie, 'but I thought we should be returning to London soon. Your visitors will be leaving the day after tomorrow, so I wondered...'

'I don't think there is any need for me to leave here just yet unless there are any real problems. Perhaps, if you feel inclined, Laurie, you ought to return for a couple of days to see if everything is as it should be and the staff there are still in harmony with each other. By the way,' asked Alex as he prepared to open the door, 'do you know if Miss Elliss is ill?'

Laurie looked startled. 'Not as I know of, sir. Why?'

'No matter.' Alex left the room leaving Laurie staring after him, a puzzled frown on his brow.

Chapter Thirteen

THE FOLLOWING MORNING Alex and Chris decided to go riding for a short while, as Chris said that on the morrow he would be cooped up in the carriage for some time going home to Derbyshire. The girls asked if they could walk to the village, but Alex wasn't too happy about this especially as Miss Hunt wasn't able to accompany them. Phoebe asked if Miss Elliss would go with them. Alex frowned. It wasn't her responsibility to chaperone the girls, but he couldn't expect the twins to stay indoors while he and Chris were out enjoying themselves. He pulled the bell cord and told the answering servant to ask Miss Elliss to come to the morning room immediately.

Kate was busy in the kitchen, as usual, while Mrs Watson was telling her how to find the house of Mr Berry, the author. 'He will be pleased to see you, Miss Kate, I was told to say, whenever you can get away.'

'We are rather busy today,' said Kate. 'Being as it is the visitors' last day here, we shall have to present some extra nice dishes. It would be best perhaps if I postponed seeing Mr Berry until tomorrow. It wouldn't matter, would it?'

Before Mrs Watson could answer there was a knock on the door. Peg answered it. 'Miss Elliss, Mr Sheldon wishes to see you in the morning room,' she said.

'Oh, dear,' said Kate, 'now what's the matter? Is my cap on straight?' She was told it was, amidst giggles from the girls, and hurried out, following the servant.

As she entered the room the twins looked smilingly at her. 'Miss Elliss,' began Mr Sheldon, 'could you be free to accompany these two young ladies to the village this morning?'

'Yes, sir, of course, but...' she said slowly. What other answer could she give? Besides, perhaps she could visit Mr Berry while the twins were looking in a shop or something.

'But?'

'Mrs Watson can cope if I can organise things in the kitchen before I go, if that is all right?'

Mr Sheldon looked at her. 'What you are really saying is that you can go in about half an hour's time but not immediately?'

Why did he have to be so picky? Something of her thoughts crossed her face, which made Alex grin. 'I like to know exactly the time it will take you to organise things. So shall we say half an hour?'

'If possible, yes,' said Kate, not committing herself.

Alex was about to reply but the twins forestalled him. 'Thank you, Miss Elliss,' they said. Chloe nudged Phoebe. 'Oh, yes, when we were out yesterday we bought this for you as a little thank you.' They gave her the card.

Kate blinked and looked at them. 'For me?' she asked, as though she couldn't believe it.

'Yes,' said Chloe, 'you are so kind to us, playing for us dancing and everything.'

Kate had taken the little card and read: 'To Miss Elliss, Thank you for everything, Love Phoebe and Chloe.' She noticed the forget-me-nots and ribbon and the carefully written message. It had taken her by surprise to think that two young girls, whom she had never met before this week, could spend their pin money on her. She felt very emotional and a tear found its way down her cheek. She brushed it away, swallowing hard. She managed to smile at the girls who were looking at her anxiously. 'Thank you. How very kind of you. I haven't had a gift like it since I was a little girl. I shall treasure it, thank you.'

'Oh, poor Miss Elliss,' said Chloe and went and placed her arms around her.

Alex looked on, a frown on his face. All this was beyond him. He couldn't understand why a small piece of paper created such emotion. Phoebe unwittingly enlightened him. 'It is so sad, Uncle, isn't it?' she whispered, 'that someone as old as Miss Elliss has never had a gift of any kind given to her while being an adult?'

Alex bit his lip. He wondered how old Phoebe thought Miss Elliss, who, he was sure, wouldn't be too pleased to realise that she was looked upon as someone of advanced years. All the same, if what she said was true, it was sad. He was still watching Kate and he noticed her smiling valiantly at Chloe, saying she was sorry to be so stupid. 'I – I must go. I will meet you both in half an hour.'

'Thank you,' the girls chorused.

Kate gave a curtsey to Mr Sheldon, avoiding his eyes, which she felt, correctly, were upon her. 'Just a moment, Miss Elliss,' he said as she was turning to leave the room.

'Yes, sir?' She still felt she couldn't look at him.

He moved towards her. 'Are you all right? You're not ill?'

'No, sir.' She wished he would be quiet and let her leave the room, otherwise she wouldn't be ready in the stipulated half an hour.

'Look at me.'

Kate looked at him and felt she should say something. 'It – it is just that the young ladies were kind.'

'I see,' he said. He didn't really. Why in tears when someone was kind? But he couldn't question her further especially with the twins being present. 'Very well. Thank you for agreeing to go with these two. Come along, you have to be ready or Miss Elliss won't wait.'

At last, Kate was able to escape.

'Is there anywhere you wish to go, particularly?' Kate asked the twins as they walked through the park.

'We'd like to look at the shops,' said Phoebe, 'and perhaps we can walk further to see the church?'

'Where would you like to go, Miss Elliss?' asked Chloe, considerately.

'I do have to see a Mr Berry for a few moments, but I must find out where he lives. The address is Beech Lane, so if you see a sign, tell me please, otherwise I shall have to ask someone in the village.'

'Perhaps it is near some beech trees,' said Chloe. 'What do beech trees look like, Phe?'

'Big,' giggled Phoebe.

Kate decided they would look at a few shops, enquire about the address and then, depending where it was situated, the twins could look round the church while she saw Mr Berry. She hoped he wouldn't keep her too long.

Unfortunately, they were told that Beech Lane was at the other end of the village to the church, so after they had browsed in the book shop and bought some lemon drops in another shop, they walked to find Beech Lane. This proved to be rather pretty but there were no beech trees. There was a line of cottages and a middle-aged lady with a basket was coming out of the gate of one of them.

'Excuse me,' said Kate, 'could you tell me where Mr Berry lives?'

'I'm his sister. He lives here,' she said.

'I'm Miss Elliss. I...'

'Oh,' said Miss Berry, 'he'll be delighted to see you, Miss Elliss. I will take you inside. Perhaps these young ladies would like to sit in the garden with a cooling drink?'

'Yes, please,' chorused the twins.

While they were occupied, Kate went indoors to meet Mr Berry.

'Here's Miss Elliss to see you, Arnold,' said Miss Berry.

Mr Berry was older than his sister but quite spry. He wore a pair of spectacles and his greying hair was carelessly tied back. He was very round shouldered, probably, Kate thought, from poring over his literature. But for all that he had a kind smile and a twinkle in his eye.

'Let me show you my work, Miss Elliss, and then you can see if you are able to do what is necessary.' He showed her a pile of papers with lists on them of names and places. There were plenty of words crossed out and others put in their place but for all the muddle, Kate could read it. 'I think I could manage to sort this out, Mr Berry,' she said.

'Good, good. Would you be kind enough to write something for me now, just a little, so that I could see if it would be suitable for the publishers?'

'Yes, of course.'

'Please sit here,' he indicated his desk then placed a small piece of paper in front of her. 'Try this pen and here is the ink.'

Kate took the quill pen and carefully dipped it in the ink and began to write. She copied a little off the paper Mr Berry had shown her. 'Is this all right, Mr Berry?' she asked anxiously.

'Oh!' he said looking carefully at what she had written, 'That is excellent. If all of it could be like that I would be very pleased.'

Kate smiled, happy that she had given satisfaction.

'Now, if I gave you these pages to begin with, and when you bring them back, I will pay you for what you have done and then you can take the remainder, if you are agreeable.'

'Yes, Mr Berry, I am quite agreeable and I will do my best. Do I have a time limit or...'

'No-o, but as soon as possible, please. I know you have other work to do but please do your best.' He smiled at her. 'I am very grateful to you for your assistance and I'm sure the publishers will be pleased too as you write so clearly.'

Kate was given some good quality blank paper and noticed that she wouldn't have to make mistakes otherwise she wouldn't have enough. Paper was expensive, she knew, but she could only do her best. With her parcel placed in her basket, she was taken to the garden to find the girls. She hoped they hadn't been bored waiting for her. She needn't have worried, as they had found that Miss Berry had a dear little tortoiseshell kitten and they had been playing with it, nursing it and watching it lap some milk.

'Isn't it sweet?' said Chloe. 'I'm going to ask Papa if we can have one like it. It is so pretty.'

They finally left the cottage and Kate was relieved the twins had enjoyed their visit. They were walking towards the church at the opposite end of the village when Chloe noticed that Kate was limping slightly. 'Are you all right, Miss Elliss? Have you hurt yourself?' she asked.

'No, no, but I think I must have picked up a pebble when we were at the cottage,' she said.

'Shall we take off your shoe for you?' asked Phoebe.

'Not in the middle of the street with all these people around,' smiled Kate.

'We could enter a shop...' said Chloe.

'No, no, I can manage until we go inside the church, then I can sit down.'

The church of St Peter was plain inside and quite chilly but it was different on a Sunday when the vicar, choir and congregation were present.

Kate liked to go when she could but as everyone at The Hall wanted a cooked meal it was difficult. She knew Mr Sheldon attended when possible and had a special pew near the front. Kate always sat at the back so that she could leave at the earliest opportunity and return to work.

Kate and the twins didn't stay long but Kate managed to dislodge the errant pebble and quickly pack the paper back over the hole in her shoe.

Outside once again, Kate would have liked to have visited Will but felt she couldn't with the girls in tow. Not only would they be liable to take the infection, but she didn't want her connection to Will and Matty to become known to Mr Sheldon. He was beginning to be more curious about her as it was, so she didn't want him to be told anything else.

Unfortunately, as they were passing the cottages, Dr Pearce came out, evidently having been to visit Will. 'Good morning, Miss Elliss,' he called.

Kate could do nothing but return the greeting.

'I expect you would like to know how Mr Stokes is?' he said courteously.

'Of course,' Kate said, 'but please may I introduce you to my companions, Miss Phoebe Johnston and Miss Chloe Johnston.'

The girls gave a curtsey and smiled into Dr Pearce's handsome face. He bowed and smiled at them.

'Charming,' he said, 'two identical pretty young ladies with the beautiful Miss Elliss. I am lucky indeed this morning.'

The twins grinned at him and at each other. They remembered seeing Dr Pearce speaking to Miss Elliss when they rode out the other day.

Kate ignored the pleasantries. 'And how is Mr Stokes, Doctor?'

'Improving, improving. I need not visit so often now but he can call on me if there is a relapse, of course.'

'Thank you,' said Kate. 'Come, ladies, we must go back to The Hall. Good day, Dr Pearce.'

He bowed and crossed the road to go to his next patient.

'Ooh, isn't he handsome, Miss Elliss? Do you know him well?'

'No,' said Kate.

'And is his patient well known to you?'

'Yes, why?'

'No reason. You just seem a popular person.'

'No, not really. Now have you seen everything you wanted? I must go back to the kitchen.'

'Yes, let us go back. We can sit by the trees, Clo, can't we? You don't mind if we do, do you, Miss Elliss?'

'No, but you won't go back to the village without me, will you?'

'No, of course not. But why are you so worried?' asked Phoebe.

'You were placed in my care and I should be in trouble with your uncle if you went to the village without me.'

'I don't think he would be really cross with you, Miss Elliss. We think he likes you.' The girls smiled mischievously at each other.

'Maybe,' said Kate quickly, 'but I cook his food so he has to like me. I must leave you now, it is getting late.'

The twins sat on the seat beneath the trees to suck their lemon drops and discuss what they thought of Miss Elliss, their uncle, and what they would tell him about their expedition.

Chapter Fourteen

MRS WATSON had done well in the kitchen. All the dishes that should be were cooking and others were waiting. A rich syllabub and fruit dishes were ready and Tommy's jam tarts were made.

'Thank you,' said Kate, 'you all have done really well.'

'Did you see Mr Berry?' asked Mrs Watson.

'Yes, a nice man. I have here the work I have to do. Perhaps it would be better to take the papers upstairs out of the heat and steam. I shall be back directly.'

'Where will you do your writing?' asked Mrs Watson, when Kate had returned and was busy making some pastries for the twins to take on their journey next day.

'I've been thinking about that. The kitchen isn't really a good place, is it? And my bedroom doesn't have enough light. I did wonder if Mr Ward would let me go in to his office in the evening when he has finished there. I shall have to go and see him as soon as possible.'

'Don't let Mr Sheldon catch you,' tittered the girls.

'I don't suppose he's bothered about seeing Mr Ward in an evening. I wouldn't have thought he worked then, anyway.'

As Kate had been out during the morning, she suggested Mrs Watson would like to return home early that afternoon. Kate didn't want her to think she was taking advantage of her and although she enjoyed taking the twins out she had had no choice in the matter. She had been unable to refuse. But to keep harmony in the kitchen, she thought it diplomatic to offer Mrs Watson a kindness. It was appreciated and Kate managed quite well working only with Peg and Tilly.

Phoebe and Chloe, looking clean and neat, sat down to their meal with their uncle, brother and Laurie. The talk was of horses and manly things, Phoebe whispered to Chloe, so the girls concentrated on their meal, made no comment and waited their turn when they would be asked about their walk to the village.

'Well, you two,' said Alex, eventually, 'and what have you been up to? You're both looking very demure and good and when you look like that, I'm worried.'

'Well!' said Phoebe, 'of all the things to say, Uncle. You sound like Papa.'

'We've been very good,' said Chloe, 'we went to the village with Miss Elliss and we did as we were told.'

She looked so prim and proper that Alex's lips twitched but before he could say anything Chris interrupted. 'Oh dear, when they look and say they've behaved we shall find it is just the opposite. Come along, you two, what have you been up to?'

This is just what they had been waiting for. 'We had better tell them,' said Chloe. She noticed Laurie looking at her, a gleam in his eye. Was he laughing at her? 'We left here with Miss Elliss and we went to look at the village shops. Then we had to find Beech Lane, as Miss Elliss had to see someone who lived there. We looked for some beech trees but finally we had to ask the way. It was a pretty lane with cottages, but there were no beech trees, would you believe? Fortunately we saw a lady coming out of one of the cottages and luckily it was the one we wanted. She was kind and gave us lemonade, and while Miss Elliss went inside to see the gentleman, we sat in the garden and played with a dear little tortoiseshell kitten. Do you think we could have one at home, Chris?'

Phoebe took up the tale, not allowing her brother to answer. 'After that, Miss Elliss came out with a parcel in her basket and as we wished to look at the church we walked the length of the village to Saint – um…oh, yes, Saint Peter's. Well, on the way, Miss Elliss started to limp and said she had a pebble in her shoe. We said we would take her shoe off for her but she declined as she said it would make everyone stare. So she limped along until we came to the church. We sat on one of the seats and Miss Elliss took off her shoe and found the pebble. She had paper in her shoe too for some reason, which she wouldn't tell us. Anyway, we didn't stay long as it was dark and chilly. As we came out we met Dr – Dr – ?' Phoebe looked at Chloe.

'Pearce,' supplied Chloe.

'Oh, yes, Dr Pearce. He seemed to know Miss Elliss quite well. She introduced us and he said he was lucky to meet such pretty young ladies and the beautiful Miss Elliss. Or did he say we were beautiful and Miss Elliss pretty? I don't remember, do you, Clo?' Without waiting for an answer, Phoebe turned to Alex, saying, 'Which is best, Uncle, beautiful or pretty?'

'Don't ask me,' said Alex, 'ask Laurie, he'll know.'

Grinning, Laurie replied diplomatically, 'I think they are both very nice compliments.'

'Yes, well,' Phoebe went on, 'Miss Elliss asked after his patient, who she knew, evidently, and he said that he was improving. She thanked him...'

'Profusely,' interrupted Chloe.

'Yes, profusely, and then she said we must return as she had to see that everything was well in the kitchen. We sat on the seat in the park and she made us promise not to go back to the village.'

'And did you?' asked Chris, knowing his sisters well.

'Certainly not,' said Phoebe indignantly, 'we should have caused trouble for Miss Elliss, shouldn't we, Uncle?'

Alex had continued to eat while this diatribe had taken place. Laurie noticed that sometimes he glanced at the girls, frowning, but he neither smiled nor commented. For one thing he was wondering why fruit fritters were served at the evening meal yesterday? Was Miss Elliss aware of how he felt when he saw her with the doctor? And if so, how could she know?

Laurie wondered if Mr Sheldon realised the twins had particularly stressed the part Miss Elliss played in the outing. But all he said when they had finished was that he was glad they had enjoyed themselves. He continued to take part in the general conversation over the meal but Laurie knew his thoughts were elsewhere.

When the meal was over the girls and Chris said they must pack their things, and also see that Miss Hunt had done the same and that she would be ready to depart after breakfast the next day. Chris accompanied his sisters upstairs. 'Now, you two little gypsies,' he said, 'will you stop roasting Uncle Alex?'

'We don't know what you mean,' said Phoebe.

'Oh, yes you do. No doubt what you said was true but there was no need to elaborate quite so much. I know you think he likes Miss Elliss but that is his business and not ours.'

'Well, I think he needs a little help, perhaps,' ventured Chloe.

'Nonsense. Now promise, no more.'

'All right,' said Phoebe, 'we won't say another thing about the beautiful Miss Elliss, unless…' she grinned mischievously at her brother and began to run up the stairs away from him.

Chris followed, laughing.

Later, when there was a lull in the work in the kitchen, Kate went to find Mr Figgis. She explained she wished to speak to Mr Ward and could he suggest a suitable time for her to see him. It would be for only a moment. He came back with the information that Mr Ward would call at the kitchen when he was free.

Sometime later there was a knock on the kitchen door, which Peg answered, but Kate saw it was Mr Ward so she stepped into the corridor. She asked if it was possible for her to use his office for a short while in an evening, perhaps when he had finished his work, as she had some writing to do. It would take a few evenings.

Laurie looked at her. 'Yes, of course. I'm sure we can arrange something.'

'I would need only ink and a pen and possibly the pounce box. I have paper,' said Kate. 'I will be very careful and not touch or disturb anything of yours. It would be only for a few evenings after I have finished in the kitchen.'

'Does Mr Sheldon know?' asked Laurie.

'No and I would rather he didn't, if you don't mind. I'm not doing anything wrong but he might want to know all the details and I wish…'

'Yes, I know exactly what you mean. Don't worry, I know you can be trusted,' said Laurie. 'Come along to my room when you're ready. If I'm not there I will leave my desk all in order for you.'

'Thank you, I'm really very grateful.' She went back to the kitchen pleased at how things were working out.

That night Kate went to bed feeling satisfied with the writing she had accomplished. It had been pleasant to sit quietly in Mr Ward's room, which was beautifully furnished and it made her feel that she was a lady again and not a servant. She made sure she left everything as it was when she found it and quietly walked to the back stairs that led to her bedroom. Her eyes and her body were tired but things would be a little easier on the morrow as four people were returning home and did not have to be fed, apart from breakfast. However, she had to be up at six o'clock as usual and as soon as her head was on her pillow she was asleep.

The twins were sorry to be leaving the next day, 'just as things were becoming interesting' they said. They had enjoyed their stay and they had had fun that last evening playing various games, in which Laurie had joined them. Chloe said she would be sorry to leave him but she hoped he would write to her. Chris had enjoyed his stay, too, but he hoped to be back in London soon if an architect was interested in seeing him. Therefore, he hoped he would see Uncle Alex in the not too distant future.

Laurie had enjoyed the companionship of the younger people for a change and he thought Chloe was sweet. Perhaps if she remembered him when she came again and was older, he could easily continue to give her his attention. As it was there was work to be done and Miss Elliss to help and also to keep Mr Sheldon happy. Laurie liked him and the work wasn't difficult. Mr Sheldon was easy going up to a point but recently he found him more reserved and thoughtful. Perhaps he would feel better after his visitors had gone, and although Laurie was sure he had enjoyed their company, perhaps he wanted to revert back to his usual solitary state. The twins had certainly teased him, the minxes, but he hadn't risen to their bait. It had been nice to have the visitors, but it would be good to be back to the usual routines. He must prepare himself to go to London for a short while to see if all was well there. It seemed, from what he had said, that Mr Sheldon would remain at The Hall for a while. Laurie wondered why, as he usually preferred meeting his friends in London and the round of dinners, theatres and social gatherings; he was popular, partly because he was still single, of course.

As Alex sat in his favourite place in his library, nursing his brandy glass, he relaxed, thinking of his visitors. He was sure they had enjoyed themselves and he had taken pleasure in their company too. He hoped to see Chris again soon and he would do all he could to help him, and the twins had been fun. What did disturb him were their stories about Miss Elliss. Who was she? Why was she a cook? She was a good one and he hoped she would continue to cook at The Hall. What were these papers she had collected? Who was ill whom she knew? And why could she play the harpsichord so well? Her manners and speech were not those of a servant, either. Laurie had said perhaps she had fallen on hard times. It was possible. So why was she visiting people in the village and how friendly was she really with Dr Pearce? According to the twins, very friendly, but was that true? She was certainly attractive with that hair, her bearing and her speech. Was she beautiful? No, she was too slim. That was probably because she worked too hard and didn't eat enough. And why was he worried about her? He wasn't, Alex told himself, it was just that… He tossed off the remains of his brandy, arose from his chair and went to bed.

Breakfast the following morning was a lively affair. The twins, although sorry to leave dear Uncle Alex, were looking forward to seeing their parents again and renewing their social life at home once more. A box of pastries and fruit had been left on the table for them to take on their journey, for which they said they must go and thank dear Miss Elliss before they departed.

Their coach was brought round, servants deposited their luggage outside, Miss Hunt was escorted by Mrs Sharpe, the housekeeper, and delivered to be with the twins once more and Chris carefully helped her up the steps into the coach. The twins hugged Alex and Laurie kissed their hands. Chris thanked Alex once more, shook hands and took his place inside the coach while Alex told them to remember him to their mother and father. The steps were lifted, the door closed and they were away, Chris leaning out of the window to wave until a bend in the drive obscured his view.

Chapter Fifteen

AFTER HIS VISITORS had departed Alex went to visit Laurie in his office. 'Have you any problems or is there anything I should know about?' Alex asked. He sat down in a chair. 'It will be nice to be back to normal again,' he said, stretching out his long legs. 'Not that the visitors were not welcome, of course. They're bright and fun, but a trifle wearying at times. I must ask my brother-in-law how he copes. And will you miss Chloe, Laurie?'

'Well, yes,' answered Laurie carefully, 'but both girls are young. If Chloe and I feel attracted to each other at a later date, then things might change.'

'You don't think you should secure her while you can?' enquired Alex.

'No, sir, it is too soon and we both could change our minds.'

'Very wise,' said Alex gravely. 'Now is there any business for me to attend to or have you coped with it all?'

'There are a few things on which I need your yea or nay,' smiled Laurie.

Alex quickly sorted out the papers that Laurie gave to him, and handed two piles back. 'And when do you go to London?' asked Alex.

'I thought at the beginning of next week, if that is convenient to you.'

'As you please,' nodded Alex. 'There are a few business people I wish you to see for me while you are there.'

'Certainly,' said Laurie. 'Are there any friends or acquaintances to whom I have to carry any messages as well?'

'No. If anyone enquires, just say I'm staying here for health reasons,' said Alex, grinning as he got up and left the room.

He decided to go riding to visit acquaintances around the area and whom he hadn't seen since he had been back in Ashleigh. He found the air was pleasant and fresh. He was trying to clear his head, as he hadn't slept well which was unusual. He told himself he didn't know the reason for this but at the back of his mind was the thought that Miss Elliss was to blame. How ridiculous, he told himself, it was more likely the brandy. All the conjecture was forgotten, however, when he was astride his horse and he gave himself up to a pleasurable gallop before his visits.

In the kitchen, Mrs Watson was anxious. She asked Kate if she knew how much longer she would be employed at The Hall. 'I was only brought in because there were visitors. Peg was too,' she said.

'No-one has said anything to me,' said Kate. 'I feel we should all carry on as usual and hope they have forgotten about it. We are all working well together and I should miss you, Mrs Watson. We have plenty to do between us and I feel even if only one left, the extra work would be noticed.' Everyone decided to say nothing and await events.

Much to the girls' delight, Laurie decided to visit the kitchen to have a word with Kate. She walked with him in the corridor outside. 'I shall be away at the beginning of next week, Miss Elliss, but please use my room as we planned. If there is anything you wish to ask me before I go, please do so.'

Kate thanked him and returned to the kitchen, Mrs Watson pleased to learn that the conversation was not about her leaving. Lunch was an easy meal to get ready, as apart from the staff, there was only Mr Ward. Mr Sheldon would be eating elsewhere. They prepared everything as far as they could for the evening meal so that it would just mean placing various pots on to cook at the right time, which was easily done. Kate said if it was convenient she thought she would take an hour off that afternoon to buy two candles and also visit Will and Matty. Mrs Watson agreed to supervise while she was away and Kate suggested that when she returned Mrs Watson could go home early.

Kate liked being in the fresh air but somehow the walk through the park to the gates took longer than usual. She tried to pull herself together and quicken her pace otherwise she wouldn't have so much time to spend with Will and Matty.

The shopping was soon done, as she only bought the two candles. She felt she couldn't expect to use Mr Ward's and not replace them. She hurried to the cottage.

It was a pleasant day and apparently Will thought he could manage a little fresh air. Kate was delighted to see him out in the garden. 'Will, Will, you look much better than when I saw you last!' she said, smiling at him.

Will was delighted to see her and took her inside the cottage. 'Come here, Matty,' he called. 'See who is here.'

Matty came quickly and, of course, she too was pleased to see Kate. They went into the parlour and Kate listened to Will telling her how wonderful the doctor was. Emma was home, too, and brought tea for them all as a treat.

When Will had finished telling Kate about his illness, Emma wanted to know how things were at The Hall. Kate was able to tell her about the visitors and how Mrs Watson and the girls were helping in the kitchen.

Time sped by and Kate finally said she must leave. She had stayed longer than she intended but they all were so pleased to see her and to hear all the news that they didn't want to let her go. 'I will come again as soon as I can,' she said. She kissed them all and hurried down the path and through the gateway, where she gave them a final wave. Then, walking as fast as possible, she returned to the park through the large gates.

It wouldn't take her long to reach the kitchen, she told herself, and wished she could run. She wanted Mrs Watson to return home early as she had promised her. She thought how surprising it was that when you were with people you knew and there was so much to talk about, how the time seemed to pass by more quickly. She began to be a little agitated and decided to risk a run and hoped there was no one around to see her. But she hadn't allowed for her wretched shoe. Somehow the paper she had placed inside to cover the hole had moved and she inadvertently trod on a large stone, with the result that she ended in twisting her ankle as she ran and fell headlong on to the path. She didn't cry out as she was too surprised. She had never fallen like that before. All she could think was that it was such a silly thing to do. She was a while getting her breath back and then she tried to sit up. That was when she realised the pain in her left ankle was worse and not better when she did this.

A figure appeared in the shape of Tommy. 'Tommy help,' he said, holding down his hands. But Kate couldn't rely on him being strong enough to pull her up.

'Tommy,' said Kate in a small voice, 'could you ask Mr Figgis to come to help me, please?'

Tommy nodded and left. He rushed through the side door nearly bumping into Alex as he stood talking to Laurie. Tommy was breathing hard. 'Got to get Mr Figgis,' he said. 'Miss Elliss…' and he tried to push past them.

'Just a moment,' said Laurie, used to Tommy's mental state, 'What about Miss Elliss, Tommy?'

'Can't get up. Wants Mr Figgis.'

'Where is she?' asked Laurie.

'Path,' said Tommy as he disappeared at speed.

Laurie and Alex hurried outside and saw Kate on the ground. 'What the devil are you doing down there?' asked Alex. Then he saw her white face. Without more ado he bent down and picked her up easily, just as Mr Figgis and Tommy appeared.

'What happened, sir?' asked Mr Figgis.

'I'm sorry,' Kate managed to say, 'I just slipped, that's all. I've lost my shoe.'

'I have it, Miss Elliss,' Laurie said, picking it up.

'I'm sorry to cause all this trouble,' said Kate, seeing four people gathered around her. 'If you will set me on my feet, Mr Sheldon, I shall…'

'Oh, be quiet,' he said and marched on into the house. He went to the morning room, where there was a couch, and placed her gently down upon it.

'Brandy, sir?' asked Mr Figgis.

'Please, and ask Mrs Sharpe to come here.'

'I don't like brandy,' Kate managed to say. She was surprised how queer she felt after just such a simple fall. She tried to pull herself together but her left ankle was aching badly. She looked up and found Mr Sheldon frowning down at her.

She ignored him. 'Is Mr Ward here?' she asked.

'I'm here, Miss Elliss.'

'Would you be so kind and see Mrs Watson and tell her I shall be in the kitchen in a few minutes and that she can leave as planned, please?'

'Yes, of course,' Laurie said, with a meaningful look at Mr Sheldon, and left the room.

Mrs Sharpe came in with the brandy that Mr Figgis had given her.

'I don't want it, thank you,' said Kate.

'But...' began Mrs Sharpe.

'Remind me to ask you what you want sometime, Miss Elliss. At the moment I'm not interested. Now drink it,' said Mr Sheldon roughly.

Kate took the glass and had a sip. It didn't taste too bad and Kate suspected Mrs Sharpe had added water to it. She drank it down and gave the glass back, saying: 'Thank you. Now I feel better. I must go back to work.' She tried to move herself round to enable her to stand up.

'Stay where you are. Mrs Sharpe, would you feel Miss Elliss's ankle and see what needs to be done? If you think it broken we must send for the doctor,' said Alex.

While he stood and looked out of the window, Mrs Sharpe carefully felt Kate's ankle, asking her if it hurt when she pressed it.

'I can move it,' said Kate, 'there is nothing broken.'

'I think a wet bandage would be best,' said Mrs Sharpe.

'We can go through to the kitchen, then,' said Kate, 'we can't have wet bandages in here. Now where are my shoes?' She swung her legs down off the couch, keeping her feet covered with her dress as far as she could, and wished her head didn't swim so much. But she persevered. 'Where are my shoes?' she asked again.

'I have them,' said Alex. 'Will you go and prepare the bandages, Mrs Sharpe, and I will see you back here in a few minutes?'

'No,' said Kate, looking up. 'I can get up and walk to the kitchen.'

Alex nodded to Mrs Sharpe who scuttled out of the room.

'I think you are forgetting yourself, Miss Elliss. You are still one of my staff, you know. Now, your shoes. This one I will pass, but this one...' He held up her shoe with his finger through the hole. 'What the devil do you mean by wearing this which looks as though it should have been thrown away months ago?'

Kate didn't know what to say. All she could think of was to say she was sorry.

'But that isn't an answer,' Alex said.

She shook her head and found it ached now. What she would like to do was to take a strong dose of laudanum to take away the pain and curl up in bed and sleep. This was a nightmare. She had tried so hard to do what was right and keep going and look after Will and Matty. If only she had walked home as usual and not hurried. Tears began to fall and she brushed them away with trembling fingers.

A handkerchief was placed in her lap. 'Poor Kate,' Alex said softly.

The door opened and Mrs Sharpe came back with an enamel basin of water and bandages. She also brought a covering for the carpet.

Alex nodded to her and left. Outside he went to find Laurie.

'Well, what happened in the kitchen?'

'I asked to talk to Mrs Watson and took her into my room away from the two young girls. She looked really worried – I think she thought I was going to tell her to leave. However, I explained the situation about Miss Elliss and she was quite upset as she said they got on so well together in the kitchen. She said the meal was cooking as they had all worked hard so that Miss Elliss could have an hour off to visit someone and then she, Mrs Watson that is, would go home early. But she said in the circumstances it didn't matter and she would stay as long as she was wanted.'

'I can't help but feel that Miss Elliss is up to something,' said Alex. 'She's well paid and yet she has a great hole in her shoe. Her own clothes are old and her working ones are always clean but of hardly good quality. She knows someone who is ill and visits this man who gives her paper of some kind. What is that all about?'

'I do know,' said Laurie, 'but I promised not to say anything to you.'

'You'd better tell me, you know. I shall find out eventually.'

Laurie thought hard. He didn't like betraying a trust but Mr Sheldon paid him his wages and he couldn't really refuse to tell him. 'Perhaps you would be kind enough not to tell Miss Elliss you know.'

'Very well,' said Alex.

'She is copying notes made by someone into a fair copy so that it can be sent to the publishers. She asked me if she might use my room in an evening when I'm not here. I said she could, that is all.'

'As if she hasn't enough to do,' mused Alex. 'It looks to me as though she needs more money for something. Is there someone, a relation or a child, whom she has to pay for? What do we know about her, anyway? Anything?'

'Not really,' said Laurie. 'She was introduced by the previous cook but how she knew her I didn't enquire and she seemed popular with everyone and pleasant. She cooks well, which is the main thing.'

Alex nodded, frowning.

A step sounded behind him. It was Mrs Sharpe. 'Excuse me, sir,' she said, 'but I've bound up Miss Elliss's foot. I think it is only sprained and I've cleared everything away. Tommy gave me this which he said he found lying on the ground.'

'Thank you,' said Alex. He took the parcel, which was nearly undone and found the two candles Kate had bought, but now they were broken with pieces of wax loose in the paper. 'Candles? Why would she want to buy candles? Don't we provide candles for all rooms, Laurie?'

'Of course we do. I can't answer that, I'm afraid, unless she was going to replace the ones she was using here.'

'Well, I'll go and find out,' said Alex. He left Laurie feeling uneasy. He hoped Mr Sheldon would be kind to poor Miss Elliss.

Kate felt her ankle a little easier now it was bound and she decided to see if she could stand up. She hoped to get to the kitchen before Mr Sheldon returned. If she could put her right shoe on, it wouldn't matter about the left. She gritted her teeth and leaning on her right foot only, pushed herself up. She managed to stand without going dizzy and looked round for her shoes. She found Mr Sheldon had placed them on the floor near the couch. The difficult thing was to get her right foot into the shoe while standing on her bound foot. She decided to leave the shoes and hopefully get someone to return them to her later. Now she must endeavour to walk towards the door. Perhaps if she held on to the furniture she could manage it. Her ankle was painful but she was determined to get to the kitchen.

Alas for her plans. The door opened and Alex stood there, but only for a moment. 'Where do you think you're going?' he said, at the same time lifting her off her feet and depositing her back on the couch.

'I was going to the kitchen where I should have been long ago,' Kate managed to say.

'Instead of which you are going to talk to me,' said Alex. He picked up a chair and moved it nearer to her.

'Am – am I?' frowned Kate.

'Yes, and don't frown at me. I deduce by the state of your shoes that you don't have enough money to buy any more. So, tell me, if you please, why you haven't enough money. Are the wages you are paid inadequate or are you doing something else with them?'

'The – the money you give me is perfectly adequate, and yes, I am doing something else with it other than buying new shoes,' Kate said carefully.

'And are you going to tell me what you are doing with your money?'

'No, I think that is my business.'

'My good girl, it is very much my business when you damage yourself and make it impossible for you to do your work, for which I am paying you.'

'I keep trying to go to the kitchen to do my work, but you keep stopping me,' Kate spat back at him.

Alex looked at her. 'You know very well you wouldn't be able to do any good if you were there. And I believe all you would like to do at this moment is to go to your bed,' he said, trying to keep his temper on a tight rein.

What Mr Sheldon said was only too right, Kate thought resignedly. She would love to go to her bed, but she was trying to do her best and he wasn't helping. She swallowed. 'Yes,' she said, 'I would like to go to bed but I'm endeavouring to do what I'm paid for and go to the kitchen – but you keep stopping me. Sir,' she added, as an afterthought.

Alex looked at her. She looked so pale and tired that he kept his temper and refrained from asking more questions. No doubt he would find out eventually, he thought, but it would be cruel to continue questioning her. In one way he admired her. She was trying to be fair to everyone, but she seemed to have forgotten about herself. His face softened. He got up and pulled the bell pull. A servant answered immediately. 'Mrs Sharpe, please,' said Alex.

Kate was pleased he wasn't going to persevere. It was difficult to concentrate on the right answers when her ankle and her head throbbed in unison.

Mrs Sharpe arrived. 'Miss Ellis is going to her bed,' Alex informed her. 'Would you lead the way, please?'

'Yes sir, of course.'

'There is no need, I can…' began Kate.

'Oh, do be quiet,' said Alex, at the end of his tether. He strode forward and easily picked her up. 'Lead on, Mrs Sharpe,' he said. He managed the two flights of steps to the servants' quarters and the walk along the corridor to Kate's room. Mrs Sharpe, having duplicate keys to all doors, opened Kate's door wide so that Mr Sheldon could walk in and deposit Kate onto her bed. He did this, turned and walked out again, but not before his keen eyes had taken in the clean and tidy but poor condition of the room. Were all the servants' rooms like this? He must look into the matter and have a word with Laurie.

Chapter Sixteen

ALEX WAS UP EARLY, and as it was a bright morning he thought it just the time for a quick gallop in the fresh air before breakfast. He went to the stables and was soon mounted on his favourite horse, Samson.

On their way back half an hour later, as Samson was trotting carefully up the drive, Alex noticed a small figure walking slowly towards the door.

Alex stopped. 'Good morning,' he said, 'Can I help you?'

The small girl dropped a curtsey and held up a piece of folded and sealed paper. 'I was told to deliver this, sir,' she said.

'Who is it for?'

'I – I don't know, sir, I can't read. The doctor gave it to me to deliver.'

Leaning down, Alex said: 'I own this house so I will give it to whomever it is addressed.'

'Thank you, sir,' she said and turned to go.

'Here you are,' said Alex, bending down and handing her a coin. 'Have you walked from the village?'

'Yes, sir.'

'And are you hungry?'

'Oh, yes, sir.'

'Go round the corner there,' said Alex, pointing, 'and call in the kitchen and say Mr Sheldon told you to ask for food. Then follow the path through the park to the gates and you will be in the village.'

The girl smiled up at him. 'Oh sir, thank you, thank you.'

Alex nodded and rode away, looking forward to his own breakfast.

Kate awoke and wondered what the time was. She had slept well which was surprising, she supposed, when her ankle had been so painful. She moved her foot experimentally whilst lying down. It still felt sore but she hoped, when she placed it on the floor, she would be able to stand on it. She still felt sleepy and didn't really want to get up, but she made a big effort, sat on the side of the bed and experimentally placed both feet on the floor. Although the left one was painful, she gritted her teeth and rose, and then immediately fell back onto the bed again. How was she going to manage to get downstairs? She swallowed hard and made another attempt, hoping it would be better this time. It wasn't.

Just as she was wondering what to do, there was a knock on the door. It opened and one of the maids appeared carrying a tray.

'Oh, Miss,' she said, 'you're not to get up, Mrs Sharpe says, and I've brought your breakfast.'

'Why, thank you Lizzie, but I must get up.'

'Mrs Sharpe said I was to tell you to have your breakfast and she would then come up and see you, Miss,' said Lizzie, placing the tray on the bed.

'Do you know what time it is, Lizzie?'

'I don't know the exact time but it is after half past seven.'

'Good gracious, I should have been in the kitchen long ago,' said Kate, horrified to think that all the responsibility was on poor Mrs Watson's shoulders.

'Well, Mrs Sharpe said you was to have your breakfast in bed, Miss, and then she would come up to see you. I must go.'

'Thank you, Lizzie,' called Kate as the young maid disappeared round the door.

Kate had her breakfast in bed for the first time in her life. She didn't know whether she liked it or not but it was certainly different. Mrs Sharpe visited a little while after. 'How are you feeling, Miss Kate?'

'I feel better but I don't know how I am going to get down the stairs. I can't place my weight on my foot. It is so ridiculous and such a stupid thing to have happened.'

'I will send up some water for you and perhaps you could manage to wash if you put your weight on your right foot. Then you must go back to bed and stay there until tomorrow and see if it is any better. I will bandage it again for you later.'

'But I can't stay in bed. I must go down to the kitchen. Poor Mrs Watson…'

'I'm sorry,' said Mrs Sharpe 'but I'm only obeying orders and so must you. Mr Sheldon said you were to stay in bed for two days at least.'

'I never heard of such a thing, Mrs Sharpe,' said Kate. 'I'm not ill.'

'Nevertheless, Mr Sheldon thinks you are tired out and need to rest, so that is what you'll do.'

'Very well,' said Kate with a sigh. But after she had washed herself with the help of Lizzie, she was pleased to go back to bed. Surprising herself, she went to sleep again.

Kate had to admit that after two days in bed she felt much better. Not only had her ankle improved but she felt better in herself. She managed the stairs with help from Mr Figgis, and she sat on a stool in the kitchen some of the time to do her work. Mrs Watson and the girls were pleased to see her again and told her of the meals they had made. Mr Sheldon had seemed satisfied with the food they had cooked for him, as there had been no complaints. Kate thought there would have been plenty if he hadn't liked his food.

Sometime she would have to see him, as that morning Lizzie had helped her to dress and had brought with her a mended pair of shoes. Evidently Mr Sheldon had had them repaired for her. She was pleased to have them once more, of course, but she must see him, she felt, to thank him and offer to pay for them. After their last meeting, though, she didn't feel much inclined to seek him out.

She didn't have to, as after the next meal she was summoned to the dining room. She felt apprehensive, but comforted herself with the thought that Mr Ward would be there to help her out of any difficulties. But when she entered the dining room Mr Sheldon was alone. Kate remembered then that Mr Ward had gone to London.

'Miss Elliss, come with me into the withdrawing room,' said Alex. He didn't ask her if she could walk or if it was convenient, he just pushed open the intervening door and expected her to follow.

He sat down and indicated a chair opposite. Kate stood. 'I don't think I should, sir,' she said. What would the servants clearing the dining table think if she sat with Mr Sheldon? What would they think of her being alone with him anyway?

'For goodness sake sit down and do as you're told,' said Alex, irritably.

'But the servants, sir,' she said, trying to be reasonable.

'Miss Elliss, must I keep reminding you that this is my house and, servants, including yourself, do as they are told? Now sit.'

Kate sat.

'Thank you,' said Alex. 'Now, how is your ankle?'

'Much better, thank you, and I must thank you for having my shoes mended. Would you be kind enough to deduct the cost from my next wages, please?'

'No, I wouldn't. The shoemaker in the village is making you another pair, so at some stage you will have to go and try them. I suppose he will let you know when. And you don't pay for those either,' Alex finished.

Kate, twisting her fingers together, looked at him with misty eyes. 'Thank you, you are very kind, I don't know what to say, what to tell you...'

Alex interrupted. 'You can tell me who this is from.' He gave her the sealed note that the girl had brought earlier that morning. He noticed that Kate's hands weren't quite steady as she took it.

She knew what it was, but how she was going to explain it she didn't know.

'It is from Dr Pearce,' Kate said.

'And?'

Kate frowned at him. He had been very kind about her shoes but he had no right to demand to know the content of her letters. 'And what?' she asked.

'Open it.'

Kate opened it and Alex, watching her, saw her face whiten and the missive drop to the floor from her nerveless fingers.

Without hesitation he picked it up and saw it was a large bill for medicines and eight visits from Dr Pearce.

'This can't be for you,' said Alex gently. 'You haven't been ill, have you?'

'No,' said Kate, so quietly that he could hardly hear her. 'No, it is for a friend, a very dear friend. He had the influenza, you see.'

'And will you tell me who it is?' asked Alex.

'I've known Will and his wife all my life. I had to help him otherwise he would have died and it would be because of me.'

Alex frowned. That didn't make sense. 'I assume they have little money to pay for this,' he said.

'They rely on me to look after them to a certain extent, although they do work in the village where and when they can.'

'I know Dr Pearce is a good doctor by reputation,' said Alex, 'so I don't suppose this is out of the way expensive. Would you like me to pay it for you?'

'Thank you, but why should you? It is not fair that you should – but I don't know what to do otherwise. I will certainly pay you back eventually. I will keep a note of everything.' She rubbed her hands across her face, thankful that her immediate problems were solved. Nothing was said but when she looked up at Mr Sheldon again she found he was frowning at her. 'What is it?' she asked anxiously.

'I just wondered if you are worried that I would take my payment in another way – like expecting you to share my bed,' he said. 'Forgive me if I speak bluntly.'

Kate looked horrified. 'No, no, I didn't, honestly. No, why should I think that, you have never given me cause, no, oh, no!'

Alex smiled. 'Very well, let's leave it there. Is there anything else you want to tell me?'

'No, I don't think so.'

Alex was disappointed. He had hoped she would confide in him and tell him more. Had he handled her wrongly? It was like drawing water out of a well with the bucket suspended half way up, he thought. Obviously, there had been unhappiness in her life and she was trying to right some wrongs, somehow. She also had a great awareness of what was fair and just. Did that mean she had been treated in quite the opposite way? Poor girl, he hoped not.

'Very well,' he said at last, looking at her as she anxiously watched him. Then he smiled. 'Do you think I deserve fruit fritters for my dinner?' he asked, as he stood up.

Kate, with a sigh of relief, gave an answering smile. 'You deserve them every day, I think, but you would tire of them that way. But I do thank you, sir. I don't mean to be troublesome.' She stood up and carefully walked to the door.

Kate went back to the kitchen feeling a weight lifted from her shoulders. The money problem was still there, of course, but the desperate and immediate need for it had receded and it meant that now she could rest in an evening instead of doing more work. She had Mr Berry's writing to finish, of course. She could not let him down, but given one more evening she should be able to complete her task. Dr Pearce's bill would be paid, she had a pair of mended shoes to wear and another pair being made. She realised Mr Sheldon had money, quite a lot in fact, as he had a house in London as well as The Hall, and the amount that Kate needed was nothing to him, but she believed that if he was kind enough to help her he should be repaid whatever the circumstances. So it was with a lighter heart that she returned to the kitchen.

'I have to make fruit fritters again, ladies,' she said. 'Could one of you go and see the gardener and see what fruit is available. If you bring plenty, we can all share them.'

'I'll go,' Peg and Tilly chorused together.

'Why don't you both go – but not for long, mind.'

Laughing, they took off their aprons, found a basket and left.

Mrs Watson eyed Kate. 'Do we have good news or something?' she asked.

'Well, in a way,' said Kate. 'Mr Sheldon has paid for my shoes to be mended and for a doctor's bill for my friend, on the understanding that I pay him back later.'

'Mm,' said Mrs Watson, 'will you bother?'

'Oh, yes,' said Kate. 'And I shall finish Mr Berry's work this evening, so he will pay me for that. So I feel as if a weight has been taken off me. Hence the fritters,' she added.

Mrs Watson gave her a measured look but said no more.

That evening Kate went quietly to Mr Ward's room and worked on Mr Berry's book. Tomorrow she would take the finished pages back to him if her ankle would let her. As soon as she was finished, she would go to bed to rest it and hopefully sleep well.

Alex, passing by Laurie's room some time later, saw the flicker of candlelight beneath the door. He smiled. Should he go and surprise Miss Elliss and tell her he knew what she was doing? On second thoughts, he decided not. It would be better for her to finish her writing and then go and rest. He would go to the library for his usual nightcap and hopefully finish reading his book.

Chapter Seventeen

THE FOLLOWING WEEK was uneventful for Kate. She felt happier than she had done for some time and although she was determined to repay Mr Sheldon the money she owed him, she felt as though a weight had been lifted from her. She did wonder why he was so concerned about her. Would he treat all his staff as he had treated her? She had noticed how kindly he had looked at her sometimes and although what he said was law in The Hall, she felt there was a warmth about him that she hadn't been aware of before. She liked him, she told herself, but it was more than that, wasn't it? If she was honest she was a little bit in love with him. She smiled to herself. Was that because he was just being kind to her in so many ways, which she had never known before from anyone? She didn't know.

Her ankle was back to normal if she was careful where she walked and the work for Mr Berry had been finished and returned to him. He was pleased with her and had paid her, so she was able to visit Matty and Will and leave them a little of the money. She had been for a fitting of her new shoes, which would be a boon when the winter weather arrived. The work in the kitchen was still hard but she was in pleasant company. Even the weather was kind at the moment, apart from a few showers, which was no bad thing as they refreshed the gardens and created a sweet smell. She hadn't spoken to Mr Sheldon since their conversation in the withdrawing room and although Mr Ward was back from London, she hadn't seen him to speak to either.

One late morning, as Alex was with Laurie in his room going through some papers with him, the knocker sounded on the main door. Ben went to answer it. As he opened the door he saw a travelling coach standing outside in the driveway, so he assumed the man who stood before him had travelled far.

'Good morning, sir,' said Ben. 'Can I help you?' For some reason he didn't like the look of the gentleman. He was tall and dark, but carelessly dressed and his face had a gaunt look.

'Is a Miss Elliss living here?' he asked abruptly, with no accompanying smile.

'We do have a Miss Elliss here, sir,' acknowledged Ben.

'Well, can I see her?' the man said irritably. 'Don't keep me waiting out here. I've travelled a long way.'

'If you step inside then, sir, and wait here,' Ben indicated the entrance hall, 'I will see if she is available. Who shall I say has called?'

'No name,' said the man. Then, as Ben frowned, he added: 'I wish to surprise her.'

Ben thought this most odd and that something wasn't quite right; the man didn't seem very pleasant. He thought it best if he went in search of Mr Sheldon or Mr Ward first, before sending the man round to the kitchen. He knocked on Mr Ward's door. When he was told to enter Ben apologised for the interruption and was pleased to see Mr Sheldon there. 'A gentleman has called asking for Miss Elliss, sir. He wouldn't give me his name and I – I really didn't like the look of him so I thought it best not to send him round to the kitchen before I asked you, sir. He looks as though he's travelled a long way.'

Alex raised his eyebrows. 'Mm. You were quite right to let me know first, Ben. Show him into the morning room. I will see him there in a few minutes when I've sorted something out here with Mr Ward. Don't tell Miss Elliss at the moment, but wait outside the room.'

'Yes, sir.'

The gentleman was taken to the morning room but he refused the sherry Ben offered him. Five minutes later Alex entered to find his visitor looking out of the window. As he heard the door opening he turned saying: 'You've taken your time, haven't...' He stopped mid sentence when he saw Alex.

'Good morning,' said Alex smoothly, disliking his visitor on sight. 'May I help you?'

'I told that servant I wished to speak to Miss Elliss,' complained the man.

'Did you?' asked Alex. 'But this is my house. I'm Alexander Sheldon and I give the orders here. Before I ask Miss Elliss to join us, I wish to know your name.'

'I'm Daniel Elliss, her brother.'

'Thank you,' said Alex. 'Have you been offered a drink?'

'I refused. I don't have much time.'

Alex inclined his head. 'Please sit down,' he said as he walked to the door, thinking how uncouth and rude this man was. Was he really Miss Elliss's brother? Ben was outside. 'Please ask Miss Elliss to join me here,' he said quietly.

'Yes, sir,' said Ben and went quickly to the kitchen. He knocked on the door, which Tilly opened. 'Mr Sheldon requests Miss Elliss to come to the morning room now, please,' said Ben.

'Thank you,' called Kate, 'I won't be a moment.' She had just finished dressing two chickens ready for the next meal. She quickly washed her hands, smoothed down her apron, made sure her cap was on straight and hurried after Ben.

She knocked on the door, opened it and entered, saying: 'You wished to....?'

She got no further as her gaze was riveted on her brother. Her face paled. All she could say was: 'You!'

'Mm,' thought Alex, 'Do I gather she's not pleased to see him?'

Daniel faced her, his lip curling, as he looked her up and down. He had found her at last and it was easy to see the role she was playing in this establishment. He thought there may be money to be had here. Meanwhile Alex stood to one side, not intending to leave the room unless he thought Miss Elliss wished him to. At the moment he doubted she did.

'You've done rather well for yourself, haven't you?' sneered Daniel.

Kate tried to pull herself together. 'Well?' she said. 'Why are you here and what do you want?'

'I would have thought you could guess,' said Daniel, with an unpleasant smile.

'Well I can't and as I'm not in the mood for playing games, say what you have come to say and go.'

'That's told him,' thought Alex.

'There's no need to be so sharp. I've had the devil of a time finding you. Fanny and I came to London to my father's house to find it all locked up. You should have let me know about that – and I had to guess where the keys were.'

'Dear, dear, what a puzzle for your poor brain,' said Kate sarcastically.

'And,' Daniel emphasised the word, 'and the house was dirty and just abandoned.'

'Did you expect me to clean it and look after Father as well? It's about time Fanny got her hands dirty and cleaned it herself.'

'She couldn't...' began Daniel, shocked.

'No, not couldn't, she just wouldn't,' said Kate.

'Anyway, I had to go to Mr Fawcett to obtain the keys. Also I had to enquire about coaches and bribe the man to look up his passenger list at round about that time. So that's how I come to be here and I've found you at last.'

'So now you've found me you can leave,' said Kate.

Alex admired her, standing up to this unpleasant brother of hers. 'But if he doesn't soon go I shall have to step in and do something about it,' he thought.

'Now I am here,' went on Daniel, 'I must tell you that you owe me money.'

'Rubbish!' said Kate. 'The shoe is on the other foot, I think.'

'You sold many items from the house. Everything was left to me and me only.' Daniel thrust out his chin. How Alex longed to punch it.

'The contents were not left to you. You forget, I think, that I read the will for myself,' said Kate.

'So,' said Daniel nastily, 'it's just your word against mine.' He thought the money he had hoped to obtain from Kate would not be so easy to get hold of after all. He went on: 'And I know that in a court of law whose word they would take. Me and Fawcett against you, it would be. But you mistake, dear sister, you cannot have read the will properly. It says plainly, house, money and contents. Therefore you owe me money – a lot of money.'

'I don't believe you,' said Kate. 'I know what I read. It said 'house and money' only and not the contents. I expect you've been to Child's bank?'

'Of course.'

'Well then, you have enough money. You have the house and all the money. I will not and indeed I cannot give you the money from the contents, as they raised barely enough to provide for Will and Matty, nothing more.'

'Well said,' thought Alex. 'Stand up to him.'

'Very well,' said Daniel, 'I have given you a fair chance to pay me back and you refuse, so I shall take you to court. You wouldn't like that, would you? Just think of yourself stood there, accused of theft from your own brother. No one would believe you against me.'

Kate must have heard Alex's thoughts. 'Don't be silly,' she said, trying to battle on. 'Show me this will that you think I misread.'

'It is you who are silly,' said Daniel, 'you don't think I carry important documents with me, do you?'

'No, because there isn't one,' said Kate. 'If you have no more to say, you had better leave Mr Sheldon's house.'

'In that case I will go to my lawyer and I will bring this matter to court. You have done wrong, Kate, and I will have that money.'

'I see what it is. Fanny needs more money to bring out your two daughters so that they marry well. She cannot mix with the rich without it. Tell her she's living beyond her means. She's behind all this and you, like her little lapdog, do what she says otherwise life is uncomfortable for you. Well, find your money elsewhere, I don't have any. You won't take me to court as that would cost you money and you wouldn't be stupid enough to go that far,' said Kate, hoping she sounded confident.

Daniel laughed and it wasn't very pleasant. 'Oh, wouldn't I? I will have you in court, you know, charged with theft and there are many other charges I can think of, too. You will go to gaol or be transported or branded. How would you, or your protector here, like that?'

Kate had paled but she still stood straight in front of him. 'Daniel Elliss, if you take me to court, you would lose as I know I am right about the will. You wouldn't get as far as court procedure, anyway. You would lose.'

'Nonsense, I know what I'm talking about. But if you don't want that to happen, give me the money and…'

Kate interrupted pettishly. 'I have no money. I work here as a cook for my living.'

Daniel looked at her, his lip curling nastily. 'I can see you do. At least you are dressed as a cook today. You never cooked in your life. What will you dress as tomorrow? You are a whore, Kate, and he…' Daniel pointed to Alex, but before he could say anything more Kate had rushed up to him and struck him a stinging blow across his face with the flat of her hand. 'How dare you insult a gentleman in his own home?' she cried.

Alex by this time had shouted for Ben who opened the door. Alex quickly grabbed Daniel by the collar and the seat of his breeches and part lifted, part dragged him through the door. They both were tall men but Alex had the advantage, as he was more heavily built and stronger. 'Door!' yelled Alex to Ben, who rushed to open the front door, where Alex with one big effort heaved Daniel out on to the driveway.

The door was shut, Alex dusted his hands and Ben said, with a grin: 'Well done, sir.'

Alex acknowledged this with an answering grin. 'Would you see no one disturbs me unless it's urgent?'

'Yes sir.'

Alex walked back to the morning room.

It took Daniel some minutes before he could pick himself up off the ground. Not only were his clothes dusty, his nose was bleeding. He managed to find his handkerchief and, holding this to his abused face, climbed into the waiting coach with the words 'Drive, damn you' to the smirking coachman.

Alex opened the door quietly to find Kate stood as if turned to stone. One hand clasped the back of the chair otherwise she would have fallen. Her face was white and her eyes looked into the distance.

'Kate,' said Alex softly.

She turned her head to look at him but she seemed not to see him. He placed his hand over her one gripping the chair. 'Come,' he said softly. She didn't move.

'Hold my hand, Kate, now,' Alex said quietly but firmly.

She looked at her hand as though it didn't belong to her, but she unclasped it and as she did so her knees began to buckle. Alex quickly caught her, lifted her and sat her on the couch. He dropped his handkerchief into her lap while he poured two glasses of sherry, which he placed on a small table. He looked at Kate. Her fingers were playing nervously with the handkerchief.

Alex sat down beside her. 'Do you think you could drink some sherry?' he asked, holding a glass in front of her. She shook her head slightly.

'Try,' he said.

Kate felt numb – she just wanted to die. Perhaps if she didn't eat or drink anything it would be best. She shook her head once more.

'Stop it, Kate,' Alex said in a louder voice. 'Now do as you're told and drink this.'

She looked at him then. He sounded like Dr Roberts when she was little and ill in bed. She placed her hand over Alex's and guided the glass to her lips where she was going to take a sip. But Alex tipped the glass so that she had a mouthful. She coughed and spluttered and pressed the handkerchief to her lips. Over it she saw Alex smiling at her. The spell was broken.

'I – I'm sorry,' Kate murmured. 'I expect you would like me to leave after what happened this morning.'

'Certainly not. Who would make my fruit fritters?'

There was no answering gleam in Kate's eyes. She just looked down at her hands. 'I seem to be always in a scrape,' she sighed. 'I thought I tried so hard but evidently I don't try hard enough.'

'Well, I don't know about that,' said Alex, 'but what I do know is that you and I are going to have a talk right now and sort things out. But first you will take off that cap and apron and throw them somewhere. I will not talk to my cook sat next to me, but I will talk to Miss Kate Elliss.'

Kate did as she was told and looked nervously at Alex as he sat down beside her. She felt he radiated warmth, security and reliability, and she would have loved to cuddle up against him and go to sleep like a trusting kitten.

'Well, what I would like to know is why an accomplished young lady like yourself is working for me in my kitchen. And how is it you have no money when your brother thinks you have? Who are Will and Matty? Please tell me your story from the beginning, if I am to help you. I do intend to help you, but only if you are honest with me,' said Alex.

'It's a long story, but I'll try and tell you as concisely as possible,' said Kate. There was a pause while Alex waited patiently and Kate gathered her thoughts. 'My father,' she began 'wasn't at all a nice man to know and how Mama came to marry him, I've no idea. She had six children, who consisted of five sons, and then I came along. My father had no time for me as I was a girl, but Mama and I were everything to one another. When I reached the age of eighteen, I was presented along with my friends and went to balls and things. I remember Mama making my dresses, as they were too expensive to buy. My father wasn't interested. During that time Mama became sickly. She had had too many children, the doctor said.' Kate paused, as the past she had buried now resurfaced. She went on: 'I was taken to dances with my friends and their mamas. Once, I was invited to Derbyshire for a holiday with my youngest brother, Daniel, whom you met today. I looked forward to seeing the countryside there but all he and the family wanted me for was to look after their children while they went out and enjoyed themselves. I remember I returned to London after two days. After that, my other brothers left at some time. I never really knew them. They weren't interested in Mama or me. We did have Matty and Will Stokes, though. They came and stayed with us and Matty cooked and helped Mama and Will worked around the house. Dr Roberts was helpful to Mama, too, and kind to me, like a father should be. I wished he had been my father. When Mama died I kept house and Matty and I cooked and worked together. I kept away from my father as much as possible. Then the drink caught up with him and he was confined to his bed. I looked after him, with help from Dr Roberts, and, of course, from Matty and Will. Daniel came nowhere near. When my father died earlier this year, I expected I should be left the house. I promised Matty and Will that I would sell it and divide the money between us. The day before the funeral Daniel and Fanny, his wife, turned up unexpectedly. I think the lawyer must have let them know. After the funeral, Mr Fawcett came to read the will and the house and money in the bank was left to Daniel and I was expected to live with them. I knew what that would entail, so I refused. I did ask to see the will and it was the house and money only left to Daniel and not the contents. Afterwards, Will and I sold anything that was valuable so that we could move away. Matty said we could come to Ashleigh and stay with her sister Emma Moss, who was your cook. We travelled by stagecoach as it was the cheapest way and Emma was very kind to me. But, of course, I had to find work and I couldn't stay with them forever as there was little room. Then, as Emma wished to leave here as she felt she was getting too old, she taught me how to cook in the kitchen and I gradually took over. I have also tried to give Matty and Will a little money as I promised. And I will pay you back somehow, I promise, Mr Sheldon. But if Daniel takes me to court, I – I don't...'

Alex mercifully broke in. 'Maybe it was all bluster on your brother's part. But first you would go to the local magistrate whom I know, so don't worry. Forget what your brother said until you get a summons to attend the court; then if you do, we will think what is to be done. I'm going to help you, you know, I shan't forsake you. I can always think of something and I know many people, so don't worry about it.'

'I can't help it. Fanny will push him to find money somehow.'

'Well, you and I will not be popular with either of them. I threw him out, you know, and he landed on his nose on the driveway.'

This drew a quick smile from her. 'I'm pleased you did, sir, he was very rude to you and I'm sorry...'

'You have nothing to be sorry about. Now tell me, was one of your brothers called Gideon?'

Kate thought for a moment. 'I believe so,' she said. 'The boys were all named from the Old Testament in the bible, like my father. Why I don't know. Perhaps he thought if he did name them as such it would exonerate him from any wrongdoing. He left my Mama to name me, thank goodness. But did you know Gideon, sir?'

'Briefly. He ran off with the girl I was hoping to marry,' said Alex.

Kate looked quickly at him. 'Oh, no, I am so sorry. How could he?'

'Easily, evidently. However, as it happens, perhaps it was a good thing. I always thought if ever I met him I would kill him. But it was all a long time ago.'

'Was – was she very beautiful, sir?' Kate asked wistfully.

'I believe I thought so at the time, but to be honest, I can't remember what she looked like now.' He suddenly smiled, looking down at her. 'Now I think we should carry on as usual until we hear something more. It is no use planning further if there is no need to. If we do hear something, that will be the time to discuss what to do next.' Alex stood up and moved to the door. 'And drink your sherry,' he said as he left the room.

Chapter Eighteen

THE FOLLOWING MORNING, after a substantial breakfast, Alex mounted Samson and rode to visit Sir Percy Croft who lived two villages away. Alex had thought long and hard the previous night about everything Kate had told him and, although he didn't think her brother would be able to take things further, he was just the type of person to cause trouble if he could. Alex decided to be beforehand with the world and place Kate's case in front of his friend to see what he had to say. Alex rode up to the old house, which was large and grand and surrounded by trees of oak and sycamore.

Fortunately, Sir Percy was at home and after the preliminaries, Alex asked him if he would kindly advise him on a certain matter. Sir Percy was willing to listen and so Alex told him the story as briefly as he could and as he knew it, to his friend.

'We didn't see the will, of course, and as far as I can see it is Miss Elliss's word against her brother's. She told me she was sure it only said 'house and money' and it didn't include contents. Could another will have been written, do you think?'

'Seems unlikely,' said Sir Percy. 'I mean it would have the father's signature on it and that would be difficult to forge. Of course, it could have been a middle page which could have been forged, I suppose. Who are the lawyers that are involved?'

'A Mr Fawcett, I believe.'

'And this is in London, I presume?'

'Yes. I've never heard of him,' said Alex, 'but then there are many lawyers.'

'Mmm. Also some dishonest ones.'

'I suppose so. But if it came that Miss Elliss was arrested, she would be tried only by a magistrate such as yourself, wouldn't she?' asked Alex.

Sir Percy looked at him and smiled. 'I infer she means a lot to you, apart from being your cook,' he said.

'Let us say she is the type of person who likes things to be right and fair. She has done no wrong as far as I can see and the brother who is accusing her is a nasty piece of work. So much so that I evicted him from my house by the seat of his breeches.'

'I see,' said Sir Percy. 'I suppose you are talking of your house in Ashleigh. But where did the lady live before residing at The Hall?'

'In London. I don't know the address,' said Alex.

'In that case, if the brother took it further, I'm afraid it would have to be heard in a magistrate's house in London, or more publicly in a rotation office like Bow Street. I'm afraid I could do nothing to help, other than advise you. I'm sorry,' Sir Percy added kindly. 'If you do hear further, I would be pleased to know what the charge is and I could perhaps tell you how to proceed. But let us hope the brother will think better of it and keep quiet.'

Kate was hoping the same, of course. She was worried, which was only natural, but knowing Daniel, with Fanny demanding money, she wouldn't be surprised if things became unpleasant. She was comforted to know Mr Sheldon was behind her, to advise and help her. She couldn't have wished for anyone better. He had been so kind to her and even called her Kate. She didn't feel so alone in the world.

On returning to the kitchen, she had apologised to Mrs Watson, who had valiantly carried on organising the food and at a convenient moment she told her briefly what had happened. She said how Daniel had visited and what he said he proposed doing. Mrs Watson was shocked, but delighted that Mr Sheldon had thrown him out, and after discussing this part some more, they made it sound so funny that even Kate laughed. She said she felt much better.

Alex had a word with Laurie, to tell him what had happened. Most of the servants knew of Daniel's eviction, as told to them with relish by Ben, and they grinned to think that Mr Sheldon had done such a thing; it did him no wrong in their eyes. They also knew it was something to do with

Miss Kate and they wondered what would happen next. Occurrences like this helped to break the monotony of everyday work.

It was two weeks later, when Kate had recovered from Daniel's visit and the worries that went with it, that Mr Sheldon sent for her. She knocked and entered the morning room as usual. She looked anxious, Alex noticed, so he smiled at her.

'Come and sit down,' he said. He pointed to the couch. Sitting beside her, he handed her a sealed document. 'This has just come by special courier,' he said. 'It is addressed to you.'

'Is – is it from...?' She couldn't go on. With trembling fingers, she broke the seal and spread out the page. It was a legal document but she couldn't read it as the words danced before her eyes. 'Please,' she whispered.

Alex took the document from her and read it through to himself. He looked at her, at the same time placing a comforting arm around her. 'I'm afraid it is a summons to attend the magistrate's own house in London. This means that he will hear the charge against you and then he will either throw the case out or decide the next step.'

'I see. When do I have to be there, does it say?'

'Yes, next Friday at ten o'clock. Is there anyone you could stay with in London? There would be talk, not least from your brother, if you stayed in my house, it being a bachelor residence.'

Kate rubbed her eyes. 'I – I could go to Dr Roberts if he would have me, I suppose. He used to be like a father to me.'

'Could you write to him and ask him? Laurie will go up to London to prepare my staff for my arrival and he could see Dr Roberts, tell him our problem and give him your letter?'

'Yes, I could do that.' Kate nodded, trying to pull herself together.

'Good,' said Alex. 'Now look at me. Good girl,' he smiled at her as she obeyed. 'I shall see you through this unpleasantness, so don't worry. I will advise you what to do. It may turn nasty but you will be strong, as I know you can be, and some day we will look back on all this as just a bad dream. Do you think you can be cool and calm through it all?'

'I don't know, but I'll try,' said Kate.

'Good. Don't get flustered, just answer the questions put to you honestly and I shall be somewhere near at all times.'

'Thank you. You are very good to me.'

'Now I think you must prepare for London and we must buy you a suitable dress to appear in. Nothing too fancy, just a plain serviceable dress of a dark blue or grey that befits a cook. Perhaps the dressmaker in the village might be able to supply it. I suggest you take Mrs Sharpe with you.'

'The servants will wonder what is going on, you know,' said Kate.

'I propose telling them a little and why we are leaving. In that way, they will be pleased to help if they feel we are one happy family. And they are very fond of you, you know,' said Alex.

'Are they?' asked Kate. 'I wonder why? Oh, Mrs Watson and the girls will be able to carry on very well in the kitchen on their own.'

'Good,' said Alex, businesslike once more. 'I will talk to the staff after I've chatted to Laurie. You go back to the kitchen when you're ready and I will send for you eventually.' He gave her a quick hug before rising to his feet and leaving her to sit or go back to the kitchen, whichever she felt like doing.

Alex visited Laurie next and told him the news. Laurie's reaction was as Alex expected. 'It's such a shame,' he said. 'Life is so unfair sometimes. Miss Kate works hard, bless her. Don't you think it unfair, sir?'

'Sometimes,' said Alex, 'but I must think positively and advise the poor girl. We shall have to go to London, of course, so you must organise things but I think I shall have to have a meeting of the staff here and explain some of it to them. Otherwise there will be a lot of untruthful tales going around.'

'When do you want me to organise this?' asked Laurie.

'Now? There's no time like the present, is there?'

Laurie went to see Mr Figgis and asked him to tell the rest of the servants to attend Mr Sheldon in the morning room. Mrs Watson, along with Tilly and Peg, were asked to be present and Kate said she would carry on with the cooking in the kitchen. She didn't want to be at the meeting, she had enough to think about. She told herself that with Mr Sheldon behind her to tell her what to do, everything would be all right. She would go to London and see Dr Roberts again, which would be nice, but she must see Matty and Will before she left. Perhaps she could visit them at the same time as she and Mrs Sharpe visited the dressmaker in the village later. And so she kept her mind busy, refusing to look further at what might happen.

Meanwhile, Alex began to address the rest of the staff. 'This will not take long,' he said when they were all present. 'Some of you will know what happened some mornings ago when I had the task of removing a Mr Elliss from the house. He had come to see his younger sister, whom we know as Miss Kate. He accused her of theft and this morning a summons was issued for her to appear before a magistrate in London. Miss Elliss denies the charge. Mr Ward and I, together with Miss Elliss, will travel to London the day after tomorrow. I believe her when she says she is innocent of the charge against her, but she and I thought you all should know what is going on. Mrs Watson will kindly continue to cook for you in the meantime. Now is there anything you would like to say or ask?'

Immediately, Mr Figgis cleared his throat. 'I'm sure I speak for us all, Mr Sheldon, when I say how sorry we are to hear the news. Miss Kate is such a nice and kind lady that I'm sure she would never do what she shouldn't. Is there anything we can do?'

Alex smiled. 'I cannot think of anything at the moment, Mr Figgis, thank you, but perhaps if any of you see Miss Kate, smile at her or say something nice so she knows she has your support. As you may guess, she is frightened at the prospect of facing a magistrate, and we're hoping that the case won't get as far as the courts.'

A voice spoke from the back of the room. It was Tommy. 'Please, sir, will I still have my jam tarts?'

There were a few titters and Alex looked puzzled, but Laurie said, 'Mrs Watson, will you continue to make Tommy his jam tarts?'

'Yes, of course sir,' she said, amidst grins from the girls.

'There you are, Tommy,' said Laurie.

Tommy beamed and nodded. 'Tommy likes jam tarts,' he said.

'Thank you, ladies and gentlemen,' said Alex. 'We hope to return soon but Mr Figgis will sort out any problems and Mr Ward will return at intervals to see how things are.'

The next day, after a near sleepless night, Kate and Mrs Sharpe walked to the village to visit the dressmakers. Kate wasn't really interested but Mrs Sharpe took charge kindly but firmly, and after looking at materials they found a bluey-grey fabric which would make up well. The dressmaker took Kate's measurements and, as it was to be a plain dress with no embellishments, she said she and her two daughters would have it ready for the following day. 'It has to be plain and neat, please,' said Mrs Sharpe. When they had finished, Kate told Mrs Sharpe she had to visit Mr and Mrs Stokes and let them know that she was going to London. Mrs Sharpe suggested they met up again at the park gates in half an hour as she could quite happily spend the time looking at the shops and chatting with friends.

Kate dreaded seeing Matty and Will to tell them the news, but when they opened the door to her knock and saw her standing there they immediately knew something was wrong. 'Come in,' said Matty, looking searchingly at Kate's white face. 'What is the matter, love?'

She sat down and tears began to fall as she told them what had happened. Matty and Will were horrified. 'But we heard what was read out,' said Will.

'And I saw it,' said Kate. 'It said nothing about contents.'

'It sounds to me as though Daniel is up to something dishonest.'

'But how can I prove it?' asked Kate.

'If we can be witnesses, we'll gladly come to London, Miss Kate,' said Will.

'Dear Will, I know you would but Mr Sheldon has it all arranged. But I will tell him what you say and if you are needed he or Mr Ward will fetch you.'

'Whatever we can do, we will do it,' said Matty, stoutly.

'I'm hoping to stay with Dr Roberts, but Mr Sheldon and Mr Ward are organising everything so I haven't to bother my head.'

'It's a shame,' said Matty. 'Let's hope that brother of yours comes by his just desserts.'

'Mr Sheldon did throw him out the front door,' said Kate.

'Oh, good,' said Will. 'I wish I had seen it.' He laughed.

They kissed Kate goodbye, telling her to let them know how everything turned out and that they were there for her if they were needed. She kissed them both hurriedly and dried her eyes before meeting Mrs Sharpe at the park gates for the walk back to The Hall.

Chapter Nineteen

KATE WAS READY to leave The Hall on Wednesday morning. She felt sad and apprehensive of the future, and annoyed that Daniel had turned up again like a bad penny just when she had started to feel that everything was going along so happily. The coach stood ready and Mr Sheldon, aware of the proprieties, had decided to accompany it riding on Samson. As Kate came out of the front door, held open for her by Ben, she was amazed to see all the staff standing outside waiting for her. Mr Figgis stepped forward, saying briefly: 'We would all like to wish you well, Miss Kate. Come back to us soon.'

Everyone shouted 'Yes, yes!' and clapped.

Mrs Watson stepped forward. 'Please take this, Miss Kate, it is for luck.' She pressed a tiny iron horseshoe into her hand.

'Thank you, thank you,' said Kate. 'You are all very kind and I hope that I shall be back with you all very soon too.'

They cheered and waved and shouted 'good luck' to her, and Kate waved back to them. The coach door was shut and the horses began to move away. Alex had a final word with Mr Figgis, mounted Samson and followed the coach.

Kate dabbed away a few tears and clasped the little horseshoe in her hand. It would bring her luck, she vowed to herself, it would! Eventually she was able to look at the scenery and she wondered if she would see it again soon. She hoped so. She relaxed a little and compared this journey that she was taking in such a comfortable coach to the one in the stagecoach with Matty and Will. At least she felt that she could face whatever was to come with Mr Sheldon's support. He was so good to her, she thought, and still wondered why. Perhaps he liked things to be right and fair. He certainly treated all his staff well, but she did wonder why he was being so helpful to her. She supposed, apart from disliking Daniel, he felt that being her employer he should help her. She was pleased he was; there was no one else. And so the thoughts went round and round in her mind until after a while she was able to doze.

She was awakened by the coach coming to a standstill. Alex opened the door and invited her into the hostelry, the Red Lion, for refreshments while the horses were fed and watered. He looked at Kate and was pleased to see she was calm and even smiling at him. 'Feeling all right?' he asked, as they sat in the pleasant little inn room.

'Of course,' Kate said, hoping he wasn't going to ask further.

'Good,' he replied in a businesslike way. 'We shall travel straight to my house where Laurie will give the coachman Dr Roberts' address, and I will go with you to him.'

'But I know the doctor's address,' said Kate.

'But we don't know if he can accommodate you, do we?'

'Oh, I see,' said Kate. 'What shall I do if he is ill or – or…?'

'We'll think of something else, of course,' Alex said, matter-of-factly. Kate said no more.

When they arrived eventually at Dr Robert's house, he was there waiting for them, the dear, friendly father figure who Kate remembered so well. As soon as they were indoors, he folded her into his arms and said she was very welcome to stay as long as she wanted. He welcomed Alex too with a shake of the hand.

Mrs Walker, the doctor's housekeeper, appeared and took Kate to her bedroom while Alex sat with the doctor and briefly told him what had happened.

The doctor shook his head. 'It is such a shame,' he said. 'Kate has always shouldered her burdens with fortitude. I'm afraid her father and brothers were all rotters. But Kate and her mother were lovely people. I will certainly look after her while she is here, but I don't like this trial business. The law is not wonderful, I'm afraid. What happens if they find her guilty, irrespective of whether she is or not?'

'Then I shall have to exert myself with a little bribery in the right places, perhaps,' said Alex. 'But I feel determined that that brother of hers will not have the upper hand. I don't know yet how I'm going to do it; we shall have to see what verdict the magistrate gives on Friday.'

'Well, if I can help in any way, Mr Sheldon, do let me know, won't you?' Nothing more was said as Kate rejoined them.

'Is everything all right my dear?' asked Dr Roberts.

'Everything is lovely, thank you.'

'Will you stay and eat with us, Mr Sheldon? You are very welcome.'

'Thank you, no. I must see my secretary and hear what he has found out, if anything, and decide what action we have to take. Goodbye, sir, and thank you for your help.' He clasped Kate's hand briefly. 'Be good,' was all he said to her, and left.

Being with Dr Roberts, Kate was able to relax and tell him what she had been doing since she saw him last, and also about Matty and Will. He said he was proud of her that she had done so well, but he deplored the fact that Daniel had been so rude and unfeeling. He was concerned about the will, though. 'Are you sure you read it properly, Kate?'

'Oh yes. I checked it because I expected to be left the house. It did say the house and my father's money went to Daniel, but there was no mention of contents. They didn't fetch that much anyway, but it was enough to take the three of us to Matty's sister and give us a little to live on for a short while. Why Daniel is so keen to make trouble, I don't know. Maybe Fanny is behind it all because she wants to cut a dash now they have a new house in London. I just know that Daniel has spoiled things for me as I was happy at The Hall, although I worked hard.'

'I'm sure everything will be all right in the end, my dear,' said Dr Roberts. 'But there could be unpleasantness before that. You must prepare yourself and remain strong and resolute. You have me behind you, and Mr Sheldon, and he's a power to be reckoned with, I think.'

Kate was comforted up to a point but still felt very apprehensive at appearing before a magistrate.

Meanwhile, Alex was talking to Laurie. There was a pile of correspondence for him to go through but nothing of great importance, he thought, as he quickly sorted through the invitations to soirees, dinners and balls. The season for such entertainments was just beginning, but Alex felt no regrets. Perhaps after all the worry about Miss Elliss was over he would be pleased to attend such functions, but somehow the prospect didn't thrill him.

The staff had been busy preparing for him to return and his French cook had spared no effort in the welcoming dinner provided. After Alex and Laurie had eaten, they discussed what was to be done about Miss Elliss.

'I've located the magistrate's house, sir. He is Sir Alan Peabody. I made a few discreet enquiries about him and I'm afraid I wasn't terribly impressed. But it still may turn out all right anyway. Also, I located the lawyer, Mr Fawcett, who has an office in a rather unfashionable part of town.'

'Mm, I expect so. The thing is, Laurie, that it is just Miss Elliss's word against her brother's unless he has the document to prove he is right. And if he has it, there is no more to be said. But she is adamant that she read just 'house and money'. I realise she feels she should fight for her rights, but is it worth it? Would it be better if I pay him off and be finished with it all?'

'But,' said Laurie, 'would it be the finish, sir? I think that's just what he's after. He thinks you might pay to protect her from the scandal, and he'd try to bleed you dry. You don't want that. I think this is what Miss Elliss thinks too, so that is why she is determined to see things through. She's a remarkable woman.'

'I agree,' said Alex with a rueful smile.

The day of Kate's preliminary trial came all too quickly. Kate, looking neat and clean in her new dress of grey blue and wearing her old bonnet and shawl, said goodbye to Dr Roberts and climbed inside Mr Sheldon's light town coach. She was surprised to see Mr Ward inside with Mr Sheldon but was pleased of their reassuring presence. Nothing much was said, and soon they approached St. Paul's Cathedral, and Sir Alan Peabody's house situated nearby. It was a large town house, rather ugly and grey, and it would have looked more welcoming if some attention to cleanliness had been administered. The coach was driven round the back of the house and, as Kate alighted, Alex told her he would be waiting for her whatever happened.

A gentleman in black looked at Kate as she entered and told her to wait on a wooden seat next to some other people. Kate looked surreptitiously at them and saw a depressing sight of undernourished men and women, some quiet, but some noisy and with the smell of gin about them. One or two took swigs from a dirty bottle. Fortunately there were guards around so Kate felt a little comforted, but as she sat and waited the time went slowly. Those sitting with her seemed to be used to it all and probably had been there many times before. They were all of the poorer classes, whether by their own fault or not, and they were raucous as they continued passing round the gin bottle. The guards took no notice but if anyone moved they were soon pushed back on their seat.

Kate sat and just thought of her time at The Hall, anything to avoid looking at the assembled company. Eventually, she heard her name and looked up. One of the guards stood before her. 'Follow me,' he instructed her. As Kate followed him, another followed her. She was led into a large room.

Kate's initial thought was that it looked just as ugly as the outside. Ceiling and walls were of a dirty cream with dull red curtains that had seen better days dragged back anyhow from unwashed windows. In the centre of the room was a large heavy oak desk, behind which was an oak chair on which sat, Kate supposed, Sir Alan Peabody. Kate looked at him and saw what appeared to be a short man who ate well, if the size of his stomach was anything to go by. Kate didn't think he looked particularly bright, but hoped she was wrong. He had a plump red face, which proclaimed the drinker, and a small beak of a nose that really looked incongruous on his large face. He was a snuff taker, as shown by the stains on his fingers and coat. Kate realised she didn't like him. By Sir Alan's side sat a grey haired man dressed in black, who wrote continuously in a large book, his quill pen moving from side to side with splutters and squeaks. Obviously he was a secretary. Behind stood two men in black. Were they servants or protectors of some kind?

Two chairs, set wide apart, faced Sir Alan's desk. Daniel was already sitting on one and Kate was told to sit on the other. Again, two men in black stood behind them. Sir Alan cleared his throat. 'Your name, madam,' he asked.

'Miss Katherine Elliss, sir,' Kate said clearly, and felt pleased with herself that she hadn't mumbled.

'This is a case of dishonest acquisition of money, which comes under the heading of deception, over the will of Mr Abraham Elliss, I believe. How do you plead?'

'I plead not guilty, sir,' said Kate.

'Mm.' Sir Alan looked at Daniel. 'And you are?'

'Daniel Elliss, sir, son of Mr Abraham Elliss.'

'Carry on,' said Sir Alan, looking at Daniel.

'My father's will says that his house, his money and the contents of the house are mine. I have the house and the money but my sister sold the contents so obtaining money for herself, sir.'

'Is this true, Miss Elliss?'

'I sold some of the contents as it only said house and money were left to my brother. I thought it was right, therefore, to sell some of the contents to pay for the wages and expenses of myself and the servants.'

'So what it all comes down to is the wording of the will. Did you see it, Miss Elliss?'

'Yes, sir. I took it from the lawyer, as I was so shocked that nothing had been left to me. And it distinctly said "house and money" only and not contents.'

'You can read then, Miss Elliss?'

'Yes, sir.'

Sir Alan gave a paper to the servant standing behind him. He brought it over to Kate. 'Please read the first sentence aloud,' Sir Alan said.

Kate obliged.

'Thank you. We've established you can read. Now, Mr Elliss, what have you to say to that?'

'Only that she must have read it wrongly, sir. It definitely states "and contents" sir.'

'Do you have the will with you?'

'Of course, sir.'

The servant collected the will Daniel held out to him and gave it to Sir Alan, who placed it on his desk and read it through from beginning to end. He took his time and Kate wanted to scream at the delay.

At last he folded it up. 'There is nothing wrong with this will. It definitely says "and contents".'

'May I see the will, sir?' asked Kate. 'The one I read did not mention contents.'

Sir Alan frowned but handed it to the servant who took it to Kate. He stood in front of her ready to take it back from her quickly if she decided to tear it up. Kate looked at the will. It definitely wasn't the same. 'This is not the one I saw, sir,' she said calmly. 'I suggest this is a forgery.'

'What do you say to that, Mr Elliss?' asked Sir Alan.

'That she is wrong. How could this be a forgery? I saw it at the reading of the will with the lawyer present.'

'If there's a vestige of suspicion that it might be a forgery, it must be looked into,' said Sir Alan.

'I would like it to be investigated further, sir,' said Kate. 'I am not wrong.'

'And can you pay the expenses for this investigation?' asked Sir Alan.

'No sir,' said Kate.

Sir Alan sighed. 'Miss Elliss, this will, which looks perfectly all right to me, says "and contents." I suggest you are trying to be clever to cover up the wrong you have done and throw suspicion on innocent persons who…'

'No, sir,' interrupted Kate. 'If I have money then why am I working?'

'That is nothing to the point. If you are working you have money to pay your brother.'

'No, sir, I…'

Sir Alan was tired of the case. He interrupted her. 'Enough. You will be detained at His Majesty's pleasure in Newgate prison until your case and trial come to the Old Bailey courthouse,' he said.

'But…' began Kate, panicking.

'My word is law,' said Sir Alan, waving a dismissive hand.

'Very well,' said Kate, pale but resolute.

The guard behind Kate led her out of the room, holding her arm. Meanwhile, Daniel fawned on Sir Alan as he retrieved the will and then left the room with a jaunty air.

After Alex had waited for nearly an hour and Kate still did not appear, he climbed out of the coach and went to the door where he had seen Kate enter. He saw the guards talking together and asked the whereabouts of

Miss Elliss. One said he would find out, and he soon returned saying that she had been sent to prison to await trial. Alex, his face like thunder, went back to Laurie and they decided to go round to Newgate prison to see what could be done to make Kate's life a little more palatable.

Evidently, the new inmates had just been taken inside, according to the men at the gate and when Alex asked if he could see one of the prisoners he said he didn't really think so. The jangle of coins altered the situation dramatically and he said he would take Alex only inside the prison. Alex followed where he led and saw a slatternly woman. The gatekeeper went to speak to her. Alex heard her say: 'Oh, the gentry mort.' The gatekeeper nodded to Alex and left, while the woman looked at him. 'Could I see Miss Elliss, please?' he asked.

'Maybe,' said the woman, eyeing him.

'Perhaps she could be in a private cell?' asked Alex politely, but this time proffering a small bag of coins.

The woman grabbed the bag and looked inside. She gave him a grin, which showed rotten teeth and gaps. 'Won't keep you a minute,' she muttered, and left. She returned shortly and favoured Alex with another brown and gappy smile. 'Come with me,' she mumbled.

Alex followed her to find Kate in a cell on her own. It had a small window, which was high up on the wall, apart from which there was no light. A small rough wooden table stood in a corner, on which stood a candle stub pushed into a bottle. A rickety chair was beside it and blankets of some kind were thrown on the floor for a bed. In what condition these were, Kate hadn't time to find out. When the key was inserted she looked round quickly. At the sight of Alex, she didn't know whether to laugh or cry. He strode across quickly to her and took her hands, watched interestedly by the woman outside.

'Mr Sheldon, I'm so pleased to see you,' said Kate with a large sigh.

'We won't have long, so tell me what's happened,' said Alex.

As concisely as possible she told him. 'Are you sure that wasn't the will you saw?' asked Alex.

'I'm positive,' said Kate.

'And the signatures?'

'I don't really know. I couldn't tell.'

'Right, that gives us something to work on. Now, my dear, you are going to be uncomfortable here. Are you sure you can cope with it all? Can you be strong? I will send Laurie with food and blankets. If I bribe the woman I'm sure she will let you have them. Perhaps you can share a little food with her or something. Anything you want, tell Laurie, and I will send it to you if I can.'

'Thank you,' said Kate. 'I – I can manage. I was with some people who drank gin but, thank goodness, I was put in here away from them. I expect she thought she would benefit from the gesture,' whispered Kate.

Alex took hold of her hands. 'Remember, Laurie and I will do our best, but whatever happens in court, I will get you away somehow. But I think it won't come to that. So be of good cheer, my dear.'

'Thank you for coming,' said Kate. 'I feel better now.' She managed to smile. He pressed her cold hands between his warm ones and turned as the door was opened to let him out. It was shut with a bang behind him and locked.

Chapter Twenty

ALEX WENT BACK to the coach and told Laurie what had happened. 'Right,' said Laurie, trying to sound businesslike as he saw how distressed Mr Sheldon was. 'We have to find out about this will somehow. Meanwhile, I can take in food and wine to Miss Kate every day if you want me to.'

'Thank you, Laurie. I wish I could see my way clear about what to do next. I'm hoping the trial will be soon but we shall have to work fast to prove that Kate is innocent.'

Laurie noticed the use of Miss Kate's first name. 'Shall we call at Dr Roberts' house to let him know the outcome, sir?'

'Yes, we should, of course,' agreed Alex.

He went in to see the doctor alone. Poor Dr Roberts was upset at the news but he realised nothing could be done about Kate's situation immediately. 'But if you can think of anything that would help, then I would be pleased if you will tell me,' Alex said.

'I don't think there is anything more, Mr Sheldon, but, of course, I will let you know if there is. The lawyer is Mr Fawcett. I don't know whether it is worth seeing him. I don't particularly like the firm. It is typical of Kate's father to choose someone like him.'

'Are you saying they are crooked?' asked Alex.

'No, not exactly, but I wouldn't use them,' said the doctor.

'Well, if Miss Elliss's brother has bribed them to forge another will, he would have to pay heavily for it so he is not going to be much better off financially. And, according to Miss Elliss, she sold only a few pieces of furniture to enable her and the two servants to go to Hertfordshire,' said Alex.

'Did you see the will when Daniel visited you, Mr Sheldon?' asked the doctor.

'No, he didn't have it with him. He just mentioned it.'

'Well, perhaps after he saw you he thought he could get money from you through Kate.'

'Yes,' nodded Alex. 'Laurie thought that might be a possibility.'

Dr Roberts continued: 'So he invented the story of the will including contents, and when he went back to town, he asked Fawcett to forge one. If Kate saw it this morning, that is obviously what he has done.'

'Yes, it's possible,' said Alex, 'and it is certainly an idea. Thank you, Dr Roberts. I must try and find this will or a copy or someone who knows about it. It doesn't sound likely that I can, but you never know, something may emerge.'

Alex left the doctor then, promising to keep in touch with any fresh ideas or developments.

On Alex's and Laurie's return to Brook Street, they were met with the information that a gentleman awaited Mr Sheldon in the library. Alex frowned. He didn't really want to be bothered with visitors. He had enough to think about, but after he had handed his hat, stick and gloves to the servant, he went to see who was waiting to see him.

As soon as he entered the room a smile spread over his face. 'Chris, what brings you here?'

'Sir!' said Chris grinning, 'I hope you don't mind – I thought you would be back in London by now and....'

'Only just,' said Alex, 'but tell me why you are here. Have you heard from...?'

'Yes, I have,' grinned Chris, not waiting for Alex to finish. 'And they want to interview me. The architects, I mean. They're pleased with the work I've submitted so there is hope for me. I came here as I thought you would advise me where to stay, if it's not convenient for me to stay with you.'

'Of course you can stay here. There's plenty of room. Now tell me how your family has been since I last saw you.'

'Well, thank you sir. I promise not to be any trouble.' And Chris went on to tell of his parents' and sisters' activities at long length. Then he asked politely after his uncle's welfare and if Laurie was with him.

'Yes, Chris, he is. In fact, we have a problem to solve.'

Chris looked at him and saw the pain and worry on his uncle's face. 'I'm sorry, you shouldn't have let me bore you with what we've been doing at home. I see now that you are concerned about something. Can I help or…?'

Alex smiled. 'No, no, I was interested in what you told me, but we have a court case on our hands. You see, Kate, Miss Elliss that is, is in prison.'

Chris looked shocked. When he could speak he said: 'But she can't be. Why? No, no, I don't believe it.'

'Unfortunately, it is true. She has done no wrong, I hasten to add. Let me tell you the story.'

Chris, with his eyes fixed on Alex's face, followed his every word. 'Good gracious, the despicable man! How could he?' exclaimed Chris when Alex had finished. 'How can I help?' He pushed his hand through his hair, disordering it. 'I just can't believe anyone would do that, especially to a sister. She is such a lovely lady, isn't she, sir?'

'Yes, Chris, I believe she is,' said Alex sadly, and, Chris told his mother later, it nearly broke your heart to hear him.

'Well,' said Chris, matter-of-factly, 'I'm here to help if possible. Why don't you, I and Laurie discuss things and see if we can come to a decision.'

Alex looked at him and smiled at the concerned young face. 'We can try, Chris. We have to think of something.'

Later, Laurie joined them. He was able to report that Kate was coping well and he had had no trouble in seeing her. She said she was eating the food that he took and the book, which Mr Sheldon had sent to her, had kept her occupied and amused. The slattern who looked after her was behaving and looked forward to her coin when he appeared. Laurie had to tell Mr Sheldon not to worry.

Alex said little, only thanking Laurie for going.

'So,' said Chris, 'what do we do next?'

Alex smiled. 'I should tell you what Dr Roberts thought – and he could be right.' When he had finished telling them, they were quiet, thinking, until Chris broke the silence, saying enthusiastically: 'Right, we think there is forgery going on. Shall I go and visit this Mr Fawcett and ask him? No, I know, I'll go and ask if he will forge some papers for me, but not straight out, of course.'

Alex couldn't help but smile. 'I think we have to be more subtle than that,' he said.

'Yes,' said Laurie slowly. 'We can't go to the office, but we could watch and see who comes out. There must be someone who does the lowly work who might like to earn a few pennies for information.'

'They'll probably all be old men,' said Chris, 'who have worked there for years. You know, dressed in old shiny black clothes, looking like beetles. I bet if they took them off they would stand up on their own,' he finished with a grin.

'Well,' said Laurie, 'if Dr Roberts doesn't trust them, perhaps we can find someone, somehow. Are you free to go and find this office with me sometime, Chris? Two heads are better than one.'

'Yes, of course,' Chris said immediately, 'but not when I have my interview. It's the day after tomorrow.'

'Shall we go out later today, then, when they should be leaving to go home, and see who there is?' asked Laurie.

'Good idea,' said Chris. 'What is the address? Can we walk there? '

'From what information I know,' said Laurie, 'it is in a back street near St Paul's. So we'll take a hack and then walk the streets.'

Leaving the young men to their plans, Alex prepared to go out. He had an acquaintance, Sir Joshua Mansell, who was some years older than Alex, and although he hadn't seen him for a while, he had often met him at social gatherings in the past. He was a charming gentleman to talk to and more to the point he knew the law, having been a Justice of the Peace. Alex travelled in his light town coach to Berkeley Square and was fortunate to find Sir Joshua at home. He was still straight and tall and a commanding figure and everything about him was neat. He spoke clearly and precisely and above all he had a presence about him.

'Alexander,' he said now in his deep cultured voice, 'how nice to see you. Come and sit down. We haven't met for some time, have we? Wine?'

'Thank you,' said Alex.' I haven't long been back in Brook Street. I have been at The Hall, you know, and had visitors.'

'And very nice too.' They proceeded to talk of family and mutual friends until Alex admitted that he hoped Sir Joshua would advise him on a legal matter.

'I will do my best,' Sir Joshua said. 'What has been happening?'

Alex explained, as briefly as he could, all that had gone on.

Sir Joshua frowned. 'She should never have been sent to Newgate. It surely could have been settled out of court. What an unfortunate thing for poor Miss Elliss. And you want me to act for this lady?'

'Well, I really don't know what the next step is.' Alex explained that Laurie and Chris were trying to find someone from Mr Fawcett's office who would be prepared to help.

'Ah! Fawcett is Mr Elliss's lawyer, is he?' Sir Joshua smiled. 'It would give me great pleasure to discredit such a man as Fawcett. It is people like him who give the rest a bad name. Mmm. The trouble is, I cannot do anything unless there is someone who can state a forgery took place. If not, I will try and see Miss Elliss and perhaps she can plead benefit of clergy and be handed over to the church to deal with. But hopefully it won't come to that. She would be branded on the thumb if found guilty and the trials are not always as they should be. Can I ask you a delicate question, Alexander?'

Alex smiled and looked at him. 'Certainly, but I can guess what it is.'

'Ah, so what does Miss Elliss mean to you?' Sir Joshua smiled.

'Well, it's a long story, but I met her when she came to The Hall as a cook. She worked well but there was something about her that didn't really fit. She was too much a lady.' Alex continued with Kate's story and finished by saying: 'I admire her for her fairness, courage and determination to do the right thing. After all this business is over, well, I shall have to tread carefully, I think.'

'I see exactly what you mean,' smiled Sir Joshua, 'but take your time. After all this unpleasantness is over, think carefully.'

Alex smiled. 'Yes, of course. I'm a bit too old to rush into anything, you know.'

'Rubbish,' laughed Sir Joshua, 'you're just as vulnerable as when you were a boy of twenty. How old are you, anyway?'

'Thirty-five,' came the answer.

'Well, there you are. If I didn't have a wonderful wife, I might be tempted by your Miss Elliss, but as I'm another fifteen years older than you, there wouldn't be much hope, would there? However, this isn't a time for joking. Keep me in touch with what is happening and I will think of something.'

Alex took his leave, feeling happier. The next thing was to see what Laurie and Chris had managed to find out.

Whilst Alex was with Sir Joshua, Laurie and Chris talked over what their plan would be when they found Mr Fawcett's offices. It didn't take long.

'Now,' said Laurie. 'I'll just leave a message for Mr Sheldon telling him we will be out for a while if he wishes to know where we are when he returns. Then we'll find a hack to take us to somewhere near St Paul's, and we can walk the rest of the way, if you are agreeable, Chris?'

'Oh, yes,' he said. 'Travelling always makes me stiff.'

Laurie smiled. 'Well, you are young and healthy, living where you do, so I'm not surprised.'

When they alighted from the hackney in the shadow of St Paul's Cathedral and they began to walk, Chris asked Laurie if he thought his uncle was in love with Miss Elliss.

'I don't know,' said Laurie, thinking it wasn't his place to gossip about his employer. 'I know he doesn't like her being where she is, and he will do his best for her, I'm sure, as he would do the same for any of his staff if he found them innocent of a crime and in trouble.'

'I suppose so,' said Chris. 'Oh, I forgot to say the twins send their love to you. Chloe said it first, I must tell you, and for mischief, I think, Phoebe endorsed her words.'

Laurie just smiled. 'Thank you, I'm pleased they are well,' was all he would say.

No more was said as they concentrated on finding their way, walking through the back streets. 'Ugh,' said Chris, 'London has some foul smelling streets and they're so dismal.'

'Don't you have back streets in Derbyshire?' smiled Laurie.

'Ye-s, but I suppose there is more fresh air, and apart from the large towns like Derby there is more countryside with trees and fields. We do get cattle smells and suchlike, of course.'

'Now,' said Laurie looking about him, 'I think Mr Fawcett's offices are down here somewhere.' They had come to Law Street, a dismal, uninspiring part of London where there were no sounds except the distant cries of vendors or the clip-clop of horses' hooves.

'How depressing,' said Chris, 'and where is everyone?'

'Inside working, I expect,' said Laurie. 'Now keep you eyes open for names.'

They walked the length of the street down one side and although most of the buildings had names on plaques, they couldn't find the one they were looking for. They carefully picked their way over to the opposite side of the street, as there were no boys to sweep a crossing for them. Fortunately it wasn't like a main road apart from some horse droppings, which they carefully avoided, and the usual dust and grime from the chimneys. Walking back up the other side of the street, they met two young men walking the opposite way. 'Excuse me,' said Laurie, 'would you know where Mr Fawcett's offices are?'

The men smirked. 'The fourth one along,' one said, pointing.

Laurie thanked him and he and Chris walked on. They saw the office. It had dirty windows and steps up to the door.

'What shall we do now?' asked Chris.

'I think we shall have to walk a little way away and wait and see who comes out. Perhaps other people will be leaving from other offices soon and we won't look so out of place.'

They decided to hold a conversation, or look as though they were, but always keeping an eye on Mr Fawcett's door. Other men were leaving their offices along the street. 'No doubt Mr Fawcett is a dragon and no staff are allowed to leave until they have finished their work, tidied their desk, polished their shoes, bowed three times to god Fawcett and crawled to the door,' Chris was saying when Laurie interrupted him.

'Look,' he said, 'someone's appeared.'

'It's a beetle,' said Chris. 'I told you so.'

Then they saw another black coated individual walking down the steps and by their posture they looked elderly. Two younger men grinning and laughing at each other came down next, followed by a single figure. The two who were laughing went on their way while the last figure deliberately walked slowly behind them, or so it seemed to Laurie and

Chris. Laurie poked Chris and nodded towards the solitary figure. They walked slowly and followed him. When the two noisy young men came to the street corner, they crossed the road with neither a look nor a nod to the figure behind them. He turned the corner and walked away from them. Laurie and Chris followed and after a few minutes caught up with him.

'Excuse me,' began Laurie.

The figure turned quickly, showing Laurie and Chris a young face.

'Sir?' he said, his expression wary. Then seeing the two of them, fear came into his eyes.

Immediately, Chris grinned at him and said: 'Don't worry, we mean you no harm.'

'No, of course not,' said Laurie. 'All we would like to do is to ask you a few questions about where you work.'

'Oh,' said the young man. He looked to be about eighteen but his pale face showed lines of worry appropriate to an older person.

'Is there somewhere round here where we can buy a drink?' asked Laurie. 'Then we could sit in comfort and ask you a few questions and tell you why.'

'I – I know of a place, but I'm sorry, I don't have any money to spare,' the boy said desperately, looking from one to the other.

'Take us to this place and I will pay,' said Laurie. 'And if you can supply us with some information, I am willing to pay for that too.'

The boy walked a short way and turned a corner. 'Will this be all right?' he asked nervously, indicating a small tavern as they came to the next street.

'This will do very well,' said Laurie. He wasn't too happy about it but thought hopefully that they wouldn't be long. Fortunately, there weren't many men inside, but nevertheless he made sure that they sat at a table in a corner where no one passed by. Pickpockets and worse abounded in such places.

Laurie ordered and paid for a bottle of wine, which he shared between the three of them. Then he introduced himself. 'My name is Laurence Ward and I am secretary to Mr Alexander Sheldon who lives in Brook Street. This is Christopher Johnston who is Mr Sheldon's nephew. May we know your name?'

'It's Sam Carter. I live not far from here. You – you won't know it. I live with my mother.'

'Thank you,' said Laurie. 'Tell me how long you have worked for Mr Fawcett?'

'About two years.'

'Do you like the work?' Laurie smiled.

'To be honest, not very much.'

'Why is that? Did you not choose to work there?'

'No, not really. I can write and I like numbers, and I would like to be in a nicer place with more prospects. But I have an uncle who found the place at Fawcett's for me so I'm duty bound to stay there. Also my mother is poor and she relies on my wages, so I'm really stuck in this job, unless I can find something else, of course. But by the time I leave the office in the evening, there is nothing much I can do, is there?'

'Who were the other two young men who came out just ahead of you?' asked Chris.

'Oh, their fathers are friends of Mr Fawcett, and they are privileged,' Sam said bitterly. 'Any rubbish thing there is to do, I get the job, not them. I'm just a dogsbody, really.'

'Tell me,' said Laurie, 'in the strictest confidence, of course, does anything go on in the office that shouldn't?'

Sam frowned. 'In what way, sir?' he asked.

'Well, to put it bluntly, forgery.'

Sam frowned. 'I haven't known of it but then I wouldn't, would I? Why?'

'Well, we have reason to believe someone's will has been forged and we would like to get our hands on the original.'

'Oh,' said Sam flatly.

'Let me tell you a little more,' said Laurie. 'Someone died by the name of Elliss. Mr Fawcett went and read the will to the brother and sister. The brother received everything apart from the contents of the house, even though he hadn't seen his father for years. The sister, who had nursed her father for years, sold the contents, but they amounted to very little money. The brother afterwards produced a will for the magistrate to see in which he received the contents as well. The sister is now in gaol because of it. So we have to prove her innocence, otherwise she will suffer. And if she's proved innocent, Mr Fawcett would be up before the judges, convicted of forgery. Mr Sheldon is willing to pay for help in any way.'

'Don't people keep their own wills, though?' frowned Sam.

'Sometimes,' said Laurie, 'but if Mr Elliss has a will that Mr Fawcett forged, would Mr Fawcett give him back the original one to keep as well?'

'Oh, I see, you think perhaps he would keep the original to safeguard himself. Or,' said Sam, slowly, 'to produce at a later date and use it to blackmail Mr Elliss. But I don't know,' he sighed. 'No one ever tells me anything. If Mr Fawcett did keep any important documents, they would be in his safe and no one is allowed to open it but him.'

'If you had an opportunity, could you see if a will in the name of Elliss is there and let us have it?' asked Laurie.

Sam ran his hand over his face. 'I – I don't know. You see, my mother relies on me for money. I can't risk losing my job, even though it's not a very good one.'

'Would you think about it at least? But we haven't much time as the trial will be soon.'

'Supposing I did find it. I wouldn't have to appear in court or anything, would I?'

'No, no. How I see it is, if we are in possession of the original will, that's all the proof we need. I mean, someone could have broken in and found it, couldn't they?' said Laurie.

'But if Mr Fawcett is arrested, I shan't have a job, shall I? I mean…'

'Don't worry about that. Mr Sheldon will see you don't lose by it. He will help you. If you like, I can always take you to meet him.'

'I could go round to Fawcett's office and say I'm Mr Elliss's secretary and he wants me to collect the original will. I wonder if that would work. I can say Mr Elliss now prefers to keep it in his safe,' said Chris. 'But we're up against time, aren't we?'

'Well,' said Sam, beginning to enter into the spirit of things, 'shall I see what I can do first? Sometimes when Mr Fawcett goes out of his office, I might be able to slip in.'

'But what about all the others there, would they see you?' asked Laurie.

'I know it won't be easy, but if I do manage something, how can I contact you?' said Sam.

'Take a hack to Mr Sheldon's. We are there,' said Laurie. 'If you don't appear, I will come with a letter releasing the will into my hands. Now we must go. Can we rely on you, Mr Carter?' asked Laurie.

'Yes, yes of course.'

'Well, here is money for the hack if you use one and this is for your help today.'

'Thank you. G-good gracious,' Sam whispered as Laurie handed over some coins.

'As I said, Mr Sheldon pays well. Here is his card. Don't lose it. Be sure to do your bit if you can and keep in touch.'

'Yes, yes, of course.'

'Let us hope he does,' said Chris, as they returned to Brook Street.

Chapter Twenty-One

WHILST EVERY EFFORT was being made on Kate's behalf, Kate herself was heartily sick of her prison cell. Mr Ward had told her briefly of the things they were doing for her when he brought in her food from Mr Sheldon's kitchen. Mr Sheldon hadn't visited her again and she wished he would. But thinking about it further, she was sure she looked a fright and perhaps it was as well that he didn't. She found nights and days were beginning to be mixed, so she slept when she felt like it. The small window gave a very dim light and Kate thought of other people and animals kept in the same conditions. It was depressing not to see the sky and feel the clean air on one's face. She was thinking, of course, not of the dirty streets of London, but the more open spaces of Hertfordshire. In fact, she found herself living the time she had spent at The Hall all over again. She remembered her first meeting with Mr Sheldon, when she hadn't recognised who he was. It made her smile to think how cross he had been. He had turned out to be overbearing and he had annoyed her many times and made her angry. But he had bothered about her and helped her and not many would trouble themselves for a servant, as he was doing now. She smiled to herself. He really was kind and she loved him for it. She must not think this way, she thought sadly. She would never be more to him than a cook who he felt he should help. She thought she really did love him and her eyes filled with tears knowing that he wouldn't think the same. Besides she was only a servant and now a jailbird. She was lucky he was helping her at all.

She dashed away the tears and concentrated thinking of the servants at The Hall who were pleasant, and how dear young Tommy had asked her to make jam tarts for him. She thought of Matty, Will and Emma in their little cottage and how she visited them and how they were pleased to see her. She remembered that she had said she would love a little cottage to live in when she was in London, but how that dream had vanished when she had seen The Hall, a real dream house, and had had the privilege of working there. Then the twins and their brother came and she had played for their dancing and they had bought her a little gift. In her mind, Kate went through it all, time and time again. What an idyllic summer it had been, although hard work in the kitchen. It had been such a different life to her previous one. If everything went wrong, and this indeed was a house of horrors, she had had those few precious months to treasure and now she could do nothing except resign herself until the trial came and hope all went well then. She wouldn't think of anything further as it would be all conjecture. She thought instead of the trees and flowers and the fruit for Mr Sheldon's fritters.

Kate would have been surprised to know that another player had entered the fray by the name of Sam Carter. After his meeting with Laurie and Chris, he had gone home feeling better about himself and decided that if he could help them, then he would, but he must be careful. It was good to feel he was relied on and trusted. He would like to meet this Mr Sheldon. Perhaps he could help him find some better work than with Mr Fawcett. It was a risk for Sam to take. He didn't know if he was doing right and even if Mr Sheldon existed, apart from the card he'd been given. He wished to better himself and he certainly wouldn't be able to if he stayed where he was. So he thought he would take the risk, and if nothing came of it he would find some other work somehow.

Not only were Mr Fawcett's offices dirty on the outside, the rooms inside were just as bad. As the windows weren't washed, except by the rain, inside was dim even on the brightest morning. Candles were in evidence, but only the cheapest were used, giving the place a rather sickly smell of animal fat. One gets used to it, thought Sam, but how much better it would be for everyone if the place were clean and bright. No wonder the two older men peered through their spectacles, looking closely at the pages they were writing.

The morning began for Sam in the usual way. The older men hardly spoke. The two younger men made faces behind their backs, didn't do much work, and all the jobs they didn't like doing, such as sharpening quill pens and emptying out rubbish, were given to Sam to do. During this particular morning, Mr Fawcett went out, probably to visit a client, leaving old Mr Plimton in charge. It had happened before and really didn't make much difference. They all performed their usual tasks. Sam tried to think how he could get into Mr Fawcett's room. He had left it unlocked as usual when he had gone out, as sometimes the older men had to use the books and papers on the shelves in there. During the morning, however, Mr Plimton slowly rose from his desk and made his way to Mr Fawcett's office. He was in there a little while when there was a cry. Next came, 'Sam, Sam!' This was not unusual. Mr Plimton often picked up a heavy book and tried to carry it out of the office and, being very shortsighted, he would catch his foot in the threadbare carpet and fall.

The two younger men, with grins on their faces, said: 'Go and pick up the old sod, Sam.'

Sam rushed into the room to find, not Mr Plimton on the floor, but a whole sheaf of papers instead. 'Are you all right, sir?' asked Sam.

'Yes, yes,' said Mr Plimton, tetchily. 'Pick up all these papers, do, and put them in order. They live on that shelf.' He pointed.

'Yes, Mr Plimton,' said Sam, gathering up the papers into a heap. 'Shall I stay here and sort them out?'

'Yes, yes, where else would you go? And hurry. Mr Fawcett won't be pleased.'

'No, he won't,' thought Sam, 'and if he sees me in here, I shall be blamed for everything.' He sorted the piles of papers he had picked up as best he could and he kept an eye open for the name of Elliss, but there was nothing. The last set of papers he picked up, though, comprised a will in the name of Browne. Sam had an idea. He went to Mr Plimton. 'Sir,' said Sam, respectfully, 'I've organised the papers, but this was amongst them. Shouldn't it be in the safe?'

'Mm, mm?' said Mr Plimton, looking closely at the papers Sam was holding out. 'Yes, yes, put it in at once and be quick. Oh dear, I meant to do that yesterday.'

'Yes, Mr Plimton. Where is the key?' asked Sam.

'Top drawer of Mr Fawcett's desk. Hurry.'

Sam wasted no time. Would he be lucky and find the Elliss will or would he be caught and lose his job? Sam hurried. The key was in the top drawer and as he opened the safe door he saw more wills spread across two shelves. He looked quickly through the wills on first shelf, which were arranged in alphabetical order, but could not find anything with the name of Elliss. On the second shelf he found more wills arranged alphabetically, but this time some had little cryptic notes attached. Here, the name of Elliss was not hard to find. Sam took the papers out and placed them in his inside pocket. He dithered over the Browne will but finally decided to file it on the second shelf. He closed the safe door, locked it and replaced the key in Mr Fawcett's drawer. He left the room, closing the door quietly behind him, and sat at his desk and reshuffled his own papers, his heart beating fast. Five minutes later, Mr Fawcett returned.

Sam managed to get through the rest of the day. He performed all the odd jobs anyone asked him to do without complaint. He only hoped Mr Plimton wouldn't suspect his theft, if Mr Fawcett discovered the Elliss will was missing or he found the Browne will in the wrong place. What puzzled Sam were the two separate shelves of wills, some with the little notes. He hadn't had much chance to look at the notes, but thought he remembered one that said 'Bennett, £200' and another 'not brother'. Was this evidence of forgery? Was Mr Fawcett hoping to blackmail these people? On the other hand it was not unreasonable for a lawyer to retain wills for safekeeping. And what was Mr Plimton writing? Could he be a forger? Sam began to be really interested, and without making his movements obvious, tried to see if he could glean any information from the files he could manage to see.

The day seemed long to Sam, but at last six o'clock came and he was allowed to leave. Instead of going home, he walked until he found a hackney carriage. After convincing the driver he really did want to go to Brook Street and had the fare, Sam relaxed and enjoyed the ride. He was set down outside Mr Sheldon's house and felt very out of place. The street was quiet with the trees just turning into autumn colours and there were no unpleasant smells. He took a deep breath, trod up the steps and lifted the knocker. He hoped everything the two gentlemen had told him was true and he wasn't getting himself into something that would result in trouble.

The door opened. 'Could I see Mr Sheldon, please?' Sam asked politely.

Jean Morley 163

The servant invited him indoors. 'Please wait here sir,' he said. 'What name shall I give?'

'My name is Carter. He won't know me.'

The servant knew Mr Sheldon was in the library. He knocked and opened the door. 'Yes?' asked Alex, looking up. He was seated in a chair in front of a small fire, trying to think what to do next for Kate.

'A young gentleman by the name of Carter is here to see you sir.'

Alex frowned. 'Show him in.'

The servant took Sam to the library and announced him. Alex looked surprised at such a young man and wondered what he wanted. He stood. 'Mr Carter, how can I help you?' he said courteously.

Sam was impressed by Mr Sheldon's house and the figure standing before him. 'I – I was told to come here and see you, sir. I was given your card.'

He showed it to Alex, who nodded. 'And who gave it to you?'

'Two nice young gentlemen. They needed my help and I think, I hope, I've done the right thing and I've brought you this.' Sam took out the will from his pocket and offered it to Alex.

Alex looked sharply at him. 'Thank you,' he said, taking it. 'Do sit down.'

Sam sat, looking round the most elegant room he had ever been in and wondering if Mr Sheldon had read all the books here. Alex quickly opened the will. It was in the name of Elliss and it was as Kate had said. There was no mention of 'contents', only 'house and money'.

'Mr Carter,' said Alex, 'you don't know how much pleasure you have given me. Thank you.' He pulled the bell cord and Sam stood, thinking he was to be shown out, but Alex waved him back to his seat. When the servant appeared, Alex asked if Mr Ward was in.

'Yes, sir, he is in his office.'

'Ask him to come here, please.'

'Yessir.'

'A glass of Madeira or sherry, Mr Carter?'

'Thank you, sir,' said Sam, surprised. 'I don't mind which.'

Alex smiled at him. 'You work for Mr Fawcett, I believe?'

'Yes, sir. Do – do you know him?'

'No, thank goodness. Do you like working there, Mr Carter?' asked Alex.

'Not really,' said Sam and he explained how he came to be there.

There was a knock on the door and Laurie walked in. When he saw Sam, he grinned at him. 'Oh, Sam, did you find out anything?'

'Laurie, sit down and tell me why Mr Carter is here and how you know him. More to the point, he has brought me this.'

'Oh, well done, Sam, well done!' said Laurie, inspecting the will. 'How did you manage it?'

Over his Madeira, Sam told how it all came about. He also told them of the other wills in the safe.

'Sir, I know I don't know much about such things, but those notes are odd, aren't they?'

'Yes, they are,' said Alex, 'which makes me wonder what game Mr Fawcett is playing. Maybe some wills are genuine but others are forged. Might he blackmail his clients, and was he going to blackmail Mr Elliss, I wonder?'

'It would serve him right if he was,' said Laurie. 'What is your next move, sir?'

'I shall go back to Sir Joshua and he will advise me. I think Mr Fielding at Bow Street should know about Mr Fawcett, too. However, the most pressing problem is our young friend here. What do you suggest, Laurie? I don't want him in any trouble.'

'Do you have to go back to work for Mr Fawcett, Sam?' asked Laurie.

'I don't have to but it will look suspicious if I don't, won't it? And I have to be paid.'

'Could I suggest that you go back as usual,' said Alex. 'If you are accused of anything, deny it. If the law descends on Mr Fawcett, you won't be involved, I assure you, as I will have words in the right places.'

Alex stood up and held out his hand. 'Thank you, Mr Carter. If you are worried about anything let me know or come and see me. Now I have to see Sir Joshua. You go with Laurie and he will make all right with you.'

'Thank you very much, sir,' said Sam, bowing.

Alex lost no time and he soon arrived at Sir Joshua's house, fortunately finding that gentleman at home.

'You have news?' Sir Joshua asked, smiling.

'I have what I think is the original will. What do you think?' Alex handed it over.

'Ah, I see an absence of contents,' he mused. 'How did you get hold of this?'

Alex told him how Laurie and Chris found Sam Carter and he had risked everything to obtain the will. Also he had noticed other wills in the safe.

'Mm, it looks suspiciously like bad practice is going on in Mr Fawcett's office. It seems likely they forge some of the wills, but keep the originals as safeguards. They probably blackmail the clients afterwards. Your Miss Elliss's brother would be bled white eventually. I think I had better have a word with Mr Fielding of Bow Street. Also, I'll find a lawyer for Miss Elliss for the trial.'

'I am willing to pay any expenses,' said Alex.

'Oh, pooh,' said Sir Joshua, handing the will back to Alex. 'Perhaps the lawyer, but that is all. I'm quite enjoying myself. I'll let you know the outcome.'

'I don't want the young boy Carter in trouble in any way,' said Alex. 'He wishes to leave Fawcetts' as he's not happy there. He has a mother to support, too.'

'I'm sure there is plenty of work for a hardworking young man in other offices. I'll write a list of places for him to try,' said Sir Joshua.

Alex returned home full of hope and feeling happier than he had for quite a while. He found Chris awaiting him.

Chapter Twenty-Two

'CHRIS!' exclaimed Alex, when he saw his nephew, 'How are you? How was the interview?'

Chris grinned. 'Oh, would you believe it sir, I can't yet, but they said they would be pleased to have me and I'm to start next month. They said it would give me time to organise my accommodation and everything. I shall have to go back home to tell my family.'

Alex shook his nephew by the hand. 'Well done, well done, you should be proud of yourself. You can stay here as long as you like as I've said before, which would be cheaper for you, but if you wish to move at anytime, it is your choice.'

'Thank you, perhaps to begin with anyway and until I know my way around. Now, how are things going with Miss Elliss? Did that young man do anything at all?'

'Yes, he did and I must thank you and Laurie for that. He managed to find the original will. We wonder if Fawcett is keeping the originals so that he can blackmail his clients later. Anyway, I've put it in the hands of Sir Joshua Mansell who is going to have a word with Mr Fielding at Bow Street.'

'Everything is going well then. I wish I could stay and help but I think Papa would like to know how I have fared. I could come straight back again, Uncle, if you think I can be of help.'

Alex smiled. 'Thank you, Chris. How about if I send you home in my travelling coach? I don't need it at the moment and I have my town coach I can use. It will be quicker and more comfortable than the stage for you and then you can return in a day or two.'

'I say, what a wonderful idea! I shan't miss much of the news about Miss Elliss, either.'

'Well, we think things are going well, now, anyway,' smiled Alex, not wishing to dampen Chris's happiness.

Sam Carter went back to work the following day as usual. He felt a little apprehensive but when he arrived everything looked the same, a dismal place with dismal people. He relaxed and worked and did the jobs he was given without complaint. Mr Fawcett was in his office and at one time called in Mr Plimton, and Sam's heart beat faster, but it was nothing, just routine work as Mr Plimton came out muttering to himself as usual and carrying some papers.

A young man came in setting the doorbell ringing. 'Can I help you, sir?' asked Sam with his usual welcome. The young man said he had an appointment with Mr Fawcett and his name was Babcock. Sam knocked on Mr Fawcett's door and announced the newcomer, showing him inside. Some minutes later the young man left looking pale and worried like so many before him. Later in the morning the door opened again and another gentleman came in. He was rather large and burly. Sam couldn't imagine this gentleman leaving the office looking pale and worried, somehow. Sam, as usual, asked the man if he could help him. He asked to see Mr Fawcett.

'Have you an appointment, sir?'

'No.'

'I'll ask, and what name shall I say, sir?'

'Smith,' said the man pleasantly.

'Thank you, sir.' Sam knocked on Mr Fawcett's door once more.

'Come in,' was the tetchy reply.

'There's a Mr Smith to see you, sir,' said Sam.

'Smith, Smith,' he pondered grumpily. 'I don't know…'

'It's John Smith, Mr Fawcett,' said a voice behind Sam. He was pushed to one side. Mr Smith entered Mr Fawcett's office and closed the door firmly behind him.

Sam went back to his desk, frowning. The other young men smirked. Sam ignored them as usual. After twenty minutes Mr Smith was still with Mr Fawcett. Evidently he had a lot of business to discuss.

Another gentleman came in. 'Business is looking good for Mr Fawcett. I wonder if it's honest business,' thought Sam, as he asked the gentleman if he could help him.

'Has a Mr Smith come in here?' he asked.

'Yes sir. He's with Mr Fawcett,' Sam said, indicating the door.

'Good. I'll just wait for him then.'

Sam thought this odd but he offered the man his chair. He was much smaller than Mr Smith, with a smile on his face that didn't match his eyes. Sam thought him shifty. He refused the chair with a shake of his head and wandered round the office instead. The two elderly scribes looked at him suspiciously and began opening drawers and placing their papers inside. The small man said he would like to see their work. Mr Plimton refused, but the man pushed him to one side and snatched up all the papers from both of them. He looked at them, grinned to himself, rolled them up and placed them in a leather bag he wore on his shoulder. Mr Plimton objected strongly but to no avail.

Sam wondered if he should ask the man to sit down again, or intervene in some other way, but decided not and immersed himself in his work instead. The man wandered over to the two young men and asked what work they did. He picked up their ledgers and flicked through the pages. Then he looked at Sam and asked him about his work. Sam showed him and he nodded and went back to Mr Plimton and his colleague again.

The door of Mr Fawcett's office opened. Mr Fawcett was saying, 'You can't do this. You have no authority. You…'

'Oh, but I have,' said Mr Smith. He nodded to the man waiting for him. 'Found anything, Phil?'

'These two are dodgy,' he said, pointing to Mr Plimton and his colleague.

'Let's take them away, then,' said Mr Smith.

The little man called Phil went outside and blew a whistle and in no time a dark carriage was at the door drawn by black horses. Mr Fawcett and his two staff were bundled inside with Mr Smith, while the man called Phil locked Mr Fawcett's office and told the three young men to leave. Sam quickly gathered up his belongings and left with the others while Phil locked and chained the outer door.

The following morning Kate had a visitor. He introduced himself as John Brent. 'I am a lawyer, Miss Elliss, and I've been asked to represent you this coming Thursday when you will be on trial for deception.'

'Oh,' said Kate. 'I didn't know. Th-thank you.' She didn't really know why she thanked him but somehow it only seemed the polite thing to do.

Mr Brent was a large, older man with a pleasant smile, which was reassuring. 'I have been asked to represent you by Sir Joshua Mansell, at the request of Mr Sheldon, who you know, I think.'

'Oh, I see,' said Kate relieved. 'Yes, of course I know Mr Sheldon. Thank you, Mr Brent, I'm so pleased to see you. I would ask you to sit down but the chair is rather rickety.'

'So I see,' he said.

John Brent liked to do things properly. He banged on the door. It was opened by the usual woman. 'I need two decent chairs, now,' he barked, tossing her a coin.

She nodded and disappeared while a seedy individual stood guard. Mr Brent thought if he wanted to escape with Miss Elliss, this character wouldn't stand a chance as he could knock him down with one punch. He wouldn't, of course, as it would do no good in the long term, so he waited patiently. Eventually the woman came back dragging two chairs, which had seen better days but looked as though they would take his weight. He took them from her and she locked the door once more, leaving Mr Brent and Kate to sit down either side of the little table.

'Now,' he said with a smile, 'tell me your story. I want to know about the will left by your father, also about your brother Daniel. I don't need to know personal details if you don't wish to tell them.'

Kate nodded. She told him about the reading of the will and what her expectations were. She told him how she sold some of the contents to pay for her servants' wages and to enable them and herself to travel to Ashleigh. She explained how she obtained work as a cook for Mr Sheldon and while she was there how Daniel had reappeared, telling her the will said 'and contents' and how he wanted her to give him the equivalent value in money.

'Thank you,' said John Brent. 'I can tell you that the original will was found in Mr Fawcett's safe and he will be arrested together with two of his staff who we believe are forgers. I believe that the will your brother produced for the magistrate was a forgery. When your case comes to court on Thursday I shall have a gentleman with me who will look at the two wills. He will inspect them against your father's signature, if we can find one. Do you know where he banked? We should be able to find a document there with his signature.'

'Oh, yes, of course. It was Child's Bank.'

'Good, good, I'll go along there now and have everything put together for Thursday. Try not to worry. Be cool and calm and answer each question as concisely and honestly as you can. Goodbye, Miss Elliss, I shall see you on Thursday.'

John Brent bowed, banged on the door to be let out and left without a backward glance.

Kate sat, feeling a little happier now that she had met her lawyer. She thought he was a reliable one and felt he would do his best for her. She thought through everything he had said. Why did Mr Fawcett have her father's will? Surely Daniel can't have been so silly as to let him keep it? Really, he had no sense whatsoever. Even if he won his case on Thursday, Mr Fawcett could blackmail him. Hadn't he thought of that? He would lose any money he had gained from his father, as Mr Fawcett was the type who would take as much as he could. How could Daniel be as stupid as that, she wondered. If it all went well on Thursday and the two wills were compared with her father's signature from the bank documents, Mr Fawcett would be in trouble. Would Daniel? Would he plead ignorance of a switch? But Kate decided she didn't care as long as her innocence was proved. She had no control over what happened otherwise and therefore she tried to dismiss everything else from her mind.

When Laurie visited her next, his face was wreathed in smiles. 'Here's your meal, Miss Kate, and I think everything is in place for Thursday. Have you had a visit from Mr Brent, the lawyer, yet?'

'Yes, I have. He seems a very nice gentleman and knows what he is doing. He is going to Child's bank to see if he can find my father's signature on another paper. If he does, he said he can give the two wills and the paper to a gentleman who will detect which is the forgery. It all sounds so easy, but I'm afraid something might go wrong.' Kate tried to smile.

'Please don't worry,' said Laurie. 'Mr Sheldon will be present and he said even if for some reason things go wrong – but we don't think they will – but if they do he will still get you out of the court and into a carriage. He is determined you won't go back to prison.'

Kate smiled tremulously. 'He is very good. I don't honestly know why he bothers. I've been most troublesome.'

'He likes to see fair play, I believe,' was all Laurie could think of saying. He couldn't very well tell Miss Kate what his employer's real thoughts might be. 'Oh, Chris is with us again but he is going home briefly to tell them all his good news. He has been accepted by the architects so will start work next month. He was horrified to know you were here,' Laurie smiled.

'I'm pleased he has been successful. I liked him and his sisters very much. Please wish him well for me.'

Laurie smiled and thanked her, said he would see her in court with Mr Sheldon and that she wasn't to worry. He gave her hand a squeeze and left.

Kate felt quite cheered after his visit and hoped everything went to plan on Thursday.

Chapter Twenty-Three

ALEX TOOK HIS TOWN COACH to the Old Bailey courthouse on the morning of Kate's trial, and Laurie went with him. Neither of them were looking forward to the prospect and both were worried about Kate. Breakfast had been a hurried affair, much to Pierre the cook's surprise, as he had tried to produce a particularly appetising meal for both gentlemen. He shrugged, telling himself that there were more appreciative mortals who would have eaten it all and enjoyed it, and he felt his artistic talents were, on this occasion, wasted.

London's central criminal court was an imposing building situated north west of St Paul's Cathedral. It was named after the original fortified wall or 'bailey' of the city. Alex knew that Newgate prison was connected to the courthouse by a passageway to the basement, which made it easy for transporting prisoners for trial. Kate and all the other prisoners would use it. He wasn't aware, however, that they would all be gathered prior to the sessions in a primitive, cold room in the basement of the courthouse, which was thought quite adequate for any prisoner. Alex did know that the provision made for the judges was just the opposite to that for the prisoners, which he thought was not surprising. It was said they had beautiful carpets and furniture, with elaborate meals provided from a special kitchen.

Alex and Laurie entered the courtroom, where neither had been before, and they found two seats at the back that were high up and enabled them to see everything, but from where they would be able to leave early if necessary. The courtroom held many people. They saw the judges sitting in a row high up opposite the dock for the accused, wearing long flowing wigs over their red gowns. Below them sat the clerks, lawyers and the note writers dressed in funereal black. The jury sat close together so that they could discuss their verdicts, just below where Alex and Laurie were sitting, on the defendant's right. They didn't leave the courtroom at any time and their opinions were often influenced by the spectators who had come to see what was going on out of curiosity, instead of by those taking part in the case. Sometimes the jury could be bribed by the wealthy, and Alex had come prepared for this if it seemed that the verdict to be given in Kate's case would not be acceptable to him. But he hoped he didn't have to resort to such measures.

The dock, where Kate would eventually stand, faced the judges. It had a large mirror above in order to reflect the daylight through the windows, so that facial expressions could be seen. A sounding board was above so that the defendant's voice might be heard above the clamour of the court.

On this particular day, the whole room was full of people of all descriptions and from all walks of life. The heat and odours from the crowded, unwashed bodies was appalling. This was no place for the squeamish, although sweet smelling flowers and herbs were liberally strewn over the floor, which helped at least at the start of the day. Those with no money found that the courtroom offered great free entertainment if they could squeeze in.

Kate sat with the other prisoners in the basement of the courthouse. She had had the forethought to bring both blankets with her, which Laurie had brought for her when she was first imprisoned. One of the blankets she wrapped around her shoulders over her shawl, the other she gave to a young girl who was shivering and coughing. Kate heard names being called, and then the appropriate person stood and was led upstairs. She wondered what kind of trials were going on as it seemed that names were being called with only a few minutes in between.

Then her name was called. She stood up, passed her blanket to the person next to her, clutched her smelling salts and without a backward glance she followed the gaoler upstairs. She entered the courtroom and was led to the dock. She looked round, noticing the judges, the jury and the spectators. She saw two men stand up at the back and recognised Mr Sheldon and Mr Ward. They observed that she looked composed but very pale. She nodded at them and glanced round further. She saw the branding irons and quickly averted her eyes. Where was Daniel? Before she could look further, she heard the judge speaking.

'Your name?' asked the judge.

'Katherine Elliss, my lord,' she answered.

'You are on trial for theft, I believe. How do you plead?'

'Not guilty, my lord.' Kate spoke clearly and she told herself she must be calm and collected as Mr Sheldon was watching her.

'Is someone acting for you?' The judge looked round the court.

'Yes, my lord, I am,' said the deep voice of Mr Brent, who stepped forward. He was a commanding figure and there were some shouts from the public.

'Proceed.'

'Thank you,' said Mr Brent, his rich voice booming out so that even the noisiest of onlookers were hushed. 'My client, Miss Katherine Elliss, is wrongly accused of theft. It concerns her father's will. At the reading after Mr Elliss's funeral, house and money only were left to her brother, Mr Daniel Elliss. Therefore, to enable her to pay the wages of her two elderly servants and to enable them all to move out of the house, Miss Elliss sold some of the contents. This paid for their journey to Ashleigh in Hertfordshire, where they stayed with a sister of one of the servants until Miss Elliss could find work.'

'Yes, but this case was brought up under the local magistrate, a Sir Alan Peabody, I believe.'

'That is correct, my lord. But the will shown to him by Mr Daniel Elliss said 'house, money and contents.' There was only the one will which Sir Alan was shown at the time and he saw nothing wrong with it, so he sent Miss Elliss to prison to await today's hearing.'

'So what are you saying, sir? Please explain.'

'It seems that the will Mr Daniel Elliss produced is different from the one Miss Elliss saw after the funeral of their father, my lord.' There were mumbles in the courtroom. Mr Brent continued: 'The lawyer who produced these wills is Mr Fawcett.'

'Is the brother present?' asked the judge.

'Yes, my lord.' A Mr Pyke spoke and stood up. 'I represent Mr Elliss.'

'Yes, yes,' said the judge irritably. 'Is he present?'

Daniel stood up. Kate noticed he was very pale and nervous.

'Why does the will you have differ from the other one?' asked the judge.

'My client believes,' said Mr Pyke, 'that his sister has obtained a forged one.'

Kate gasped and there were cries of 'shame' from some onlookers and laughs from others.

Mr Brent stood up. 'My lord, I think the shoe is on the other foot. On my instigation, Bow Street sent men to inspect the premises of Mr Fawcett. They found two employees engaged in copying wills and they have admitted their purpose was fraudulent. They are now in custody. The officers also found a number of wills in the safe, some with notes attached indicating blackmail potential. Perhaps Mr Fawcett told his clients he would destroy the originals. Only he didn't destroy them and we believe that he may be using them to blackmail his customers.'

'Am I to understand Mr Fawcett is also in custody?'

'Yes, my lord, and awaiting trial.'

'Good, good. And where are these two wills belonging to the late Mr Elliss?'

'I have one which I believe is the original,' said Mr Brent.

'I have the original,' countered Mr Pyke.

'Let me see both,' ordered the judge. A clerk collected both wills and handed them to him.

After looking carefully at each one for some minutes, the courtroom decided to have their say depending on whose side they had chosen to support. It became quite noisy and arguments began, until the judge called for silence.

'I cannot detect any difference apart from the wording 'and contents.' The forgery is very cleverly done, whichever will it is. And these forgers are in gaol, you say, Mr Brent?'

'Yes, my lord.'

'So how do you propose solving this case?'

Mr Brent looked round and noticed Mr Pyke and Daniel grinning to themselves. 'I took steps to find Mr Gunning, who is an expert in detecting forgeries. I also have a statement from Child's bank which has the late Mr Elliss's signature to enable Mr Gunning to compare it to the two wills.'

'I see,' said the judge. 'Is he in court?'

'No, my lord, but he is waiting outside so that he won't have any risk of bias.'

'Thank you, Mr Brent. You have conducted this sad case very well. Let Mr Gunning be brought in.'

The court could hear someone calling for Mr Gunning and after a few minutes he came in, a small, neat, gentleman dressed in black and with a serious pale face. He bowed to the judge.

'Ah, Mr Gunning, I believe we have met before?'

'Yes, my lord, it was the Shaw case, I think.'

'Ah, yes. How long will it take for you to identify which will is the original?'

'I don't know, my lord, until I see the wills.'

'Very well, we adjourn this case until you are ready. Conduct Mr Gunning to a private room,' said the judge, handing the two wills down. 'And please give the bank document to him as well, Mr Brent.'

Mr Gunning left the courtroom. Kate was taken out as well and the two lawyers left for another room.

Other cases were seen and dealt with in the meantime, which delighted the poor who had gone to keep warm as well as be entertained.

Nearly an hour later, Mr Gunning let it be known that he was ready to return. Everyone assembled as before. Kate felt tired and sick. She was worried, hungry and uncomfortable, and she found the heat and smell of the courtroom to be overpowering after the cold basement room where she had been waiting. She used her smelling salts and by sheer willpower stood in the dock for a second time. Alex notice how ill she looked.

'Well?' said the judge. 'Have you come to a conclusion, Mr Gunning?'

'Yes, my lord.'

'Then tell us, please.'

Silence descended on the courtroom, for a change. 'I examined the signatures very carefully and the one which is a forgery is very cleverly done,' began Mr Gunning.

'Yes, yes,' said the judge, irritably. 'Get on with it, man, we don't want to be here all day.'

'I beg your pardon, my lord. Comparing the two signatures against the one from the bank, this one is the original will and this a forgery,' said Mr Gunning, holding up the two wills, one in each hand.

'Bring them and let me see,' ordered the judge.

Mr Gunning went to the judge and gave him his magnifying glass, showing him the two wills and pointing out the tiny discrepancies, which were hardly visible to a layman. The room was quiet as though everyone was holding their breath, including Kate.

After some minutes, as Kate stood anxiously waiting, the judge cleared his throat. 'Very well. Thank you, Mr Gunning. Members of the jury, the original will is the one with the wording, 'house and money' only, as the accused maintained. The one with 'and contents' added is a forgery. What is your verdict?'

The spokesman for the jury stood up amidst shouts from the benches. 'We believe the accused is not guilty, milord.'

'Thank you,' said the judge. 'Miss Elliss, you are free to leave.'

Kate managed to say: 'Thank you, my lord,' but she was sure it wasn't heard amongst all the noise. As she turned to go, she paused as the judge looked at Mr Pyke and said severely: 'Your client has clearly been in partnership with Mr Fawcett over this business. He will be taken into custody and will join them at their trial.' He turned to Daniel. 'You have caused trouble and tried to obtain money illegally, Mr Elliss. Take him away.'

Daniel was led away, now a different man looking shaken, shrunken and shamed. Boos and catcalls from the crowd followed him.

Kate had already left. She felt she must have air. She staggered out of the building, looking neither to left or right. Then she saw Mr Sheldon waiting for her, and Mr Ward standing by the coach. She hurried forward and Alex caught her as she collapsed.

The coachman moved his horses as fast as he could without injuring the people leaving the court and who were walking haphazardly across the road. But at last they were away heading for Dr Roberts' house. Kate had recovered a little but she just sat with her eyes closed, trying to think of nothing after all the traumatic experience that morning and everything leading up to it. Surely she had experienced a taste of hell, she thought, and she didn't want to remember it. She was aware of Mr Sheldon sitting next to her. She could feel his warmth, and someone had placed a warm rug over her knees. Mr Sheldon and Mr Ward were talking but about what she had no idea. She didn't want to know, she felt drained of life.

Eventually the coach stopped and the men alighted. Alex looked at Kate who had not moved or opened her eyes. 'Kate,' he called imperiously to her. 'Get up!'

She didn't want to, she wanted to be left alone. The next moment, two arms went round her and succeeded in lifting her partially from her seat.

'Come along, Kate, help me. Now!'

This did have some effect and Kate opened her eyes, realising the coach had stopped. 'Oh,' was all she said, but she knew she had to help Mr Sheldon as he said so. When she was standing on the pavement outside Dr Roberts' house, she found that Laurie had already knocked on the door and the doctor was waiting for her. He saw how dazed she was,

'Do bring her in, Mr Sheldon,' he called. Alex helped her inside to find Mrs Walker, the housekeeper, waiting in the background. The doctor asked Alex to follow her, assisting Kate, until they came to a cosy room where there was a large chair.

'If you help Miss Elliss to this chair, please sir, then I can do the rest,' said Mrs Walker.

'Are you sure, I mean…'

'It is all right, sir. Dr Roberts will know what to do. She will be looked after well, sir.'

'Yes, yes, of course. Thank you.' With a last look at Kate, Alex went back to join Laurie and the doctor.

'Come and sit down for a moment,' said Dr Roberts, seeing how anxious Alex was. 'I have had a downstairs room made ready for Kate, as it is easier for me to keep an eye on her there. She is in shock at the moment, but after rest and warmth she will recover. But I must ask you not to visit until I say. You see, there is a chance she may have contracted gaol fever. Lice abound, especially in the places where she has been, but you may be sure I will take great care of her.'

Alexander smiled. 'Yes, I know, I'm sure of it. You will let me know how she goes on, won't you? And if any money is needed and…'

'I will certainly let you know. Now I must go to her. No doubt Mrs Walker has given her a hot drink so she will soon begin to feel better. Don't worry.'

'Thank you, sir,' said Alex, shaking the doctor's hand. 'I appreciate your help.'

Reluctantly, Alex and Laurie left.

Chapter Twenty-Four

'WHAT A HORRIBLE MORNING,' said Alex to Laurie on their way home to Brook Street. 'Those poor wretches. I wonder if they were all as bad as they were made out to be.'

'And poor Miss Kate mixed up with them,' said Laurie. 'She did wonderfully well, didn't she, sir?'

'Yes, Laurie, she did,' said Alex with a smile.

By this time they were back home. They alighted from the coach and trod up the steps to the door, which was opened immediately. They stepped into the hall and found bags and baggage all over the floor.

Alex frowned while Laurie smiled. 'It looks as though your nephew is back,' he grinned.

'With a hat box?' asked Alex.

'Please don't say you object to my hat box, dear,' a lady's voice said.

'Amelia!' exclaimed Alex, turning and smiling all over his face at his sister. 'How wonderful to see you.'

'You really are pleased to see me, dear, aren't you? But when you sent Chris home in your coach I couldn't resist coming back in it with him. It was so comfortable.'

Alex embraced her. 'Of course I'm pleased to see you. Oh, this is Laurie Ward.'

Laurie, trying to organise the bags and boxes, smiled and bowed to Mrs Johnston.

'Mr Ward, how nice to meet you,' said Amelia. 'I've heard you praised by all my children.'

Laurie smiled, feeling slightly embarrassed, but Chris appeared to rescue him. 'Shall I take my things into the room I occupied before, Uncle?' he asked.

'Yes, certainly, Chris. Perhaps you can organise it, Laurie. And could you ask the housekeeper to prepare a room for Mrs Johnston, too?'

'Yes, of course.'

'And see Pierre about meals and anything else that needs doing. Come into the library, Amelia. Would you like a sherry? We will eat in a short while. But tell me all the news. How are Matthew and the twins?'

'They are all well, thank you. In fact, they all wanted to come with Chris and I, but I said "no." For one thing, to have five people descend on you without notice is unkind to say the least, and besides that,' she went on, linking her arm in her brother's, 'I want you all to myself, Alex. We cannot talk properly with the twins around so I have left them with Matt. Miss Hunt is not much use to them now, poor thing, but I wouldn't turn her out. Matt is not strict with them but they do get on well together.'

'I see,' said Alex, looking at his sister. She was eighteen months older than him, but he thought her good looks were still the same as ever. She was of medium height with dark hair like her brother's and she had a laughing face, which was attractive rather than beautiful.

Amelia watched her brother as he drank his sherry. 'You look as though you needed that,' she remarked, looking at him with a question in her eyes.

Alex laughed. 'I did,' he said and replenished his glass. He offered more to his sister but she shook her head.

'Tell me why,' she said.

'Why?' said Alex, 'because I've been in a hell hole of a courtroom all this morning at the Old Bailey.'

'Gracious!' said his sister, raising her eyebrows. 'Are you so devoid of entertainment that you have to go there?'

'No, not at all,' said Alex.

'Well, I hope you're going to tell me why you went and what you saw.'

Alex looked at her measuringly. 'I saw people tried for various crimes in five minutes. I saw a jury that was bribed and noisy and couldn't really be bothered to think. But fortunately the person I went to see was acquitted.'

'And where is she now?' asked Amelia.

'She's with… How the hell did you know it was a she?'

'Because Chris has told me what he knows. And don't swear.'

A memory flashed before Alex's eyes of him saying the same thing to Kate the first time he met her sitting on the seat in the park mending sheets.

'Miss Elliss is staying with Dr Roberts, whom she has known since childhood. No one is allowed to see her until he is sure she has no fever. I hope she hasn't. She's been through enough without that.'

'Poor lady. And what is she to you?'

'She's my cook at The Hall.'

'Oh, I see,' said Amelia, who didn't see at all and suspected she wasn't being told all the truth. 'So why does a cook at The Hall get involved with the law? What has she done?'

'That's the point,' said Alex. 'She hasn't done anything wrong. Therefore, it was my place to see that she was acquitted – as far as I could.'

'And she's a cook,' persisted Amelia.

'Yes. Now can we leave the matter?'

'Of course, dear,' smiled his sister. 'And here is a servant to announce our meal is ready. How very convenient.' She looked quizzically at her brother as she rose gracefully from her chair.

Over the next week Amelia enjoyed herself. She went to look at the building where her son would be working and was impressed. She shopped, visited some old friends with her brother, saw a play at the theatre and dined with mutual acquaintances. Alex was happy enough to spend time with his sister when he wasn't talking business with Laurie. It was decided that Laurie should visit The Hall to see that preparations for the winter weather were in place and to authorise any repairs that needed doing. He would enquire, also, into any problems the staff may have and tell them the good news about Miss Elliss.

'Also,' said Alex, 'would you find the cottage belonging to my previous cook, whatever her name was? I think Miss Elliss's servants are staying with her. They will want to know the outcome of the trial. If you can't find it, ask Dr Pearce as he treated one of them.' Laurie departed the following day.

Alex received a note that day from Dr Roberts saying Miss Elliss was much better and he could visit whenever he wished. He breathed a sigh of relief to think the threat of fever hanging over Kate had disappeared. He decided to go the next day.

'I have heard from the doctor who says I can now visit Miss Elliss, Amelia. If I went over tomorrow, could you amuse yourself for a little while or perhaps Chris will be available?'

'Yes, of course I can amuse myself,' said his sister immediately. 'I don't wish to pry, dear, but...' seeing the look on his face she added hurriedly, 'but as my three children liked her and thought you did, it's not unreasonable that I would like to meet her, is it?'

Alex looked thoughtfully at her and then smiled. 'No, I suppose not. But it's a little difficult.'

'Because she's a cook?' asked Amelia.

'No, she can cook, but cooking at The Hall was the only paid work she ever did, I believe. Let me explain.' And Alex told her Kate's story as he knew it.

'She sounds wonderful,' said Amelia, when he had finished. 'And is there anything she does that isn't?' She raised her eyebrows.

'I had to stop her swearing,' said Alex with a grin.

'You?' Amelia laughed out loud. 'You are well matched then, aren't you?'

'I don't know. If I ask her to marry me now, she will think I'm being kind and I'm sorry for her. I am, of course, but that is not the reason.'

'Mmm,' said Amelia, looking at him. 'Before I say any more I think I should visit her. Perhaps later in the week? You go tomorrow, dear, and then you can tell me if she is fit to receive me.' She gave her brother a quick kiss and left him to his thoughts.

The next day Alex presented himself at Dr Roberts's house in the late morning. 'Come in and sit down,' the doctor smiled. 'Kate is much better as you will see. At the moment she is helping Mrs Walker in the kitchen and I will tell her you are here in a moment. What I would like to ask you is what is she to do next? Is she to return to your house in Hertfordshire where she was working or...?'

'No,' said Alex, after a few moments thought. 'The work is hard and she should have some time to completely recover, so I don't think she should return to do that. Could I ask you to keep her here for a little while longer? I have to talk to her before anything else can be arranged.'

'Very well,' said Dr Roberts, looking thoughtfully at Alex. 'I'll tell her you are here.'

Five minutes later the door opened and Kate appeared. 'Oh, Mr Sheldon, Dr Roberts said I had a visitor but not who it was. Please sit down,' she said politely, indicating a chair.

He still stood, looking at her. She wore her blue dress that she must have had for years. It was out of fashion but Alex thought she still wore it elegantly. The doctor had obviously burned the one she had worn in prison. 'How are you, Kate? You're looking a little better than when I saw you last.'

'Thank you, I'm much better.' She wished he would sit down and not scowl at her. 'I'm pleased you have come as I wish to ask you something and I also want to thank you for all the help and support while I was – er – was in prison.' She looked down at her fingers. 'Perhaps you would be kind enough to thank Mr Ward and Mr Johnston for their help too, for me.' She looked up with a smile. 'I know I couldn't have survived the – the ordeal without your help. I am very grateful.'

Alex looked at her. There was no smile on his face. He could see she was unlike her usual self, which he could understand. One didn't recover in five minutes from the horrors she had been through.

He sat down. 'And what was it you wished to ask me?'

She cleared her throat. 'Could I...?' she began. 'Am I able to go back to The Hall as your cook? Or would you rather I didn't? I quite understand if you wouldn't like me to. But I must know, you see, as I will have to think of something else I could do. I cannot live here for ever and be a charge on dear Dr Roberts.' She looked at Alex and tried to smile.

Alex looked at her and his heart ached. She was so pale with dark patches under her eyes as though she hadn't slept. Her face was thinner and so was her body. She needed lots of love and attention, not to think about what work she could do. She wasn't fit to do anything at the moment.

'There is no point in discussing it as yet,' said Alex. 'You're not well enough to do anything at the moment. When you have recovered a little more we'll think further.'

'I think that means that you don't want me back at The Hall. I do understand,' said Kate quietly, looking down at her fingers.

'Are you listening to what I'm saying, Kate?' Alex stood and moved his chair so that he was sitting in front of her. He took her hands. 'What I'm saying is that you are not ready to do anything at the moment, apart from concentrating on getting well again.'

'But you don't understand. You see, if I don't think about it now while I'm improving, it will delay my departure when I become fully fit again. I'm trying to be practical, as I cannot disrupt Dr Roberts' life for long.'

'For once you have to think what is good for you and not anyone else. Now I'm going to change the subject, as I don't want you to argue with me any more. I must tell you that Laurie has gone to The Hall for a day or two on general business. I've also told him to give the good news to the staff about you and to go and let your servants know that you are with Dr Roberts.'

Alex was rewarded with a smile. 'Oh, thank you. I wondered how I could let them know as they will be so worried.'

'Well, you needn't worry any more now. The other thing is that Chris is back and going to live in my house for as long as he likes. He has to begin work at the architects next month.'

'I'm so pleased for him,' said Kate. 'He's a lovely young man.'

'And,' continued Alex, 'not only did he return, but he brought his Mama, my sister Amelia, back with him. She told me to ask you if she may visit you. Please say "yes", she is a lovely person and I'm sure you would like her. Perhaps if the weather is fine you would like to go out with her or something.'

'Yes, yes, of course. It is kind of her to wish to visit me.' Kate really wasn't sure whether she did want to meet Mr Sheldon's sister. Perhaps she thought her brother was too interested in his cook and she was worried. She needn't be, Kate thought sadly.

The following day was cool with a little sunshine. Amelia ordered Alex's town coach to be available for eleven o'clock to take her to visit Kate. The coachman had smiled at his colleagues in the mews, saying that the coach and horses knew their way to Dr Roberts' all by themselves, without him driving them.

Amelia was admitted into Dr Roberts's house by Mrs Walker. 'Did you need the doctor, madam?' She asked. 'I'm afraid he is out at the moment.'

'No,' said Amelia, 'I came to see Miss Elliss.'

'Oh,' said Mrs Walker, smiling, 'that will do her good. Do come in. What name shall I say, please?'

'I'm Mrs Johnston.'

Amelia followed Mrs Walker, who knocked and opened a door. 'Mrs Johnston to see you, Miss Elliss,' she announced.

Kate rose from her chair. 'Oh,' she began.

'Forgive me for calling without letting you know. I'm Alex's sister,' said Amelia forthrightly as she entered the room. She saw before her an elegant lady with auburn hair, below which was a beautiful face. No wonder Alex was interested in her.

Kate smiled. 'Mr Sheldon told me you would visit. It is nice to meet you, Mrs Johnston. I enjoyed meeting Chris and the twins earlier this year.'

'And they enjoyed meeting you, too. Chris is to stay with my brother for a while now he has found employment here in London.'

'You must be very proud of him,' said Kate.

'We all are, of course, but I really came to see you, as I wondered if you would like a little air. Would you like to go out for a while? Would you like that? The weather is pleasant and I would like a little female company for a change.' Amelia smiled at her coaxingly.

'Why, thank you, you are very kind.' Kate thought to herself that if they were in the coach no one would see her old clothes and a little fresh air would be nice. She had been cooped up for some time, first in prison and then at Dr Roberts'. Some fresh air would be wonderful.

Amelia took in at a glance the old dress Kate was wearing, and her bonnet and cloak, and decided that a visit to the shops would be a good idea. The bills would be given to her brother, of course, but she wouldn't tell Kate that.

'Before we go any further,' she said, 'my name is Amelia, and are you Kate or Katherine?'

'Usually I'm called Kate.'

'Good, now come along while the weather is nice,' said Amelia, brooking no nonsense.

Chapter Twenty-Five

IT WAS WONDERFUL to see the trees beginning to change from their summer greens to bright yellows and gold, and Kate noticed the green verges of the small area where the children played. A weight seemed to lift from her and she thought wistfully of the parkland surrounding The Hall. Eventually, the coach wended its way to a leafy suburb where the shops were small and pretty. The ladies walking there, peering in the bow windows, were dressed quite fashionably and Kate looked longingly at them. It was at this moment that Amelia knocked imperiously on the ceiling of the coach. It slackened pace and drew up outside a small shop named 'Madame Clare's'. The coachman opened the door and let down the steps.

'Come along, Kate. I need a new dress. Come and help me choose.'

'Well, I – I'm not dressed very fashionably,' said poor Kate, feeling decidedly uncomfortable.

'Nonsense,' said Amelia, 'you're dressed, that's the main thing. Come along.'

Without waiting she stepped down and went to look in the window. Seeing no help for it, Kate descended and joined Amelia. Anyone interested, thought Kate, will take me for a servant, anyway.

The coach left, the coachman having been instructed to return in two hours' time, and without more ado Amelia opened the shop door of Madame Clare's, setting the doorbell ringing.

Although the shop was small, Kate noticed the floor was clean and that there were large gold framed mirrors on the walls. Elegant chairs, which looked too delicate to sit on, were placed invitingly nearby, and there were areas curtained off where garments could be tried on. A bowl of late roses, whose perfume wafted through the shop, stood on a small table. A middle aged lady, presumably Madame Clare, curtsied before them.

'Good morning, ladies, may I help you?' She looked from one to the other and noticed one was elegantly dressed and the other rather less so.

'Good morning,' said Amelia. 'My friend is looking for a morning dress. Have you anything she would like, I wonder?'

Kate was about to protest when Amelia squeezed her arm to keep her quiet.

'May I take Madam's measurements, please?'

This was done and afterwards many dresses were brought out, which Amelia held up to see if they would suit Kate. She rejected quite a few but decided that a dark blue with cream trimmings would be the one for Kate. Not wishing to make a fuss, Kate did as she was told and tried it on. When she saw herself in the mirror she couldn't believe how well it looked. She smiled, she felt a different woman. Amelia and Madame Clare thought she looked most elegant and said so.

'It suits you beautifully,' said Amelia. 'Shall we take it?'

'How much...?' began Kate.

'We'll see about that in a moment. Now have you an afternoon dress as well, Madame, perhaps in a lighter colour?'

Madame called to a young assistant to take the unwanted dresses away while she found some pretty afternoon ones with much delicate lace around the neckline and elbow length sleeves. After picking out a pale bluey-green silk and a flowered yellow one, Amelia said the bluey-green one looked best, particularly against the colour of Kate's hair. Amelia told Kate to change into the dark blue dress and Madam would parcel the other for them to take home.

While Kate was busy changing again, Amelia found out the price of the two dresses and happily paid Madame Clare. She smiled to herself and wondered what Alex would say when she presented him with the bill.

After they had left the shop they had nearly an hour to spare, which Amelia spent quite happily buying small items for the twins with Kate's help, and then the two hours were gone and the coach came at the appointed time. Kate was relieved to see it, as she was pleased to sit down. She still felt a little weak but she had enjoyed the outing and seeing and doing something different.

'Did you enjoy that?' asked Amelia, smiling at Kate. 'I find there is nothing better to lift the spirits than a new dress.'

'Thank you, I enjoyed it very much and I love the dresses, but you cannot pay for them for me. You must let me know how much...'

'My dear, there is no need to worry. I shall give the bills to my brother and he will reimburse me. He will be delighted.'

Kate didn't think so. She decided she would take the dress off when she was back at the doctor's and then take both of them back. If the one she was wearing creased a little while she was in the coach, she would hang it up and it would look as good as new.

While she was thinking this and Amelia was feeling pleased with herself, the coach stopped and they were in Brook Street.

'Oh,' said Kate, 'I thought I was to be taken back to Dr Roberts.'

'Eventually,' said Amelia. 'I want to see my brother's reactions to you in a new dress.'

'But – but I can't...' began Kate.

Amelia didn't hear as she was being helped from the coach, so Kate had to follow suit.

'It is quite acceptable for you to visit while I am here,' said Amelia. 'Come along.' She led the way to the front door. She only had to knock once and it was opened by a servant. Kate felt a little nervous.

'Is my brother home?' asked Amelia, divesting herself and Kate of their cloaks and hats.

'Yes, madam.'

'Good, come along, Kate,' and she led the way into the library. 'Ah, there you are, Alex. I've brought you a visitor.'

Alex was looking through some messages he had just been given. It was evident he had been out riding, as he hadn't yet changed. He turned. 'Who...?' Then he saw Kate. He dropped the papers quickly on to the table and came over to her, taking her hands in his. 'How lovely to see you,' he said. 'You're looking much better.' He was smiling down at her.

'I thought she should visit us for a change,' said Amelia. 'Now, Alex, doesn't she look nice? We've been shopping, you see.'

Alex looked at the new dress. Kate didn't know what to say or do so she just stood there. 'Nice?' said Alex, smiling. 'She looks beautiful.'

'There is nothing like a new dress to cheer one up,' said Amelia, 'so I bought her two. And you can reimburse me any time, dear.'

'I might have known,' said Alex, his lips twitching. 'Why Matt isn't a pauper with you buying people dresses, I don't know.'

'Well, I shall go and find my son and you two can pull my character to shreds behind my back.' Amelia smiled at her brother and walked out of the room.

Kate didn't know what to do. 'I'm sorry,' she began. 'I didn't know Amelia meant to buy me dresses. I can take them back and…'

'For a sensible woman you say the most ridiculous things at times,' Alex said. 'Come and sit down. I'm sure you must be feeling tired. Amelia is a dear girl but she can be exhausting.' He led her to the sofa.

'She is very kind,' murmured Kate.

Alex poured out a glass of sherry and handed it to Kate. Sitting down beside her, he continued, 'Of course, I'll buy your dresses and more besides if only you'll let me.'

'But – but you must not, it would be quite wrong. Remember I am only a cook, or I was. I quite see that with all that has happened you would rather I didn't continue at The Hall.' Kate found herself wondering what would happen next. This morning was proving to be so unreal.

Alex saw the puzzled look and took her by the hand. 'I think,' he said, 'that Amelia has left us alone, not to talk about dresses, but so that we can talk about the future. And we will leave Kate the cook out of our discussion, as she is no more. Kate, my love, look at me and tell me if you feel you could marry me? I do love you, you know. I love the way you look and your good sense and above all your consideration for others. I want to protect you and to have you by my side.'

When Kate had arisen that morning she was feeling cool and calm and pleased with her progress. Now her life had changed completely, an outing, new dresses and now a marriage proposal. 'Please, I – I don't know. I never expected… I – I must think. I'm sorry.' She hid her face in her hands.

Alex placed a comforting arm around her. 'Oh, poor Kate. But I do love you dearly, you know – please say you will be my wife?'

Kate tried to pull herself together. She looked at him. She shook her head. 'Thank you, you are very kind but indeed you must not expect me to, it wouldn't be right.'

'Why wouldn't it be right? I'm afraid I'm rather dense this morning so I'm afraid you will have to explain it to me.'

'Well, I'll try. I am a servant, a cook and worse than that I have been in prison. Everyone will know and you will be open to ridicule. And – and also my brother is in prison now and people will say I am not the right wife for you.'

'Well,' said Alex, 'as far as I'm concerned people can say and think what they like. I know who you are and the problems you have had and I don't care what others say. I still wish to marry you.'

'Well then I must care for you and refuse and…'

'My darling girl, if you care for me to that extent I think you must love me. Now tell me.'

Kate looked at him wonderingly and saw the kindness and love in his eyes. 'Of course I love you. How can I not when you are so good to me?'

'Then say you will be my wife.'

Kate smiled at him. 'If you are sure – really sure – then thank you, Alex, I will be your wife.'

He kissed her gently.

'I love you, too, my dear, and to prove it I must tell you I have kept a lovely drawing of you by Chris. Do you remember?'

He went quickly to his desk and opened the top drawer, taking out the picture. He showed it to Kate, and she remembered that Chris had had his sketchbook with him that evening when she played the harpsichord for the party. 'I chose it from all the others,' said Alex. 'You looked so beautiful, you see.'

'Well,' said Kate, happily, 'I can't ask more than that, can I? Only you are so kind to your staff and I thought that is all it was with me and I was so glad of your help. I was always attracted to you, even when we first met, but, of course, I had to remember I was a servant, which at times I found very difficult.'

'You won't be a servant any more. You must leave Dr Roberts' but you can't stay here unless you're married to me. Amelia will have to return home soon so this is what I suggest we do. You and I will be married by special licence, which can soon be arranged, and Dr Roberts could give you away if you wished. And afterwards, where would you like to go?'

'Gracious, let me think. It would be nice to go back to The Hall for a while. It really is my house of dreams,' she said wistfully. 'I was very happy there, you know, and I can see Matty and Will. But not, of course, if you don't wish too.' She looked anxiously at him.

'That might be a good idea, my love,' said Alex slowly. 'I always found it a happy place in which to live, even when Amelia and I were children. Yes, I'll get Laurie working on that. Then when you are fully recovered we can go abroad for a while.'

'Abroad? Oh, where would we go?' Kate asked breathlessly.

'Paris? Venice? Where would you like to go?' Alex smiled down at her and saw the love in her eyes as she looked at him. He made sure that she wasn't able to say anything for a long time.

Amelia, peeping carefully round the door sometime later, was very pleased with what she saw.

Lightning Source UK Ltd.
Milton Keynes UK
176396UK00002B/25/P